MEDUSA'S DAUGHTERS

*MAGIC AND MONSTROSITY FROM WOMEN WRITERS
OF THE FIN-DE-SIÈCLE*

EDITED BY THEODORA GOSS

LANTERNFISH PRESS

Philadelphia, PA

MEDUSA'S DAUGHTERS

Lanternfish Press
399 Market Street, Suite 360
Philadelphia, PA 19106

lanternfishpress.com

Printed in the United States of America.
Library of Congress Control Number: 2019943335
ISBN: 978-1-941360-36-1

For my daughter Ophelia,
and all the other daughters of this new
century.

SOURCES

Ethna Carbery (Anna MacManus), "The Love-Talker" and "Niamh," *The Four Winds of Eirinn: Poems*, M. H. Gill and Son, Ltd. and Jas. Duffy and Co., Ltd., 1906.

Willa Cather, "Princess Baladina—Her Adventure," *The Home Monthly* VI, August 1896 (under the pseudonym Charles Douglass).

Nora Hopper Chesson, "A Drowned Girl to Her Lover," *The Bodley Head*, 1896. "Hertha," *Aquamarines*, Richard Grant, 1902.

Kate Chopin, "An Egyptian Cigarette," *Vogue Magazine*, April 19, 1902.

Mary Coleridge, "The Witch," "The White Women," and "The Other Side of a Mirror," *Poems by Mary E. Coleridge*, Elkin Matthews, 1908.

Olive Custance, "The White Witch," *Rainbows*, The Bodley Head, 1902. "The Changeling," *The Inn of Dreams*, The Bodley Head, 1911.

Mary Wilkins Freeman, "Luella Miller," *The Wind in the Rose-Bush and Other Stories of the Supernatural*, Doubleday, Page & Company, 1903.

Charlotte Perkins Gilman, "When I Was a Witch," *The Forerunner* I.7, May 1910. "The Yellow Wallpaper," *The New England Magazine*, January 1892.

May Kendall, "A Castle in the Air," *Songs from Dreamland*, Longmans, Green, and Co., 1894. "The Mermaid's Chapel," *Dreams to Sell*, Longmans, Green, and Co., 1887.

Vernon Lee (Violet Paget), "Dionea," *Hauntings: Fantastic Stories*, William Heinemann, 1890.

Charlotte Mew, "The Farmer's Bride" and "The Changeling," *The Farmer's Bride*, The Poetry Bookshop, 1921. "A White Night," *Temple Bar*, January 1, 1903.

E. Nesbit, "Man-Size in Marble," *Grim Tales*, A. D. Innes & Co., 1893. "The Princess and the Hedge-Pig," *The Magic World*, MacMillan and Co., 1912.

Dollie Radford, "A Ballad of Victory," *A Ballad of Victory and Other Poems by Dollie Radford*, Alston Rivers, 1907.

Lizette Woodworth Reese, "The Singer," *A Branch of May*, Cushings and Bailey, 1887. "All Hallows Night," *The Selected Poems of Lizette Woodworth Reese*, George H. Doran Company, 1926.

A. Mary F. Robinson, "The Dryads," *The Collected Poems, Narrative and Lyrical, of A. Mary F. Robinson*, T. Fisher Unwin, 1902.

Dora Sigerson Shorter, "The Watcher in the Wood" and "The White Witch," *The Collected Poems of Dora Sigerson Shorter*, Harper & Brothers Publishers, 1907.

Katherine Tynan, "The Children of Lir" and "Nymphs," *Twenty One Poems by Katharine Tynan: Selected by W. B. Yeats*, Dun Emer Press, 1907.

Rosamund Marriott Watson, "Ballad of the Bird-Bride" and "The Orchard of the Moon," *The Poems of Rosamund Marriott Watson*, The Bodley Head, 1912.

Edith Wharton, "Bewitched," *Here and Beyond*, George J. McLeod Limited, 1926. "The Hermit and the Wild Woman," *The Hermit and the Wild Woman and Other Stories*, Charles Scribner's Sons, 1908.

Virginia Woolf, "A Haunted House," *Monday or Tuesday*, The Hogarth Press, 1921.

Elinor Wylie, "Atavism," "The Fairy Goldsmith," and "Madman's Song," *Nets to Catch the Wind*, Harcourt, Brace and Company, 1921.

CONTENTS

MEDUSA'S DAUGHTERS

INTRODUCTION

THEODORA GOSS

In 1865, the prominent Pre-Raphaelite painter Dante Gabriel Rossetti, brother of Christina Rossetti, wrote a poem titled "Aspecta Medusa" to accompany a planned painting:

> Andromeda, by Perseus sav'd and wed,
> Hanker'd each day to see the Gorgon's head:
> Till o'er a fount he held it, bade her lean,
> And mirror'd in the wave was safely seen
> That death she liv'd by.
>
>   Let not thine eyes know
> Any forbidden thing itself, although
> It once should save as well as kill: but be
> Its shadow upon life enough for thee.

In the poem, Rossetti warns Andromeda against curiosity, which women have been warned against since Eve plucked an apple from the Tree of Knowledge and Pandora opened her infamous box. Charles Perrault issues a similar warning in the moral appended to "Bluebeard":

> *La curiosité malgré tous ses attraits,*
> *Coûte souvent bien des regrets;*
> *On en voit tous les jours mille exemples paraître.*
> *C'est, n'en déplaise au sexe, un plaisir bien léger;*
> *Dès qu'on le prend il cesse d'être,*
> *Et toujours il coûte trop cher.*[1]

Women cannot help succumbing to their curiosity, Perrault tells us, but it always comes at a price. Without that moral, "Bluebeard" might teach a different lesson: for example, don't marry serial killers, no matter how wealthy they are. But with Perrault's admonishment, the fairy tale warns against the sin of Eve and Pandora. Women, it implies, should not try to open secret chambers, to see what is forbidden. They should not taste apples from the Tree of Knowledge, for doing so results in death, damnation, or both. In Rossetti's poem, Andromeda is defined by her relationship to Perseus, who both saved and wed her. She is the bride rescued from the sea serpent, the hero's wife. Medusa's petrifying countenance is the instrument by which she was saved; her salvation depends on the death of another woman. Only because Medusa, the monster, died can Andromeda live.

---

1 Loosely translated: Curiosity, despite its attractions, often results in regrets; every day one sees a thousand such examples. With all due respect to the ladies, it is a slight pleasure; once it is satisfied, it ceases to be, and it always costs too much.

This dichotomy mirrors (most apposite of images!) the division Sandra Gilbert and Susan Gubar describe in *The Madwoman in the Attic* between the Victorian angel in the house and her shadow, the madwoman or monster, whose "Medusa-face," Gilbert and Gubar tell us, "kills female creativity."[2] The angel is Jane Eyre; the monstrous madwoman is Bertha Rochester, who is both her opposite and double. In his warning against curiosity, Rossetti insists that the shadow on the water is sufficient—Andromeda should not try to see more. But in both *Jane Eyre* and Charlotte Mew's "The Other Side of a Mirror," shadows are dangerous. In her essay "The Child and the Shadow," Ursula Le Guin writes that "the shadow is the other side of our psyche, the dark brother of the conscious mind. It is Cain, Caliban, Frankenstein's monster, Mr. Hyde. It is Vergil who guided Dante through hell, Gilgamesh's friend Enkidu, Frodo's enemy Gollum. It is the Doppelgänger. It is Mowgli's Grey Brother; the werewolf, the wolf, the bear, the tiger of a thousand folktales; it is the serpent, Lucifer."[3] But if Le Guin had written this essay later in her career, when her thinking had been influenced in a more significant way by feminist theory, she might have identified the shadow as a dark sister, as Lilith, Hecate, Hel, Ereshkigal. As Bertha, or Becky Sharp, or any of the other darkly unrepentant women of literature, the ones who refuse to be angels.[4] As Medusa, whose head

---

2 Sandra M. Gilbert and Susan Gubar, *The Madwoman in the Attic: The Woman Writer and the Nineteenth-Century Literary Imagination*, Yale University Press, 1979, p. 17.

3 Ursula K. Le Guin, "The Child and the Shadow," *The Quarterly Journal of the Library of Congress*, vol. 32, no. 2, 1975, p. 143.

4 Gilbert and Gubar point out that in *Vanity Fair*, Becky is described as a siren with a "hideous tail" below the water, "diabolical and slimy" like Medusa's serpents, although she is a decorous woman above, p. 29. Sometimes the angel

was eventually given to Athena, to adorn her shield. She is the other face of Athena, and when you see the guardian of Athens, the giver of laws, on one of the red amphorae that fill the halls of the British Museum, you see two faces: the goddess and the monster.[5] Those two faces are counterparts, like the Wicked Queen and little Snow White, whom Gilber and Guber tell us will eventually look into her stepmother's mirror. When she realizes that she is no longer the fairest by patriarchal social standards, will she too become wicked? Will she too try to write her own story?

This is a collection of women telling stories, whether in prose or verse. I have chosen these particular stories because they were written by women writers of the fin-de-siècle, that liminal period (approximately 1870-1910, with some fuzziness at the edges) between the Victorian age and the beginning of Modernity. This was an age when images of Medusa proliferated: Arnold Böcklin's *Medusa* (1878), Franz Von Stuck's *Head of Medusa* (1982), and Fernand Khnopff's *The Blood of Medusa* (1898) show us only her fearsome visage, although Medusa herself does not look particularly frightened—she seems rather weary of the whole snake business. In Alice Pike Barney's *Medusa* (1892), by contrast, the monster resembles a terrified Gibson Girl, aware that her face is surrounded by serpentine chaos. Mary de Morgan's sculpture *Medusa* (1900) is calm and

---

contains the monster.

5 We should not forget that the goddess created the monster. Medusa, the beautiful maiden, was raped by Poseidon in Athena's temple. As punishment, Athena gave her snakes for hair and looks that could kill. Like the angel in the house, Athena, sprung from the head of Zeus, is an upholder of patriarchal authority. Paradoxically, while patriarchy creates the female monster, she can also function as a symbol of female power and rebellion.

contemplative, her snaking hair an inventive coiffure rather than a cause for dismay. Gustav Klimt's *Pallas Athene* (1898) shows us Athena as an armored warrior, regal and severe, with an unusual breastplate: a female countenance, ludicrous, tongue sticking out at the viewer. This is a different sort of Medusa, not on Athena's shield but directly below her chin: a second face, a mirror image, a shadow, showing us once again that Medusa and Athena are two aspects of the same figure. Medusa's head was commonly featured on late Victorian pins and brooches. What did that head say about the woman wearing such an ornament? What was the wearer claiming or communicating about herself?

Rossetti's painting is not of Medusa but of Andromeda, a typically lush and beautiful Pre-Raphaelite "stunner" (as the painters of the Pre-Raphaelite Brotherhood called their models).[6] The preparatory drawing makes clear that she is gazing into a pool, seeing the reflection of Medusa rather than the head of the monster herself, the shadow rather than the reality—which is all, Rossetti tells us, we can handle. The unmediated Gorgon's head would be too much. Why were late nineteenth-century artists obsessed with Medusa? In part, I think, because she captures the dichotomous position of women at that time: the angel might still be in the house, but she might also be out on the street, riding her bicycle to a suffrage rally.

I've chosen the title *Medusa's Daughters* for this collection because the stories and poems featured here respond to that

---

6 Christina Rossetti criticized her brother's treatment of his models in the poem "In an Artist's Studio," where the artist "feeds" upon the woman whose image fills his canvases, "Not as she is, but was when hope shone bright; / Not as she is, but as she fills his dream." He is an aesthetic vampire who has sucked youth and life out of the model to create his art.

obsessive interest in the figure of the monstrous female, whom Andromeda can see only reflected, as though looking at a version of her own face. They all focus on women and the fearful or fantastic (or both). Additionally, they reveal a series of common themes that were important to women writers of that time, or at least the sorts of women writers we associate with more *avant garde* publications such as *The Yellow Book*.[7] The writers I have included were rebels, each in her own way—Mary Coleridge remained an angel in the attic bedroom she shared with her sister but taught at the Working Women's College, while Vernon Lee dared to rebel more openly against social strictures, dressing in masculine attire and having several long-term relationships with female lovers. Their writing challenges Victorian patriarchal norms and shows the way toward a more modern sensibility, which comes to full fruition in Virginia Woolf. Here are some of their common themes, which weave in and out of the stories like serpents:

1. **The silencing of women:** Coleridge's woman in the mirror "had no voice to speak her dread," but other female figures are rendered voiceless as well. No one will listen to the protagonist of "The Yellow Wallpaper," and the young bride in Charlotte Mew's terrifying "The Farmer's Bride" is "Happy enough to chat and play / With birds and rabbits and such as

---

7 *The Yellow Book* was a British journal of literature and art published from 1894 to 1897. It was considered scandalous at the time, partly because of its association with the Aesthetic movement and artists such as Aubrey Beardsley. Writers in this volume whose work appeared in *The Yellow Book* include Nora Hopper Chesson, Olive Custance, Vernon Lee, Charlotte Mew, E. Nesbit, Dollie Radford, and Rosamund Marriott Watson (both under her own name and the pseudonym Graham R. Tomson).

they, / So long as men-folk keep away." She cannot speak in the company of men. What will happen to her if her husband climbs the stair that separates them? Perhaps she will become another madwoman behind the wallpaper. Silencing is presented most starkly in Mew's "A White Night," where a woman is consigned to death by both institutional patriarchy and a male narrator who treats the event as an aesthetic experience, presuming that she has also participated in what, to him, is a fitting and even artistic end to her life. It seems no coincidence that silencing is associated with confinement: in attics, under the floors of churches, through the looking glass.

2. The violence of patriarchy: Violence is implied in "The Farmer's Bride" and Edith Wharton's "Bewitched," where we are told that witches and women who prey on men deserve the stake or burning. It is carried out frighteningly in "A White Night" and almost humorously in E. Nesbit's "Man-Size in Marble," where the narrator's wife dies when she encounters two marble knights in armor who, on a particular day of the year, leave their marble slabs and walk—the narrator's "wife," a true angel in the house, succumbs to petrified symbols of male violence. Nesbit is an imaginative and supremely humorous writer—I think she appreciated the grim joke.

3. The danger of femininity: If patriarchy is deadly, so is traditional femininity. Sweet, frail, helpless Luella Miller sucks the life out of her devoted attendants. Coleridge's pleading witch, who tells the narrator, "I am but a little maiden still, / My little white feet are sore" and asks to be lifted over the threshold (a common vampire gambit), destroys the peace of the household. In his lecture "Of Queens' Gardens" on the proper place and role of women in Victorian society, John Ruskin famously claimed that a true woman, a true wife, could make a home even in the wilderness—that this was woman's magic and power. The house existed because there was an angel to create and adorn it.[8] But in these stories and poems, women like Vernon Lee's Dionea and Coleridge's witch destroy the home rather than bringing it into being.

4. Doubling and the shadow: Female characters are presented as doubles in several of these narratives, most clearly in "The Other Side of a Mirror" and Lizette Woodworth Reese's "All Hallows Night," where the ghost that the narrator encounters is herself. But the woman behind the yellow wallpaper is also a counterpart of the woman who perceives and eventually becomes her, and Gilman makes clear that patriarchy splits a woman off from herself: doubling is in part a result of violent separation between the angel and the monster, until the speaker gazes into the mirror like Coleridge's wild-eyed narrator, hoping to deny that "I am she." A woman who is not split in that way would be defined as rebellious and a source of danger, like the female protagonist of Wharton's "The Hermit

---

8 "Of Queens' Gardens" and a companion lecture, "Of Kings' Treasuries," on the role and responsibilities of Victorian men, were published together in the volume *Sesame and Lilies* in 1865. In context, "Of Queens' Gardens" presents a complex and sometimes contradictory message: girls should be educated, Ruskin tells us, but not formally—instead, they should be allowed to roam in their fathers' libraries, somewhat like literate fauns. To give Ruskin credit, he was trying to improve the position of women in Victorian society; however, the essay also enshrined the idea of "separate spheres," in which men were supposed to act in the public world, while women were relegated to decorating the private one.

and the Wild Woman," who defies religious strictures to experience the pleasure of bathing in a forest pool. Only in the end does the hermit realize he has been harboring not a potential contaminant but a saint.

5. The deadly female gaze: There is an alternative to vampiric angels such as Luella Miller. That alternative is the witch or goddess, who is beautiful and powerful. However, she remains dangerous to men. Dionea is one of these dangerous women, but even clearer examples are found in Coleridge's "The White Women" and A. Mary F. Robinson's "The Dryads." Coleridge tells us that "One of our race, lost in an awful glade, / Saw with his human eyes a wild white maid, / And gazing, died." Robinson warns us that we should not seek out her magical women:

> Nay! Nay! For should the woodman find
>   A Dryad in a hollow tree,
> He drops his hatchet, stricken blind—
>   I know not why, unless it be
>   The maid's Immortal, and not he!"

These witchy women are Medusa's daughters indeed—their gaze kills. But rather than sending heroes to slay them, the writers of this collection celebrate the deadliness of their *femmes fatales*.[9]

---

9 The *femme fatale*, literally "deadly woman," has a long tradition in literature and art, from the sirens of *The Odyssey* to film actresses such as Theda Bara, who capitalized on the seductive iconography of the *femme fatale* to become an international star.

6. The company of women: Coleridge's "wild white women" and Robinson's dryads both live in all-female communities, as does Rosamund Marriott Watson's bird-bride before she is captured by her human husband. There is a sense, throughout the stories and poems, that these communities are liberating: that women living together experience a sort of Amazonian freedom. It is when women are isolated that they are vulnerable; if they are denied community, they will create it, even with a shadow on the other side of the wallpaper. The opposite of positive female community is the cloister, as in "The Hermit and the Wild Woman"—an unusual fable for Wharton, the chronicler of elegant New York society at the turn of the century. There, wilderness and isolation are preferable to the community of women dominated by and enforcing a social code created by men.

7. The witch and/as the goddess: We are presented with both witches and goddesses in these narratives, but the dividing line between the two seems blurry. Dionea demonstrates how easily the witch can turn out to be an incarnation of the goddess. Olive Custance's "The White Witch" is a fin-de-siècle aesthete playing at witchcraft, while Dora Sigerson Shorter's narrator in a poem with the same title warns M'Cormac, "A white witch woman is your bride: / You married for your woe." Fortunately, M'Cormac does not seem to care and only laughs at this warning. The magical woman is a witch indeed, but she has already cast her spell. Ethna Carbery's "Niamh" and Nora Hopper Chesson's "Hertha" are also of this magical company. Hertha, in particular, is a goddess figure: as she tells us, "Mortality, eternity,

/ Change, death, and life are mine—are me." Perhaps witch and goddess are two sides of the same woman, like Athena and Medusa—as M'Cormac implies, what you see depends on your interpretation. And witchcraft itself can function as social rebellion, refashioning society, at least for a while, as in Gilman's "When I Was a Witch."

8.   The problem of love: M'Cormac seems to love his witch-bride, but these stories and poems often introduce us to troubled homes. "The Farmer's Bride" could be renamed "Prelude to a Rape"—it is certainly not a positive image of marriage. Neither, for all the male narrator's nostalgia, is "Ballad of the Bird-Bride," where the seagull woman was seized and abducted from her family. Her return to the air, with her children, is in part Watson's response to Victorian divorce laws that forced women who left their husbands to abandon their children. The narrator's sad conclusion is also her liberation, her return home. Ethna Carbery's "The Love-Talker" is a deadly seducer: "Who meets the Love-Talker must weave her shroud soon." But female figures can be equally problematic, as Dionea demonstrates. The goddess of love is fundamentally a destructive figure. Perhaps one solution to the problem of love can be found in Coleridge's "white women," who reproduce partheno-genically—all it takes is a western breeze.

9.   The power of imagination: From Kate Chopin's "An Egyptian Cigarette" to Elinor Wylie's "The Fairy Goldsmith," these stories and poems celebrate the richness and power of imaginative creation. In Lizette Woodworth Reese's "The Singer," the princess remembers a song she heard years ago, which she wants to hear again in her old age. Watson's Orchard of the Moon, with its "faërie flower" and "faërie fruit," is a garden of the imagination. It is where dreams are grown, just as the princess dreams of love, or a lover, like a wild plum tree. Such enchanted dreams may not last: finally the cigarette is smoked, and fairy creations taken out of fairyland fade away. Wylie warns us:

> O, they never can last
> Though you hide them fast
>   From moth and from rust;
> In your monstrous day
> They will crumble away
>   Into quicksilver dust.

However, it is better to follow the siren song, or in this case the underwater bell described in May Kendall's "The Mermaid's Chapel," than to stay in mundane reality one's whole life. It is better to live in "A Castle of Dreams" than a house of bricks. As Wylie insists:

> Better to see your cheek grown hollow,
> Better to see your temple worn,
> Than to forget to follow, follow,
> After the sound of a silver horn.

The alternative is a world without magic, where the nymphs of Katherine Tynan's poem, "beautiful girls of the mountain, / Oreads all," no longer respond when we call to them.

10. The changeling as outsider: These stories and poems are filled with outsiders, described as changelings, or birds, or hares.[10] They are part fairy, part animal, not quite human—and the non-human world summons them. As Custance tells us in "The Changeling,"

> They stole the crying human child,
>> And left me laughing by the fire;
> And that is why my heart is wild,
>> And all my life a long desire . . .

Mew's poem with the same title tells a similar story of being abandoned in the human world. Here, however, the fairies come back for their own. At night, by firelight, the changeling child can see them at the window:

> A pinched brown face peered in—I shivered;
>> No one listened or seemed to see;
> The arms of it waved and the wings of it quivered,
>> Whoo—I knew it had come for me;
>> Some are as bad as bad can be!

Watson's bird-bride, Tynan's children of Lir, and Mew's farmer's bride are all such fantastical, half-animal figures, not quite human and therefore both magical and vulnerable. What makes them different can also make them powerful: the

---

10 These are the counterparts to Le Guin's werewolf, bear, and tiger—although they are gentler and more domestic images, they also symbolize the fantastical or animal double, the shadow self.

bird-bride finally answers the call of her own nature, return-ing to the avian sisterhood, taking her children with her. But Tynan shows that the liminal space between human and ani-mal, society and the natural world, can be problematic. The children of Lir are neither fully bird nor fully human: "Robbed alike of bird's joys and of man's are they." Like a changeling, they cannot be wholly one thing or the other—they are per-manent outsiders, an image many of these women writers must have identified with.[11]

11. The return of the (un)dead: Many of these stories and poems are haunted: by characters who return from the dead, by voices from beyond the grave, by images that refuse to die. "Bewitched" and "A Drowned Girl to Her Lover" are obvious examples, since in both, a dead woman walks and speaks. But the narrator of Wylie's "Atavism" fears an unnamed creature in the local pond, described only as presenting a "painted mask of death," and Shorter's "The Watcher in the Wood" is suf-fused with the doom that threatens the beautiful fairy dancers. It's worth remembering that in Irish folklore, fairyland and the land of the dead are more or less the same territory. "The Yellow Wallpaper," usually read as a story of depression and illness caused by its supposed cure, can also be read as a ghost story. The attic bedroom the narrator sleeps in, with its bed bolted to the wall, its bars on the widow, obviously had a pre-vious inmate. It is entirely logical in the context of the story to suppose that inmate has stayed on and is still there, trapped

---

11 As Gilbert and Gubar point out, the categories of woman and writer were symbolically incompatible in Victorian society. After all, an angel has no need to write. Therefore, a woman writer must be a monster: female above the sur-face but with a fish tale below.

within the wallpaper. Like Henry James's *The Turn of the Screw*, this is a story that can be read as a case of either hallucination or possession.

But hauntings are not always negative. Perhaps the dead girl's lover wants to share her narrow bed, and the ghostly couple in Woolf's "The Haunted House" are certainly one of the happiest in literature. As they wander the house, they rediscover the joy they once shared: "'Here we slept,' she says. And he adds, 'Kisses without number.' 'Waking in the morning—' 'Silver between the trees—' 'Upstairs—' 'In the garden—' 'When summer came—' 'In winter snowtime—' The doors go shutting far in the distance, gently knocking like the pulse of a heart."

12. The victorious fairytale heroine: Female writers at the turn of the century wrote in a variety of genres. Ghost stories were always popular, as were tales of gothic horror in general—we can see Nesbit trying her hand at one in "Man-Sized in Marble." She succeeds, although she cannot help being funny, and one gets the sense that she does not take the genre itself seriously. She is not really trying to frighten us. But her forté is the fairy tale, another genre that gave women writers the ability rewrite and challenge social norms. I have included several examples in this collection, specifically because it was in fairy tales and tales for children that women writers often showed a way forward.[12] "Man-Size in

---

12 Perhaps because fairy tales such as "Bluebeard" and "Snow White" so clearly encode patriarchal messages, women writers have found them fertile ground for feminist rewriting, from the *salonnières* of seventeenth- and eighteenth-century Paris to modern writers such as Angela Carter and Anne Sexton.

Marble" may present us with an image of the crushing weight of patriarchy, but "The Princess and the Hedge-Pig" shows that a princess can collaborate with a baker's boy turned into a hedgehog to regain her kingdom, forming a bond of equals that transcends gender, class, and perhaps species. One does not expect a story like "Princess Baladina" from a writer as serious as Willa Cather—at least, it surprised me when I came across it. But it is both a humorous children's tale and a serious critique of the fairy-tale requirement that princesses must find princes. Poor Princess Baladina can't find a prince, and so she can't get her adventure—which is for the best, because she is only a child, but what about when she grows up? Will she be able to find a prince then? Nesbit tells us a prince may not be necessary—a hedgehog may be enough. I count Dollie Radford's "A Ballad of Victory" among these fairy tales, because the protagonist here is a typical fairy-tale heroine in the middle of her quest, when all still seems lost. Nevertheless, among the crowd that wonders who she is and where she is going,

> Then spoke a youth, who long, apart,
> Had watched the people come and go,
> With clearer eyes and wiser heart,
> And cried, "Her face and name I know.
>
> "And well the passage of her flight,
> The starless plains she must ascend,
> And well the darkness of the night,
> In which her pilgrimage shall end.

"But stronger than the years that roll,
Than travail past or yet to be,
She presses to her hidden goal,
A crownless, unknown Victory."

Radford's language has a double meaning here: our heroine presses to her victory, but Victory could also be who and what she is, the name the lad knows that the crowd does not. Victory may be nameless and uncrowned for now, but she will be Victory still.

This is not Medusa, the monster, nor Athena, the goddess—this is a new and different possibility for women, a possibility dreamed up by women writers who were trying to educate themselves, live alone or with female roommates, support themselves financially, and of course vote—activities we take for granted nowadays, but that at the time seemed radical. They dreamed up a female character who was neither an angel in the house, nor a deadly *femme fatale*, nor an untouchable deity. She was a woman on a quest, and there was a very good likelihood that she would succeed. But she was just coming into being. Perhaps it was difficult to image her in any genre except the fairy tale, which is about the possibility of transformation. There were certainly women writers who challenged societal restrictions in more realistic modes. But fantasy allowed these writers to both discuss the challenges faced by women at the turn of the century and imagine alternatives to them—whether wild women who reproduced parthenogenically or smart, sensible princesses who married former hedgehogs.

The range of these stories and poems demonstrates the complex, sometimes contradictory, always fascinating ways that the work of women writers reflected the world around them, in this case through the lens of the fantastic. These narratives of ghosts and vampires, changelings and witches, tell us as much about the issues and concerns of the fin-de-siècle as more realistic works or even historical accounts. At the same time, they celebrate the power of the imagination to liberate and transform—to take us away to Orchards of the Moon that are also the very real gardens in which we labor to bring a new world into being.

AN EGYPTIAN CIGARETTE

KATE CHOPIN

My friend, the Architect, who is something of a traveler, was showing us various curios which he had gathered during a visit to the Orient. "Here is something for you," he said, picking up a small box and turning it over in his hand. "You are a cigarette-smoker; take this home with you. It was given to me in Cairo by a species of fakir,[1] who fancied I had done him a good turn."

The box was covered with glazed, yellow paper, so skill-fully gummed as to appear to be all one piece. It bore no label, no stamp—nothing to indicate its contents.

"How do you know they are cigarettes?" I asked, taking the box and turning it stupidly around as one turns a sealed letter and speculates before opening it.

---

1 The term is usually used for a Muslim ascetic or holy man, although in the nineteenth century it could also connote a street seller or beggar. It comes from the Arabic *faqīr*, meaning "poor man."

"I only know what he told me," replied the Architect, "but it is easy enough to determine the question of his integrity." He handed me a sharp, pointed paper-cutter, and with it I opened the lid as carefully as possible.

The box contained six cigarettes, evidently hand-made. The wrappers were of pale-yellow paper, and the tobacco was almost the same color. It was of finer cut than the Turkish or ordinary Egyptian, and threads of it stuck out at either end.

"Will you try one now, Madam?" asked the Architect, offering to strike a match.

"Not now and not here," I replied, "after the coffee, if you will permit me to slip into your smoking-den. Some of the women here detest the odor of cigarettes."

The smoking-room lay at the end of a short, curved passage. Its appointments were exclusively oriental. A broad, low window opened out upon a balcony that overhung the garden. From the divan upon which I reclined, only the swaying tree-tops could be seen. The maple leaves glistened in the afternoon sun. Beside the divan was a low stand which contained the complete paraphernalia of a smoker. I was feeling quite comfortable, and congratulated myself upon having escaped for a while the incessant chatter of the women that reached me faintly.

I took a cigarette and lit it, placing the box upon the stand just as the tiny clock, which was there, chimed in silvery strokes the hour of five.

I took one long inspiration of the Egyptian cigarette. The grey-green smoke arose in a small puffy column that spread and broadened, that seemed to fill the room. I could see the maple leaves dimly, as if they were veiled in a shimmer of moonlight.

A subtle, disturbing current passed through my whole body and went to my head like the fumes of disturbing wine. I took another deep inhalation of the cigarette.

"Ah! the sand has blistered my cheek! I have lain here all day with my face in the sand. Tonight, when the everlasting stars are burning, I shall drag myself to the river."

He will never come back.

Thus far I followed him; with flying feet; with stumbling feet; with hands and knees, crawling; and outstretched arms, and here I have fallen in the sand.

The sand has blistered my cheek; it has blistered all my body, and the sun is crushing me with hot torture. There is shade beneath yonder cluster of palms.

I shall stay here in the sand till the hour and the night comes.

I laughed at the oracles and scoffed at the stars when they told that after the rapture of life I would open my arms inviting death, and the waters would envelop me.

Oh! how the sand blisters my cheek! and I have no tears to quench the fire. The river is cool and the night is not far distant.

I turned from the gods and said: "There is but one; Bardja is my god." That was when I decked myself with lilies and wove flowers into a garland and held him close in the frail, sweet fetters.

He will never come back. He turned upon his camel as he rode away. He turned and looked at me crouching here and laughed, showing his gleaming white teeth.

Whenever he kissed me and went away he always came back again. Whenever he flamed with fierce anger and left me

with stinging words, he always came back. But today he neither kissed me nor was he angry. He only said:

"Oh! I am tired of fetters, and kisses, and you. I am going away. You will never see me again. I am going to the great city where men swarm like bees. I am going beyond, where the monster stones are rising heavenward in a monument for the unborn ages. Oh! I am tired. You will see me no more."

And he rode away on his camel. He smiled and showed his cruel white teeth as he turned to look at me crouching here.

How slow the hours drag! It seems to me that I have lain here for days in the sand, feeding upon despair. Despair is bitter and it nourishes resolve.

I hear the wings of a bird flapping above my head, flying low, in circles.

The sun is gone.

The sand has crept between my lips and teeth and under my parched tongue.

If I raise my head, perhaps I shall see the evening star.

Oh! the pain in my arms and legs! My body is sore and bruised as if broken. Why can I not rise and run as I did this morning? Why must I drag myself thus like a wounded serpent, twisting and writhing?

The river is near at hand. I hear it—I see it—Oh! the sand! Oh! the shine! How cool! how cold!

The water! the water! In my eyes, my ears, my throat! It strangles me! Help! will the gods not help me?

Oh! the sweet rapture of rest! There is music in the Temple. And here is fruit to taste. Bardja came with the music—The moon shines and the breeze is soft—A garland of flowers—let us go into the King's garden and look at the blue lily, Bardja.

The maple leaves looked as if a silvery shimmer enveloped them. The grey-green smoke no longer filled the room. I could hardly lift the lids of my eyes. The weight of centuries seemed to suffocate my soul that struggled to escape, to free itself and breathe.

I had tasted the depths of human despair.

The little clock upon the stand pointed to a quarter past five. The cigarettes still reposed in the yellow box. Only the stub of the one I had smoked remained. I had laid it in the ashtray.

As I looked at the cigarettes in their pale wrappers, I wondered what other visions they might hold for me; what might I not find in their mystic fumes? Perhaps a vision of celestial peace; a dream of hopes fulfilled; a taste of rapture, such as had not entered into my mind to conceive.

I took the cigarettes and crumpled them between my hands. I walked to the window and spread my palms wide. The light breeze caught up the golden threads and bore them writhing and dancing far out among the maple leaves.

My friend, the Architect, lifted the curtain and entered, bringing me a second cup of coffee.

"How pale you are!" he exclaimed, solicitously. "Are you not feeling well?"

"A little the worse for a dream," I told him.

Two poems by
Lizette Woodworth Reese

THE SINGER

With spices, wines, and silken stuffs,
    The stout ship sailèd down,
And with the ship the singer came
    Unto the old sea town.

"Peace to ye!" quoth the sailor folk,
    "A month and more have we
Been listening to his songs. Ah, God!
    None sings so sweet as he."

Up from the wharves the salt wind blew,
    And filled the steep highway;
Seven slender plum trees caught the sun
    Within a courtyard gray.

Out came the daughter of the king;
    Oh, very fair was she!
She was the whitest bough a-grow,
    So fair, so fair was she!

The singer sang, "My love," he sang,
    "Is like a white plum-tree!"
Then silence fell on house and court;
    No other word sang he.

The king's daughter, when she was old,
    Sat in a broidered gown,
And spun the flax from her fair fields—
    Oh, it was sweet in town!

Seven plum-trees stood down in the court,
    Each one was white as milk;
The king's daughter rose softly there,
    Rustling her broidered silk.

"Oh, set the wheel away, my maids,
    And sing that song to me
The singer sang!" "My love," sang they,
    "Is like a white plum-tree!"

ALL HALLOWS NIGHT

Two things I did on Hallows Night:—
Made my house April-clear;
Left open wide my door
To the ghosts of the year.

Then one came in. Across the room
It stood up long and fair—
The ghost that was myself—
And gave me stare for stare.

LUELLA MILLER

MARY WILKINS FREEMAN

Close to the village street stood the one-story house in
which Luella Miller, who had an evil name in the village,
had dwelt. She had been dead for years, yet there were those in
the village who, in spite of the clearer light which comes on a
vantage-point from a long-past danger, half believed in the tale
which they had heard from their childhood. In their hearts,
although they scarcely would have owned it, was a survival of
the wild horror and frenzied fear of their ancestors who had
dwelt in the same age with Luella Miller. Young people even
would stare with a shudder at the old house as they passed, and
children never played around it as was their wont around an
untenanted building. Not a window in the old Miller house was
broken: the panes reflected the morning sunlight in patches of
emerald and blue, and the latch of the sagging front door was
never lifted, although no bolt secured it. Since Luella Miller
had been carried out of it, the house had had no tenant except

one friendless old soul who had no choice between that and the far-off shelter of the open sky. This old woman, who had survived her kindred and friends, lived in the house one week, then one morning no smoke came out of the chimney, and a body of neighbours, a score strong, entered and found her dead in her bed. There were dark whispers as to the cause of her death, and there were those who testified to an expression of fear so exalted that it showed forth the state of the departing soul upon the dead face. The old woman had been hale and hearty when she entered the house, and in seven days she was dead; it seemed that she had fallen a victim to some uncanny power. The minister talked in the pulpit with covert severity against the sin of superstition; still the belief prevailed. Not a soul in the village but would have chosen the almshouse rather than that dwelling. No vagrant, if he heard the tale, would seek shelter beneath that old roof, unhallowed by nearly half a century of superstitious fear.

There was only one person in the village who had actually known Luella Miller. That person was a woman well over eighty, but a marvel of vitality and unextinct youth. Straight as an arrow, with the spring of one recently let loose from the bow of life, she moved about the streets, and she always went to church, rain or shine. She had never married, and had lived alone for years in a house across the road from Luella Miller's.

This woman had none of the garrulousness of age, but never in all her life had she ever held her tongue for any will save her own, and she never spared the truth when she essayed to present it. She it was who bore testimony to the life, evil, though possibly wittingly or designedly so, of Luella Miller, and to her personal appearance. When this old woman spoke—and she had the gift of description, although her thoughts were clothed in the rude vernacular of her native village—one could seem to see Luella Miller as she had really looked. According to this woman, Lydia Anderson by name, Luella Miller had been a beauty of a type rather unusual in New England. She had been a slight, pliant sort of creature, as ready with a strong yielding to fate and as unbreakable as a willow. She had glimmering lengths of straight, fair hair, which she wore softly looped round a long, lovely face. She had blue eyes full of soft pleading, little slender, clinging hands, and a wonderful grace of motion and attitude.

"Luella Miller used to sit in a way nobody else could if they sat up and studied a week of Sundays," said Lydia Anderson, "and it was a sight to see her walk. If one of them willows over there on the edge of the brook could start up and get its roots free of the ground, and move off, it would go just the way Luella Miller used to. She had a green shot silk she used to wear, too, and a hat with green ribbon streamers, and a lace veil blowing across her face and out sideways, and a green ribbon flyin' from her waist. That was what she came out bride in when she married Erastus Miller. Her name before she was married was Hill. There was always a sight of "l's" in her name, married or single. Erastus Miller was good lookin', too, better lookin' than Luella. Sometimes I used to think that Luella wa'n't so handsome after all. Erastus just about worshiped her. I used to know him pretty well. He lived next door to me, and we went to school together. Folks used to say he was waitin' on me, but he wa'n't. I never thought he was except once or twice when he said things that some girls might have suspected meant somethin'. That was before Luella came here to teach the district school. It was funny how she came to get it, for folks said she hadn't any education, and that one of the big girls, Lottie Henderson, used to do all the teachin' for her, while she sat back and did embroidery work on a cambric pocket-handkerchief. Lottie Henderson was a real smart girl, a splendid scholar, and she just set her eyes by Luella, as all the girls did. Lottie would have made a real smart woman, but she died when Luella had been here about a year—just faded away and died: nobody knew what ailed her. She dragged herself to that schoolhouse and helped Luella teach till the very last minute. The committee all knew how Luella didn't do much of the work herself, but they winked at it. It wa'n't long after Lottie died that Erastus married her. I always thought he hurried it up because she wa'n't fit to teach. One of the big boys used to help her after Lottie died, but he hadn't much government, and the school didn't do very well, and Luella might have had to give it up, for the committee couldn't have shut their eyes to things much longer. The boy that helped her was a real honest, innocent sort of fellow, and he was a good scholar, too. Folks said he overstudied, and that was the reason he was took crazy the year after Luella married, but I don't know. And I don't know what made Erastus Miller go into consumption of the blood the year after he was married: consumption wa'n't in his family. He just grew weaker and weaker, and went almost bent double when he tried to wait on Luella, and he spoke feeble, like an old man. He worked terrible hard till the last trying to save up a little to leave Luella. I've seen him out in the worst storms on a wood-sled—he used to cut and sell wood—and he was hunched up on top lookin' more dead than alive. Once I couldn't stand it: I went over and helped him pitch some wood on the cart—I was always strong in my arms. I wouldn't stop for all he told me to, and I guess he was glad enough for the help. That was only a week before he died. He fell on the kitchen floor while he was gettin' breakfast. He always got the breakfast and let Luella lay abed. He did all the sweepin' and the washin' and the ironin' and most of the cookin'. He couldn't bear to have Luella lift her finger, and she let him do for her. She lived like a queen for all the work she did. She didn't even do her sewin'. She said it made her shoulder ache to sew, and poor Erastus's sister Lily used to do all her sewin'. She wa'n't able to, either; she was never strong in her back, but she did it beautifully. She had to, to suit Luella, she was so dreadful particular. I never saw anythin' like the fagottin' and hemstitchin' that Lily Miller did for Luella. She made all Luella's weddin' outfit, and that green silk dress, after Maria Babbit cut it. Maria she cut it for nothin', and she did a lot more cuttin' and fittin' for nothin' for Luella, too. Lily Miller went to live with Luella after Erastus died. She gave up her home, though she was real attached to it and wa'n't a mite afraid to stay alone. She rented it and she went to live with Luella right away after the funeral."

Then this old woman, Lydia Anderson, who remembered Luella Miller, would go on to relate the story of Lily Miller. It seemed that on the removal of Lily Miller to the house of her dead brother, to live with his widow, the village people first began to talk. This Lily Miller had been hardly past her first youth, and a most robust and blooming woman, rosy-cheeked, with curls of strong, black hair overshadowing round, candid temples and bright dark eyes. It was not six months after she had taken up her residence with her sister-in-law that her rosy colour faded and her pretty curves became wan hollows.

White shadows began to show in the black rings of her hair, and the light died out of her eyes, her features sharpened, and there were pathetic lines at her mouth, which yet wore always an expression of utter sweetness and even happiness. She was devoted to her sister; there was no doubt that she loved her with her whole heart, and was perfectly content in her service. It was her sole anxiety lest she should die and leave her alone.

"The way Lily Miller used to talk about Luella was enough to make you mad and enough to make you cry," said Lydia Anderson. "I've been in there sometimes toward the last when she was too feeble to cook and carried her some blanc-mange or custard—somethin' I thought she might relish, and she'd thank me, and when I asked her how she was, say she felt better than she did yesterday, and asked me if I didn't think she looked better, dreadful pitiful, and say poor Luella had an awful time takin' care of her and doin' the work—she wa'n't strong enough to do anythin'—when all the time Luella wa'n't liftin' her finger and poor Lily didn't get any care except what the neighbours gave her, and Luella eat up everythin' that was carried in for Lily. I had it real straight that she did. Luella used to just sit and cry and do nothin'. She did act real fond of Lily, and she pined away considerable, too. There was those that thought she'd go into a decline herself. But after Lily died, her Aunt Abby Mixter came, and then Luella picked up and grew as fat and rosy as ever. But poor Aunt Abby begun to droop just the way Lily had, and I guess somebody wrote to her married daughter, Mrs. Sam Abbot, who lived in Barre, for she wrote her mother that she must leave right away and come and make her a visit, but Aunt Abby wouldn't go. I can see her now. She was a real good-lookin' woman, tall and large, with a big, square face and a high forehead that looked of itself kind of benevolent and good. She just tended out on Luella as if she had been a baby, and when her married daughter sent for her she wouldn't stir one inch. She'd always thought a lot of her daughter, too, but she said Luella needed her and her married daughter didn't. Her daughter kept writin' and writin', but it didn't do any good. Finally she came, and when she saw how bad her mother looked, she broke down and cried and all but went on her knees to have her come away. She spoke her mind out to Luella, too. She told her that she'd killed her husband and everybody that had anythin' to do with her, and she'd thank her to leave her mother alone. Luella went into hysterics, and Aunt Abby was so frightened that she called me after her daughter went. Mrs. Sam Abbot she went away fairly cryin' out loud in the buggy, the neighbours heard her, and well she might, for she never saw her mother again alive. I went in that night when Aunt Abby called for me, standin' in the door with her little green-checked shawl over her head. I can see her now. 'Do come over here, Miss Anderson,' she sung out, kind of gasping for breath. I didn't stop for anythin'. I put over as fast as I could, and when I got there, there was Luella laughin' and cryin' all together, and Aunt Abby trying to hush her, and all the time she herself was white as a sheet and shakin' so she could hardly stand. 'For the land sakes, Mrs. Mixter,' says I, 'you look worse than she does. You ain't fit to be up out of your bed.'

"'Oh, there ain't anythin' the matter with me,' says she. Then she went on talkin' to Luella. 'There, there, don't, don't, poor little lamb,' says she. 'Aunt Abby is here. She ain't goin' away and leave you. Don't, poor little lamb.'

"'Do leave her with me, Mrs. Mixter, and you get back to

bed,' says I, for Aunt Abby had been layin' down considerable lately, though somehow she contrived to do the work.

"'I'm well enough,' says she. 'Don't you think she had better have the doctor, Miss Anderson?'

"'The doctor,' says I, 'I think *you* had better have the doctor. I think you need him much worse than some folks I could mention.' And I looked right straight at Luella Miller laughin' and cryin' and goin' on as if she was the centre of all creation. All the time she was actin' so—seemed as if she was too sick to sense anythin'—she was keepin' a sharp lookout as to how we took it out of the corner of one eye. I see her. You could never cheat me about Luella Miller. Finally I got real mad and I run home and I got a bottle of valerian I had, and I poured some boilin' hot water on a handful of catnip, and I mixed up that catnip tea with most half a wineglass of valerian, and I went with it over to Luella's. I marched right up to Luella, a-holdin' out of that cup, all smokin'. 'Now,' says I, 'Luella Miller, *you swaller this!*'

"'What is—what is it, oh, what is it?' she sort of screeches out. Then she goes off a-laughin' enough to kill.

"'Poor lamb, poor little lamb,' says Aunt Abby, standin' over her, all kind of tottery, and tryin' to bathe her head with camphor.

"'*You swaller this right down,*' says I. And I didn't waste any ceremony. I just took hold of Luella Miller's chin and I tipped her head back, and I caught her mouth open with laughin', and I clapped that cup to her lips, and I fairly hollered at her: 'Swaller, swaller, swaller!' and she gulped it right down. She had to, and I guess it did her good. Anyhow, she stopped cryin' and laughin' and let me put her to bed, and she went to sleep like a baby inside of half an hour. That was more than poor Aunt Abby did. She lay awake all that night and I stayed with her, though she tried not to have me; said she wa'n't sick enough for watchers. But I stayed, and I made some good cornmeal gruel and I fed her a teaspoon every little while all night long. It seemed to me as if she was jest dyin' from bein' all wore out. In the mornin' as soon as it was light I run over to the Bisbees and sent Johnny Bisbee for the doctor. I told him to tell the doctor to hurry, and he come pretty quick. Poor Aunt Abby didn't seem to know much of anythin' when he got there. You couldn't hardly tell she breathed, she was so used up. When the doctor had gone, Luella came into the room lookin' like a baby in her ruffled nightgown. I can see her now. Her eyes were as blue and her face all pink and white like a blossom, and she looked at Aunt Abby in the bed sort of innocent and surprised. 'Why,' says she, 'Aunt Abby ain't got up yet?'

"'No, she ain't,' says I, pretty short.

"'I thought I didn't smell the coffee,' says Luella.

"'Coffee,' says I. 'I guess if you have coffee this mornin' you'll make it yourself.'

"'I never made the coffee in all my life,' says she, dreadful astonished. 'Erastus always made the coffee as long as he lived, and then Lily she made it, and then Aunt Abby made it. I don't believe I *can* make the coffee, Miss Anderson.'

"'You can make it or go without, jest as you please,' says I.

"'Ain't Aunt Abby goin' to get up?' says she.

"'I guess she won't get up,' says I, 'sick as she is.' I was gettin' madder and madder. There was somethin' about that little pink-and-white thing standin' there and talkin' about coffee, when she had killed so many better folks than she was, and had jest killed another, that made me feel 'most as if I wished somebody would up and kill her before she had a chance to do any more harm.

"'Is Aunt Abby sick?' says Luella, as if she was sort of aggrieved and injured.

"'Yes,' says I, 'she's sick, and she's goin' to die, and then you'll be left alone, and you'll have to do for yourself and wait on yourself, or do without things.' I don't know but I was sort of hard, but it was the truth, and if I was any harder than Luella Miller had been I'll give up. I ain't never been sorry that I said it. Well, Luella, she up and had hysterics again at that, and I jest let her have 'em. All I did was to bundle her into the room on the other side of the entry where Aunt Abby couldn't hear her, if she wa'n't past it—I don't know but she was—and set her down hard in a chair and told her not to come back into the other room, and she minded. She had her hysterics in there till she got tired. When she found out that nobody was comin' to coddle her and do for her she stopped. At least I suppose she did. I had all I could do with poor Aunt Abby tryin' to keep the breath of life in her. The doctor had told me that she was dreadful low, and give me some very strong medicine to give to her in drops real often, and told me real particular about the nourishment. Well, I did as he told me real faithful till she wa'n't able to swaller any longer. Then I had her daughter sent for. I had begun to realize that she wouldn't last any time at all. I hadn't realized it before, though I spoke to Luella the way I did. The doctor he came, and Mrs. Sam Abbot, but when she got there it was too late; her mother was dead. Aunt Abby's daughter just give one look at her mother layin' there, then she turned sort of sharp and sudden and looked at me.

"'Where is she?' says she, and I knew she meant Luella.

"'She's out in the kitchen,' says I. 'She's too nervous to see folks die. She's afraid it will make her sick.'

"The Doctor he speaks up then. He was a young man. Old Doctor Park had died the year before, and this was a young fellow just out of college. 'Mrs. Miller is not strong,' says he, kind of severe, 'and she is quite right in not agitating herself.'

"'You are another, young man; she's got her pretty claw on you,' thinks I, but I didn't say anythin' to him. I just said over to Mrs. Sam Abbot that Luella was in the kitchen, and Mrs. Sam Abbot she went out there, and I went, too, and I never heard anythin' like the way she talked to Luella Miller. I felt pretty hard to Luella myself, but this was more than I ever would have dared to say. Luella she was too scared to go into hysterics. She jest flopped. She seemed to jest shrink away to nothin' in that kitchen chair, with Mrs. Sam Abbot standin' over her and talkin' and tellin' her the truth. I guess the truth was most too much for her and no mistake, because Luella presently actually did faint away, and there wa'n't any sham about it, the way I always suspected there was about them hysterics. She fainted dead away and we had to lay her flat on the floor, and the Doctor he came runnin' out and he said somethin' about a weak heart dreadful fierce to Mrs. Sam Abbot, but she wa'n't a mite scared. She faced him jest as white as even Luella was layin' there lookin' like death and the Doctor feelin' of her pulse.

"'Weak heart,' says she, 'weak heart; weak fiddlesticks! There ain't nothin' weak about that woman. She's got strength enough to hang onto other folks till she kills 'em. Weak? It was my poor mother that was weak: this woman killed her as sure as if she had taken a knife to her.'

"But the Doctor he didn't pay much attention. He was bendin' over Luella layin' there with her yellow hair all streamin' and her pretty pink-and-white face all pale, and her blue eyes like stars gone out, and he was holdin' onto her hand and smoothin' her forehead, and tellin' me to get the brandy in Aunt Abby's room, and I was sure as I wanted to be that Luella had got somebody else to hang onto, now Aunt Abby was gone, and I thought of poor Erastus Miller, and I sort of pitied the poor young Doctor, led away by a pretty face, and I made up my mind I'd see what I could do.

"I waited till Aunt Abby had been dead and buried about a month, and the Doctor was goin' to see Luella steady and folks were beginnin' to talk; then one evenin', when I knew the Doctor had been called out of town and wouldn't be round, I went over to Luella's. I found her all dressed up in a blue muslin with white polka dots on it, and her hair curled jest as pretty, and there wa'n't a young girl in the place could compare with her. There was somethin' about Luella Miller seemed to draw the heart right out of you, but she didn't draw it out of *me*. She was settin' rocking in the chair by her sittin'-room window, and Maria Brown had gone home. Maria Brown had been in to help her, or rather to do the work, for Luella wa'n't helped when she didn't do anythin'. Maria Brown was real capable and she didn't have any ties; she wa'n't married, and lived alone, so she'd offered. I couldn't see why she should do the work any more than Luella; she wa'n't any too strong; but she seemed to think she could and Luella seemed to think so, too, so she went over and did all the work—washed, and ironed, and baked, while Luella sat and rocked. Maria didn't live long afterward. She began to fade away just the same fashion the others had. Well, she was warned, but she acted real mad when folks said anythin': said Luella was a poor, abused woman, too delicate to help herself, and they'd ought to be ashamed, and if she died helpin' them that couldn't help themselves she would—and she did.

"'I s'pose Maria has gone home,' says I to Luella, when I had gone in and sat down opposite her.

"'Yes, Maria went half an hour ago, after she had got supper and washed the dishes,' says Luella, in her pretty way.

"'I suppose she has got a lot of work to do in her own house tonight,' says I, kind of bitter, but that was all thrown away on Luella Miller. It seemed to her right that other folks that wa'n't any better able than she was herself should wait on her, and she couldn't get it through her head that anybody should think it *wa'n't* right.

"'Yes,' says Luella, real sweet and pretty, 'yes, she said she had to do her washin' tonight. She has let it go for a fortnight along of comin' over here.'

"'Why don't she stay home and do her washin' instead of comin' over here and doin' *your* work, when you are just as well able, and enough sight more so, than she is to do it?' says I.

"Then Luella she looked at me like a baby who has a rattle shook at it. She sort of laughed as innocent as you please. 'Oh, I can't do the work myself, Miss Anderson,' says she. 'I never did. Maria *has* to do it.'

"Then I spoke out: 'Has to do it!' says I. 'Has to do it!' She don't have to do it, either. Maria Brown has her own home and enough to live on. She ain't beholden to you to come over here and slave for you and kill herself.'

"Luella she jest set and stared at me for all the world like a doll-baby that was so abused that it was comin' to life.

"'Yes,' says I, 'she's killin' herself. She's goin' to die just the way Erastus did, and Lily, and your Aunt Abby. You're killin' her jest as you did them. I don't know what there is about you, but you seem to bring a curse,' says I. 'You kill everybody that is fool enough to care anythin' about you and do for you.'

"She stared at me and she was pretty pale.

"'And Maria ain't the only one you're goin' to kill,' says I. 'You're goin' to kill Doctor Malcom before you're done with him.'

"Then a red colour came flamin' all over her face. 'I ain't goin' to kill him, either,' says she, and she begun to cry.

"'Yes, you *be!*' says I. Then I spoke as I had never spoke before. You see, I felt it on account of Erastus. I told her that she hadn't any business to think of another man after she'd been married to one that had died for her: that she was a dreadful woman; and she was, that's true enough, but sometimes I have wondered lately if she knew it—if she wa'n't like a baby with scissors in its hand cuttin' everybody without knowin' what it was doin'.

"Luella she kept gettin' paler and paler, and she never took her eyes off my face. There was somethin' awful about the way she looked at me and never spoke one word. After awhile I quit talkin' and I went home. I watched that night, but her lamp went out before nine o'clock, and when Doctor Malcom came drivin' past and sort of slowed up he see there wa'n't any light and he drove along. I saw her sort of shy out of meetin' the next

Sunday, too, so he shouldn't go home with her, and I begun to think mebbe she did have some conscience after all. It was only a week after that that Maria Brown died—sort of sudden at the last, though everybody had seen it was comin'. Well, then there was a good deal of feelin' and pretty dark whispers. Folks said the days of witchcraft had come again, and they were pretty shy of Luella. She acted sort of offish to the Doctor and he didn't go there, and there wa'n't anybody to do anythin' for her. I don't know how she *did* get along. I wouldn't go in there and offer to help her—not because I was afraid of dyin' like the rest, but I thought she was just as well able to do her own work as I was to do it for her, and I thought it was about time that she did it and stopped killin' other folks. But it wa'n't very long before folks began to say that Luella herself was goin' into a decline jest the way her husband, and Lily, and Aunt Abby and the others had, and I saw myself that she looked pretty bad. I used to see her goin' past from the store with a bundle as if she could hardly crawl, but I remembered how Erastus used to wait and 'tend when he couldn't hardly put one foot before the other, and I didn't go out to help her.

"But at last one afternoon I saw the Doctor come drivin' up like mad with his medicine chest, and Mrs. Babbit came in after supper and said that Luella was real sick.

"'I'd offer to go in and nurse her,' says she, 'but I've got my children to consider, and mebbe it ain't true what they say, but it's queer how many folks that have done for her have died.'

"I didn't say anythin', but I considered how she had been Erastus's wife and how he had set his eyes by her, and I made up my mind to go in the next mornin', unless she was better, and see what I could do; but the next mornin' I see her at the window, and pretty soon she came steppin' out as spry as you please, and a little while afterward Mrs. Babbit came in and told me that the Doctor had got a girl from out of town, a Sarah Jones, to come there, and she said she was pretty sure that the Doctor was goin' to marry Luella.

"I saw him kiss her in the door that night myself, and I knew it was true. The woman came that afternoon, and the way she flew around was a caution. I don't believe Luella had swept since Maria died. She swept and dusted, and washed and ironed; wet clothes and dusters and carpets were flyin' over there all day, and every time Luella set her foot out when the Doctor wa'n't there there was that Sarah Jones helpin' of her up and down the steps, as if she hadn't learned to walk.

"Well, everybody knew that Luella and the Doctor were goin' to be married, but it wa'n't long before they began to talk about his lookin' so poorly, jest as they had about the others; and they talked about Sarah Jones, too.

"Well, the Doctor did die, and he wanted to be married first, so as to leave what little he had to Luella, but he died before the minister could get there, and Sarah Jones died a week afterward.

"Well, that wound up everything for Luella Miller. Not another soul in the whole town would lift a finger for her. There got to be a sort of panic. Then she began to droop in good earnest. She used to have to go to the store herself, for Mrs. Babbit was afraid to let Tommy go for her, and I've seen her goin' past and stoppin' every two or three steps to rest. Well, I stood it as long as I could, but one day I see her comin' with her arms full and stoppin' to lean against the Babbit fence, and

I run out and took her bundles and carried them to her house. Then I went home and never spoke one word to her though she called after me dreadful kind of pitiful. Well, that night I was taken sick with a chill, and I was sick as I wanted to be for two weeks. Mrs. Babbit had seen me run out to help Luella and she came in and told me I was goin' to die on account of it. I didn't know whether I was or not, but I considered I had done right by Erastus's wife.

"That last two weeks Luella she had a dreadful hard time, I guess. She was pretty sick, and as near as I could make out nobody dared go near her. I don't know as she was really needin' anythin' very much, for there was enough to eat in her house and it was warm weather, and she made out to cook a little flour gruel every day, I know, but I guess she had a hard time, she that had been so petted and done for all her life.

"When I got so I could go out, I went over there one morning. Mrs. Babbit had just come in to say she hadn't seen any smoke and she didn't know but it was somebody's duty to go in, but she couldn't help thinkin' of her children, and I got right up, though I hadn't been out of the house for two weeks, and I went in there, and Luella she was layin' on the bed, and she was dyin'.

"She lasted all that day and into the night. But I sat there after the new doctor had gone away. Nobody else dared to go there. It was about midnight that I left her for a minute to run home and get some medicine I had been takin', for I begun to feel rather bad.

"It was a full moon that night, and just as I started out of my door to cross the street back to Luella's, I stopped short, for I saw something."

Lydia Anderson at this juncture always said with a certain

defiance that she did not expect to be believed, and then proceeded in a hushed voice:

"I saw what I saw, and I know I saw it, and I will swear on my death bed that I saw it. I saw Luella Miller and Erastus Miller, and Lily, and Aunt Abby, and Maria, and the Doctor, and Sarah, all goin' out of her door, and all but Luella shone white in the moonlight, and they were all helpin' her along till she seemed to fairly fly in the midst of them. Then it all disappeared. I stood a minute with my heart poundin', then I went over there. I thought of goin' for Mrs. Babbit, but I thought she'd be afraid. So I went alone, though I knew what had happened. Luella was layin' real peaceful, dead on her bed."

This was the story that the old woman, Lydia Anderson, told, but the sequel was told by the people who survived her, and this is the tale which has become folklore in the village.

Lydia Anderson died when she was eighty-seven. She had continued wonderfully hale and hearty for one of her years until about two weeks before her death.

One bright moonlight evening she was sitting beside a window in her parlour when she made a sudden exclamation, and was out of the house and across the street before the neighbour who was taking care of her could stop her. She followed as fast as possible and found Lydia Anderson stretched on the ground before the door of Luella Miller's deserted house, and she was quite dead.

The next night there was a red gleam of fire athwart the moonlight and the old house of Luella Miller was burned to the ground. Nothing is now left of it except a few old cellar stones and a lilac bush, and in summer a helpless trail of morning glories among the weeds, which might be considered emblematic of Luella herself.

Three poems by Mary Coleridge

THE WITCH

I have walked a great while over the snow,
And I am not tall nor strong.
My clothes are wet, and my teeth are set,
And the way was hard and long.
I have wandered over the fruitful earth,
But I never came here before.
Oh, lift me over the threshold, and let me in at the door!

The cutting wind is a cruel foe.
I dare not stand in the blast.
My hands are stone, and my voice a groan,
And the worst of death is past.
I am but a little maiden still,
My little white feet are sore.
Oh, lift me over the threshold, and let me in at the door!

Her voice was the voice that women have,
Who plead for their heart's desire.
She came—she came—and the quivering flame
Sank and died in the fire.
It never was lit again on my hearth
Since I hurried across the floor,
To lift her over the threshold, and let her in at the door.

THE WHITE WOMEN

Where dwell the lovely, wild white women folk,
      Mortal to man?
They never bowed their necks beneath the yoke,
They dwelt alone when the first morning broke
      And Time began.

Taller are they than man, and very fair,
      Their cheeks are pale,
At sight of them the tiger in his lair,
The falcon hanging in the azure air,
      The eagles quail.

The deadly shafts their nervous hands let fly
      Are stronger than our strongest—in their form
Larger, more beauteous, carved amazingly,
And when they fight, the wild white women cry
      The war-cry of the storm.

Their words are not as ours. If man might go
      Among the waves of Ocean when they break
And hear them—hear the language of the snow
Falling on torrents—he might also know
      The tongue they speak.

Pure are they as the light; they never sinned,
      But when the rays of the eternal fire
Kindle the West, their tresses they unbind

And fling their girdles to the Western wind,
    Swept by desire.

Lo, maidens to the maidens then are born,
    Strong children of the maidens and the breeze,
Dreams are not—in the glory of the morn,
Seen through the gates of ivory and horn—[1]
    More fair than these.

And none may find their dwelling. In the shade
    Primeval of the forest oaks they hide.
One of our race, lost in an awful glade,
Saw with his human eyes a wild white maid,
    And gazing, died.

---

1 In classical Greek literature, these are the gates through which dreams come: through the gate of horn come prophetic dreams, while through the gate of ivory come dreams that deceive the dreamer. Penelope refers to these gates in *The Odyssey*.

THE OTHER SIDE OF A MIRROR

I sat before my glass one day,
    And conjured up a vision bare,
Unlike the aspects glad and gay,
    That erst were found reflected there—
The vision of a woman, wild
    With more than womanly despair.

Her hair stood back on either side
    A face bereft of loveliness.
It had no envy now to hide
    What once no man on earth could guess.
It formed the thorny aureole
    Of hard unsanctified distress.

Her lips were open—not a sound
    Came through the parted lines of red.
Whate'er it was, the hideous wound
    In silence and in secret bled.
No sigh relieved her speechless woe,
    She had no voice to speak her dread.

And in her lurid eyes there shone
    The dying flame of life's desire,
Made mad because its hope was gone,
    And kindled at the leaping fire
Of jealousy, and fierce revenge,
    And strength that could not change nor tire.

Shade of a shadow in the glass,
    O set the crystal surface free!
Pass—as the fairer visions pass—
    Nor ever more return, to be
The ghost of a distracted hour,
    That heard me whisper, "I am she!"

DIONEA

VERNON LEE (VIOLET PAGET)

*From the Letters of Doctor Alessandro De Rosis to the Lady
Evelyn Savelli, Princess of Sabina.*

MONTEMIRO LIGURE, *JUNE 29, 1873.*

I take immediate advantage of the generous offer of your
Excellency (allow an old Republican who has held you on his
knees to address you by that title sometimes, 'tis so appropriate)
to help our poor people. I never expected to come a-begging
so soon. For the olive crop has been unusually plenteous. We
semi-Genoese don't pick the olives unripe, like our Tuscan
neighbors, but let them grow big and black, when the young fellows go into the trees with long reeds and shake them down on
the grass for the women to collect—a pretty sight which your
Excellency must see some day: the grey trees with the brown,
barefoot lads craning, balanced in the branches, and the turquoise sea as background just beneath.... That sea of ours—it is

all along of it that I wish to ask for money. Looking up from my desk, I see the sea through the window, deep below and beyond the olive woods, bluish-green in the sunshine and veined with violet under the cloud-bars, like one of your Ravenna mosaics spread out as pavement for the world: a wicked sea, wicked in its loveliness, wickeder than your grey northern ones, and from which must have arisen in times gone by (when Phoenicians or Greeks built the temples at Lerici and Porto Venere) a baleful goddess of beauty, a Venus Verticordia,[1] but in the bad sense of the word, overwhelming men's lives in sudden darkness like that squall of last week.

To come to the point. I want you, dear Lady Evelyn, to promise me some money, a great deal of money, as much as would buy you a little mannish cloth frock—for the complete bringing-up, until years of discretion, of a young stranger whom the sea has laid upon our shore. Our people, kind as they are, are very poor, and overburdened with children; besides, they have got a certain repugnance for this poor little waif, cast up by that dreadful storm, and who is doubtless a heathen, for she had no little crosses or scapulars on, like proper Christian children. So, being unable to get any of our women to adopt the child, and having an old bachelor's terror of my housekeeper, I have bethought me of certain nuns, holy women, who teach little girls to say their prayers and make lace close by here; and of your dear Excellency to pay for the whole business.

Poor little brown mite! She was picked up after the storm (such a set-out of ship-models and votive candles as that storm

---

1 One of the epithets of the goddess Venus ("Changer of Hearts"), as well as the title of a painting by Dante Gabriel Rossetti. Vernon Lee, who was also an art critic influenced by the aesthetic theories of Walter Pater (1839–94), references works of art and artists throughout this story.

must have brought the Madonna at Porto Venere!) on a strip of sand between the rocks of our castle: the thing was really miraculous, for this coast is like a shark's jaw, and the bits of sand are tiny and far between. She was lashed to a plank, swaddled up close in outlandish garments; and when they brought her to me they thought she must certainly be dead: a little girl of four or five, decidedly pretty, and as brown as a berry, who, when she came to, shook her head to show she understood no kind of Italian, and jabbered some half-intelligible Eastern jabber, a few Greek words embedded in I know not what; the Superior of the College De Propaganda Fidē[2] would be puzzled to know. The child appears to be the only survivor from a ship which must have gone down in the great squall, and whose timbers have been strewing the bay for some days past; no one at Spezia or in any of our ports knows anything about her, but she was seen, apparently making for Porto Venere, by some of our sardine-fishers: a big, lumbering craft, with eyes painted on each side of the prow, which, as you know, is a peculiarity of Greek boats. She was sighted for the last time off the island of Palmaria, entering, with all sails spread, right into the thick of the storm-darkness. No bodies, strangely enough, have been washed ashore.

July 10.

I have received the money, dear Donna Evelina. There was tremendous excitement down at San Massimo when the carrier came in with a registered letter, and I was sent for, in presence

---

2 The College for the Propagation of the Faith was established in 1622 for the purpose of spreading Catholicism through missionary work.

of all the village authorities, to sign my name on the postal register.

The child has already been settled some days with the nuns; such dear little nuns (nuns always go straight to the heart of an old priest-hater and conspirator against the Pope, you know), dressed in brown robes and close, white caps, with an immense round straw-hat flapping behind their heads like a nimbus: they are called Sisters of the Stigmata, and have a convent and school at San Massimo, a little way inland, with an untidy garden full of lavender and cherry-trees. Your *protégée* has already half set the convent, the village, the Episcopal See, the Order of St. Francis, by the ears. First, because nobody could make out whether or not she had been christened. The question was a grave one, for it appears (as your uncle-in-law, the Cardinal, will tell you) that it is almost equally undesirable to be christened twice over as not to be christened at all. The first danger was finally decided upon as the less terrible; but the child, they say, had evidently been baptized before, and knew that the operation ought not to be repeated, for she kicked and plunged and yelled like twenty little devils, and positively would not let the holy water touch her. The Mother Superior, who always took for granted that the baptism had taken place before, says that the child was quite right, and that Heaven was trying to prevent a sacrilege; but the priest and the barber's wife, who had to hold her, think the occurrence fearful, and suspect the little girl of being a Protestant. Then the question of the name. Pinned to her clothes—striped Eastern things, and that kind of crinkled silk stuff they weave in Crete and Cyprus—was a piece of parchment, a scapular we thought at first, but which was found to contain only the name Διονεα—Dionea,[3] as they pronounce it here. The question was, Could such a name be fitly borne by a young lady at the Convent of the Stigmata? Half the population here have names as unchristian quite—Norma, Odoacer, Archimedes—my housemaid is called Themis—but Dionea seemed to scandalize every one, perhaps because these good folk had a mysterious instinct that the name is derived from Dione, one of the loves of Father Zeus, and mother of no less a lady than the goddess Venus. The child was very near being called Maria, although there are already twenty-three other Marias, Mariettas, Mariuccias, and so forth at the convent. But the sister-bookkeeper, who apparently detests monotony, bethought her to look out Dionea first in the Calendar, which proved useless; and then in a big vellum-bound book, printed at Venice in 1625, called *Flos Sanctorum, or Lives of the Saints, by Father Ribadeneira, S.J., with the addition of such Saints as have no assigned place in the Almanack, otherwise called the Movable or Extravagant Saints.* The zeal of Sister Anna Maddalena has been rewarded, for there, among the Extravagant Saints, sure enough, with a border of palm-branches and hour-glasses, stands the name of Saint Dionea, Virgin and Martyr, a lady of Antioch, put to death by the Emperor Decius. I know your Excellency's taste for historical information, so I forward this item. But I fear, dear Lady Evelyn, I fear that the heavenly patroness of your little sea-waif was a much more extravagant saint than that.

* * *

---

3 Another name for the Greek goddess Aphrodite (also the Roman goddess Venus), from her mother, the Titaness Dione. In the *Iliad*, Aphrodite is identified as the daughter of Dione and Zeus.

DECEMBER 21, 1879.

Many thanks, dear Donna Evelina, for the money for Dionea's schooling. Indeed, it was not wanted yet: the accomplishments of young ladies are taught at a very moderate rate at Montemirto: and as to clothes, which you mention, a pair of wooden clogs, with pretty red tips, costs sixty-five centimes, and ought to last three years, if the owner is careful to carry them on her head in a neat parcel when out walking, and to put them on again only on entering the village. The Mother Superior is greatly overcome by your Excellency's munificence towards the convent, and much perturbed at being unable to send you a specimen of your *protégée*'s skill, exemplified in an embroidered pocket-handker-chief or a pair of mittens; but the fact is that poor Dionea *has* no skill. "We will pray to the Madonna and St. Francis to make her more worthy," remarked the Superior. Perhaps, however, your Excellency, who is, I fear, but a Pagan woman (for all the Savelli Popes and St. Andrew Savelli's miracles), and insufficiently appreciative of embroidered pocket-handkerchiefs, will be quite as satisfied to hear that Dionea, instead of skill, has got the prettiest face of any little girl in Montemirto. She is tall, for her age (she is eleven) quite wonderfully well propor-tioned and extremely strong: of all the convent-full, she is the only one for whom I have never been called in. The features are very regular, the hair black, and despite all the good Sisters' efforts to keep it smooth like a Chinaman's, beautifully curly. I am glad she should be pretty, for she will more easily find a hus-band; and also because it seems fitting that your *protégée* should be beautiful. Unfortunately her character is not so satisfactory: she hates learning, sewing, washing up the dishes, all equally.

I am sorry to say she shows no natural piety. Her companions detest her, and the nuns, although they admit that she is not exactly naughty, seem to feel her as a dreadful thorn in the flesh. She spends hours and hours on the terrace overlooking the sea (her great desire, she confided to me, is to get to the sea—to get *back to the sea*, as she expressed it), and lying in the garden, under the big myrtle-bushes, and, in spring and summer, under the rose-hedge. The nuns say that rose-hedge and that myrtle-bush are growing a great deal too big, one would think from Dionea's lying under them; the fact, I suppose, has drawn attention to them. "That child makes all the useless weeds grow," remarked Sister Reparata. Another of Dionea's amusements is playing with pigeons. The number of pigeons she collects about her is quite amazing; you would never have thought that San Massimo or the neighboring hills contained as many. They flutter down like snowflakes, and strut and swell themselves out, and furl and unfurl their tails, and peck with little sharp movements of their silly, sensual heads and a little throb and gurgle in their throats, while Dionea lies stretched out full length in the sun, putting out her lips, which they come to kiss, and uttering strange, cooing sounds; or hopping about, flapping her arms slowly like wings, and raising her little head with much the same odd gesture as they;— 'tis a lovely sight, a thing fit for one of your painters, Burne Jones or Tadema,[4] with the myrtle-bushes all round, the bright, white-washed

4 Sir Edward Burne-Jones (1833–98) was an English painter and part of the Pre-Raphaelite movement, together with artists such as William Morris (1834–96) and Dante Gabriel Rossetti. He became famous for his romantic medievalism, typical of the Pre-Raphaelites. Sir Lawrence Alma-Tadema (1836–1912), originally a Dutch painter, settled in England and became known for his paintings of classical scenes, particularly from the Roman Empire.

convent walls behind, the white marble chapel steps (all steps are marble in this Carrara country) and the enamel blue sea through the ilex-branches beyond. But the good Sisters abominate these pigeons, who, it appears, are messy little creatures, and they complain that, were it not that the Reverend Director likes a pigeon in his pot on a holiday, they could not stand the bother of perpetually sweeping the chapel steps and the kitchen threshold all along of those dirty birds....

AUGUST 6, 1882.

Do not tempt me, dearest Excellency, with your invitations to Rome. I should not be happy there, and do but little honor to your friendship. My many years of exile, of wanderings in northern countries, have made me a little bit into a northern man: I cannot quite get on with my own fellow-countrymen, except with the good peasants and fishermen all round. Besides—forgive the vanity of an old man, who has learned to make triple acrostic sonnets to cheat the days and months at Theresienstadt and Spielberg—I have suffered too much for Italy to endure patiently the sight of little parliamentary cabals and municipal wranglings, although they also are necessary in this day as conspiracies and battles were in mine. I am not fit for your roomful of ministers and learned men and pretty women: the former would think me an ignoramus, and the latter—what would afflict me much more—a pedant.... Rather, if your Excellency really wants to show yourself and your children to your father's old *protégé* of Mazzinian times,[5] find a few

---

5 Giuseppe Mazzini (1805–72) was an Italian journalist and revolutionary who sought to create an independent, unified, democratic Italy. His dream

days to come here next spring. You shall have some very bare rooms with brick floors and white curtains opening out on my terrace; and a dinner of all manner of fish and milk (the white garlic flowers shall be mown away from under the olives lest my cow should eat it) and eggs cooked in herbs plucked in the hedges. Your boys can go and see the big ironclads at Spezia; and you shall come with me up our lanes fringed with delicate ferns and overhung by big olives, and into the fields where the cherry-trees shed their blossoms on to the budding vines, the fig-trees stretching out their little green gloves, where the goats nibble perched on their hind legs, and the cows low in the huts of reeds; and there rise from the ravines, with the gurgle of the brooks, from the cliffs with the boom of the surf, the voices of unseen boys and girls, singing about love and flowers and death, just as in the days of Theocritus,[6] whom your learned Excellency does well to read. Has your Excellency ever read Longus,[7] a Greek pastoral novelist? He is a trifle free, a trifle nude for us readers of Zola;[8] but the old French of Amyot[9] has a wonderful charm, and he gives one an idea, as no one else does, how folk lived in such valleys, by such sea-boards, as these in the days when daisy-chains and garlands of roses were still hung on the olive-trees for the nymphs of the grove;

---

was partially realized in 1861 with the creation of the Kingdom of Italy.

6 Theocritus (c. 300 B.C.) was a Greek poet credited with creating pastoral poetry.

7 Longus (date of birth unknown) was the author of an ancient Greek pastoral romance, *Daphnis and Chloe*.

8 Émile Zola (1840–1902) was a French novelist associated with Naturalism, considered radical at the time for his realistic depiction of contemporary social conditions.

9 Jacques Amyot (1513–93), a French writer and translator, translated Longus's *Daphnis and Chloe*.

when across the bay, at the end of the narrow neck of blue sea, there clung to the marble rocks not a church of Saint Laurence, with the sculptured martyr on his gridiron, but the temple of Venus, protecting her harbor.... Yes, dear Lady Evelyn, you have guessed aright. Your old friend has returned to his sins, and is scribbling once more. But no longer at verses or political pamphlets. I am enthralled by a tragic history, the history of the fall of the Pagan Gods.... Have you ever read of their wanderings and disguises, in my friend Heine's little book?[10]

And if you come to Montemirto, you shall see also your *protégée*, of whom you ask for news. It has just missed being disastrous. Poor Dionea! I fear that early voyage tied to the spar did no good to her wits, poor little waif! There has been a fearful row; and it has required all my influence, and all the awfulness of your Excellency's name, and the Papacy, and the Holy Roman Empire, to prevent her expulsion by the Sisters of the Stigmata. It appears that this mad creature very nearly committed a sacrilege: she was discovered handling in a suspicious manner the Madonna's gala frock and her best veil of *pizzo di Cantù*,[11] a gift of the late Marchioness Violante Vigalcila of Fornovo. One of the orphans, Zaira Barsanti, whom they call the Rossaccia, even pretends to have surprised Dionea as she was about to adorn her wicked little person with these sacred

---

10 In his essay "The Gods in Exile" ("*Die Götter im Exil*"), German poet and novelist Heinrich Heine (1797–1856) imagined the fate of the classical gods after they had been deposed by Christianity. For example, Apollo found work as a cowherd until a monk overheard his beautiful singing. Under torture, he confessed to his divine origins. After singing one final song that was so beautiful it made the women at the place of execution weep, he was put to death by the Church.

11 A fine, intricate bobbin lace made in the Italian city of Cantù and the surrounding villages.

garments; and, on another occasion, when Dionea had been sent to pass some oil and sawdust over the chapel floor (it was the eve of Easter of the Roses), to have discovered her seated on the edge of the altar, in the very place of the Most Holy Sacrament. I was sent for in hot haste, and had to assist at an ecclesiastical council in the convent parlor, where Dionea appeared, rather out of place, an amazing little beauty, dark, lithe, with an odd, ferocious gleam in her eyes, and a still odder smile, tortuous, serpentine, like that of Leonardo da Vinci's women,[12] among the plaster images of St. Francis, and the glazed and framed samplers before the little statue of the Virgin, which wears in summer a kind of mosquito-curtain to guard it from the flies, who, as you know, are creatures of Satan.

Speaking of Satan, does your Excellency know that on the inside of our little convent door, just above the little perforated plate of metal (like the rose of a watering-pot) through which the Sister-portress peeps and talks, is pasted a printed form, an arrangement of holy names and texts in triangles, and the stigmatized hands of St. Francis, and a variety of other devices, for the purpose, as is explained in a special notice, of baffling the Evil One, and preventing his entrance into that building? Had you seen Dionea, and the stolid, contemptuous way in which she took, without attempting to refute, the various shocking allegations against her, your Excellency would have reflected, as I did, that the door in question must have been accidentally absent from the premises, perhaps at the joiner's for repair, the day that your *protégée* first penetrated into the convent. The

---

12 For example, the *Mona Lisa*, who is famous for her mysterious smile. The Renaissance painter Leonardo da Vinci (1452–1519) painted many women with such enigmatic expressions.

ecclesiastical tribunal, consisting of the Mother Superior, three Sisters, the Capuchin Director, and your humble servant (who vainly attempted to be Devil's advocate), sentenced Dionea, among other things, to make the sign of the cross twenty-six times on the bare floor with her tongue. Poor little child! One might almost expect that, as happened when Dame Venus scratched her hand on the thorn-bush, red roses should sprout up between the fissures of the dirty old bricks.

OCTOBER 14, 1883.

You ask whether, now that the Sisters let Dionea go and do half a day's service now and then in the village, and that Dionea is a grown-up creature, she does not set the place by the ears with her beauty. The people here are quite aware of its existence. She is already dubbed *La bella Dionea*; but that does not bring her any nearer getting a husband, although your Excellency's generous offer of a wedding-portion is well known throughout the district of San Massimo and Montemirto. None of our boys, peasants or fishermen, seem to hang on her steps; and if they turn round to stare and whisper as she goes by straight and dainty in her wooden clogs, with the pitcher of water or the basket of linen on her beautiful crisp dark head, it is, I remark, with an expression rather of fear than of love. The women, on their side, make horns with their fingers as she passes, and as they sit by her side in the convent chapel; but that seems natural. My housekeeper tells me that down in the village she is regarded as possessing the evil eye and bringing love misery. "You mean," I said, "that a glance from her is too much for our lads' peace of mind." Veneranda shook her head, and explained, with the deference and contempt with which she always mentions any of her country-folk's superstitions to me, that the matter is different: it's not with her they are in love (they would be afraid of her eye), but wherever she goes the young people must needs fall in love with each other, and usually where it is far from desirable. "You know Sora Luisa, the blacksmith's widow? Well, Dionea did a *half-service* for her last month, to prepare for the wedding of Luisa's daughter. Well, now, the girl must say, forsooth! that she won't have Pieriho of Lerici any longer, but will have that raggamuffin Wooden Pipe from Solaro, or go into a convent. And the girl changed her mind the very day that Dionea had come into the house. Then there is the wife of Pippo, the coffee-house keeper; they say she is carrying on with one of the coastguards, and Dionea helped her to do her washing six weeks ago. The son of Sor Temistocle has just cut off a finger to avoid the conscription, because he is mad about his cousin and afraid of being taken for a soldier; and it is a fact that some of the shirts which were made for him at the Stigmata had been sewn by Dionea;"... and thus a perfect string of love misfortunes, enough to make a little *Decameron*,[13] I assure you, and all laid to Dionea's account. Certain it is that the people of San Massimo are terribly afraid of Dionea....

JULY 17, 1884.

Dionea's strange influence seems to be extending in a terrible way. I am almost beginning to think that our folk are correct in their fear of the young witch. I used to think, as physician

---

13 The *Decamerone*, by the Italian writer Giovanni Boccaccio (1313–75), contains one hundred stories within a frame narrative.

to a convent, that nothing was more erroneous than all the romancings of Diderot and Schubert[14] (your Excellency sang me his "Young Nun" once: do you recollect, just before your marriage?), and that no more humdrum creature existed than one of our little nuns, with their pink baby faces under their tight white caps. It appeared the romancing was more correct than the prose. Unknown things have sprung up in these good Sisters' hearts, as unknown flowers have sprung up among the myrtle-bushes and the rose-hedge which Dionea lies under. Did I ever mention to you a certain little Sister Giuliana, who professed only two years ago?—a funny rose and white little creature presiding over the infirmary, as prosaic a little saint as ever kissed a crucifix or scoured a saucepan. Well, Sister Giuliana has disappeared, and the same day has disappeared also a sailor-boy from the port.

AUGUST 20, 1884.

The case of Sister Giuliana seems to have been but the beginning of an extraordinary love epidemic at the Convent of the Stigmata: the elder schoolgirls have to be kept under lock and key lest they should talk over the wall in the moonlight, or steal out to the little hunchback who writes love-letters at a penny apiece, beautiful flourishes and all, under the portico by the Fishmarket. I wonder does that wicked little Dionea, whom no one pays court to, smile (her lips like a Cupid's bow or a tiny snake's curves) as she calls the pigeons down around her,

---

14 The French philosopher Denis Diderot (1713–84), best known as co-creator of the monumental *Encyclopédie*, also wrote a novel called *La Religieuse* (*The Nun*). The Austrian composer Franz Schubert (1797–1828) wrote a series of songs or *lieder* called "*Die Junge Nonne*" ("The Young Nun").

or lies fondling the cats under the myrtle-bush, when she sees the pupils going about with swollen, red eyes; the poor little nuns taking fresh penances on the cold chapel flags; and hears the long-drawn guttural vowels, *amore* and *morte* and *mio bene*, which rise up of an evening, with the boom of the surf and the scent of the lemon-flowers, as the young men wander up and down, arm-in-arm, twanging their guitars along the moonlit lanes under the olives?

OCTOBER 20, 1885.

A terrible, terrible thing has happened! I write to your Excellency with hands all a-tremble; and yet I *must* write, I must speak, or else I shall cry out. Did I ever mention to you Father Domenico of Casoria, the confessor of our Convent of the Stigmata? A young man, tall, emaciated with fasts and vigils, but handsome like the monk playing the virginal in Giorgione's *Concert*,[15] and under his brown serge still the most stalwart fellow of the country all round? One has heard of men struggling with the tempter. Well, well, Father Domenico had struggled as hard as any of the Anchorites recorded by St. Jerome, and he had conquered. I never knew anything comparable to the angelic serenity of gentleness of this victorious soul. I don't like monks, but I loved Father Domenico. I might have been his father, easily, yet I always felt a certain shyness and awe of him; and yet men have accounted me a clean-lived man in my generation; but I felt, whenever I approached him, a poor worldly

15 *Le Concert champêtre*, a pastoral painting of several musicians, including a young man playing a lute, is attributed to the Italian painter Giorgione (1477/78–1510) or his pupil Titan (c. 1488/90–1576), who may have finished the painting after Giorgione's death.

creature, debased by the knowledge of so many mean and ugly things. Of late Father Domenico had seemed to me less calm than usual: his eyes had grown strangely bright, and red spots had formed on his salient cheekbones. One day last week, taking his hand, I felt his pulse flutter, and all his strength as it were, liquefy under my touch. "You are ill," I said. "You have fever, Father Domenico. You have been overdoing yourself— some new privation, some new penance. Take care and do not tempt Heaven; remember the flesh is weak." Father Domenico withdrew his hand quickly. "Do not say that," he cried; "the flesh is strong!" and turned away his face. His eyes were glistening and he shook all over. "Some quinine," I ordered. But I felt it was no case for quinine. Prayers might be more useful, and could I have given them he should not have wanted. Last night I was suddenly sent for to Father Domenico's monastery above Montemirto: they told me he was ill. I ran up through the dim twilight of moonbeams and olives with a sinking heart. Something told me my monk was dead. He was lying in a little low whitewashed room; they had carried him there from his own cell in hopes he might still be alive. The windows were wide open; they framed some olive-branches, glistening in the moonlight, and far below, a strip of moonlit sea. When I told them that he was really dead, they brought some tapers and lit them at his head and feet, and placed a crucifix between his hands. "The Lord has been pleased to call our poor brother to Him," said the Superior. "A case of apoplexy, my dear Doctor—a case of apoplexy. You will make out the certificate for the authorities." I made out the certificate. It was weak of me. But, after all, why make a scandal? He certainly had no wish to injure the poor monks.

Next day I found the little nuns all in tears. They were gathering flowers to send as a last gift to their confessor. In the convent garden I found Dionea, standing by the side of a big basket of roses, one of the white pigeons perched on her shoulder.

"So," she said, "he has killed himself with charcoal, poor Padre Domenico!"

Something in her tone, her eyes, shocked me.

"God has called to Himself one of His most faithful servants," I said gravely.

Standing opposite this girl, magnificent, radiant in her beauty, before the rose-hedge, with the white pigeons furling and unfurling, strutting and pecking all round, I seemed to see suddenly the whitewashed room of last night, the big crucifix, that poor thin face under the yellow waxlight. I felt glad for Father Domenico; his battle was over.

"Take this to Father Domenico from me," said Dionea, breaking off a twig of myrtle starred over with white blossom; and raising her head with that smile like the twist of a young snake, she sang out in a high guttural voice a strange chant, consisting of the word *Amor—amor—amor*. I took the branch of myrtle and threw it in her face.

JANUARY 3, 1886.

It will be difficult to find a place for Dionea, and in this neighborhood well-nigh impossible. The people associate her somehow with the death of Father Domenico, which has confirmed her reputation of having the evil eye. She left the convent (being now seventeen) some two months back, and is at present gaining her bread working with the masons at our notary's new house at Lerici: the work is hard, but our women often do it, and it is magnificent to see Dionea, in her short white skirt and tight white bodice, mixing the smoking lime with her beautiful strong arms; or, an empty sack drawn over her head and shoulders, walking majestically up the cliff, up the scaffoldings with her load of bricks.... I am, however, very anxious to get Dionea out of the neighborhood, because I cannot help dreading the annoyances to which her reputation for the evil eye exposes her, and even some explosion of rage if ever she should lose the indifferent contempt with which she treats them. I hear that one of the rich men of our part of the world, a certain Sor Agostino of Sarzana, who owns a whole flank of marble mountain, is looking out for a maid for his daughter, who is about to be married; kind people and patriarchal in their riches, the old man still sitting down to table with all his servants; and his nephew, who is going to be his son-in-law, a splendid young fellow, who has worked like Jacob, in the quarry and at the saw-mill, for love of his pretty cousin. That whole house is so good, simple, and peaceful, that I hope it may tame down even Dionea. If I do not succeed in getting Dionea this place (and all your Excellency's illustriousness and all my poor eloquence will be needed to counteract the sinister reports attaching to our poor little waif), it will be best to accept your suggestion of taking the girl into your household at Rome, since you are curious to see what you call our baleful beauty. I am amused, and a little indignant at what you say about your footmen being handsome: Don Juan[16] himself, my dear Lady Evelyn, would be cowed by Dionea....

---

16 A famous fictional lover (and leaver) of women whose exploits appear in a number of artistic works, including the opera *Don Giovanni* by Wolfgang

Magic and Monstrosity

MAY 29, 1886.

Here is Dionea back upon our hands once more! but I cannot send her to your Excellency. Is it from living among these peasants and fishing-folk, or is it because, as people pretend, a skeptic is always superstitious? I could not muster courage to send you Dionea, although your boys are still in sailor-clothes and your uncle, the Cardinal, is eighty-four; and as to the Prince, why, he bears the most potent amulet against Dionea's terrible powers in your own dear capricious person. Seriously, there is something eerie in this coincidence. Poor Dionea! I feel sorry for her, exposed to the passion of a once patriarchally respectable old man. I feel even more abashed at the incredible audacity, I should almost say sacrilegious madness, of the vile old creature. But still the coincidence is strange and uncomfortable. Last week the lightning struck a huge olive in the orchard of Sor Agostino's house above Sarzana. Under the olive was Sor Agostino himself, who was killed on the spot; and opposite, not twenty paces off, drawing water from the well, unhurt and calm, was Dionea. It was the end of a sultry afternoon: I was on a terrace in one of those villages of ours, jammed, like some hardy bush, in the gash of a hill-side. I saw the storm rush down the valley, a sudden blackness, and then, like a curse, a flash, a tremendous crash, re-echoed by a dozen hills. "I told him," Dionea said very quietly, when she came to stay with me the next day (for Sor Agostino's family would not have her for another half-minute), "that if he did not leave me alone Heaven would send him an accident."

Amadeus Mozart (1756–91) and the epic poem *Don Juan* by Lord Byron (1788–1824).

JULY 15, 1886.

My book? Oh, dear Donna Evelina, do not make me blush by talking of my book! Do not make an old man, respectable, a Government functionary (communal physician of the district of San Massimo and Montemirto Ligure), confess that he is but a lazy unprofitable dreamer, collecting materials as a child picks hips out of a hedge, only to throw them away, liking them merely for the little occupation of scratching his hands and standing on tiptoe, for their pretty redness.... You remember what Balzac says about projecting any piece of work?— *"C'est fumer des cigarettes enchantées...."*[17] Well, well! The data obtainable about the ancient gods in their days of adversity are few and far between: a quotation here and there from the Fathers; two or three legends; Venus reappearing; the persecutions of Apollo in Styria; Proserpina going, in Chaucer, to reign over the fairies; a few obscure religious persecutions in the Middle Ages on the score of Paganism; some strange rites practiced till lately in the depths of a Breton forest near Lannion.... As to Tannhäuser,[18] he was a real knight, and a sorry one, and a real Minnesinger not of the best. Your Excellency will find some of his poems in Von der Hagen's[19] four immense volumes, but I

17 Honoré de Balzac (1799–1850) was a French novelist and playwright. In this phrase he compares creativity to smoking enchanted cigarettes. The phrase concludes, *"mais sans l'exécution tout s'en va en rêve et en fumée"*: without execution, everything goes up in dreams and smoke.

18 Tannhäuser was a thirteenth-century German Minnesinger, or writer and singer of love poetry. Although he was a historical figure, he became the subject of a folk ballad in which the knight Tannhäuser enters the Venusberg, the underground home of Venus, and spends a year there with the goddess.

19 Friedrich von der Hagen (1780–1856) was a German philologist who published several collections of old German poetry, including one called *Minnesinger*, in four volumes.

recommend you to take your notions of Ritter[20] Tannhäuser's poetry rather from Wagner.[21] Certain it is that the Pagan divinities lasted much longer than we suspect, sometimes in their own nakedness, sometimes in the stolen garb of the Madonna or the saints. Who knows whether they do not exist to this day? And, indeed, is it possible they should not? For the awfulness of the deep woods, with their filtered green light, the creak of the swaying, solitary reeds, exists, and is Pan; and the blue, starry May night exists, the sough of the waves, the warm wind carrying the sweetness of the lemon-blossoms, the bitterness of the myrtle on our rocks, the distant chant of the boys cleaning out their nets, of the girls sickling the grass under the olives, *Amor—amor—amor*, and all this is the great goddess Venus. And opposite to me, as I write, between the branches of the ilexes, across the blue sea, streaked like a Ravenna mosaic with purple and green, shimmer the white houses and walls, the steeple and towers, an enchanted Fata Morgana[22] city, of dim Porto Venere;... and I mumble to myself the verse of Catullus, but addressing a greater and more terrible goddess than he did:—

"*Procul a mea sit furor omnis, Hera, domo; alios; age incitatos, alios age rabidos.*"[23]

---

20 German for "Knight."

21 The folktale of Tannhäuser was incorporated into the opera *Tannhäuser* by the German composer Richard Wagner (1813–83).

22 A mirage, named after the sorceress Morgan le Fay from the Arthurian legends.

23 The last two lines of the poem "Attis" by the Roman poet Catullus. Just before these lines, Catullus has included an invocation to the goddess Cybele, who was associated with Aphrodite: "Dea, magna Dea, Cybelle, Didymi Dea domina . . ." Together, the three lines read loosely: "Goddess, great Goddess, Cybele, Lady of Dindymus, may all your fury be far from me and my house, my Queen; drive others to frenzy, drive others to madness." Dindymus or Dindymon was a mountain sacred to Cybele.

MARCH 25, 1887.

Yes; I will do everything in my power for your friends. Are you well-bred folk as well bred as we, Republican *bourgeois*, with the coarse hands (though you once told me mine were psychic hands when the mania of palmistry had not yet been succeeded by that of the Reconciliation between Church and State), I wonder, that you should apologize, you whose father fed me and housed me and clothed me in my exile, for giving me the horrid trouble of hunting for lodgings? It is like you, dear Donna Evelina, to have sent me photographs of my future friend Waldemar's statue.... I have no love for modern sculpture, for all the hours I have spent in Gibson's and Dupré's[24] studio: 'tis a dead art we should do better to bury. But your Waldemar has something of the old spirit: he seems to feel the divineness of the mere body, the spirituality of a limpid stream of mere physical life. But why among these statues only men and boys, athletes and fauns? Why only the bust of that thin, delicate-lipped little Madonna wife of his? Why no wide-shouldered Amazon or broad-flanked Aphrodite?

APRIL 10, 1887.

You ask me how poor Dionea is getting on. Not as your Excellency and I ought to have expected when we placed her with the good Sisters of the Stigmata: although I wager that, fantastic and capricious as you are, you would be better

---

24 The Welsh sculptor John Gibson (1790–1866) and the Italian sculptor Giovanni Dupré (1817–82) both worked in the Neoclassical style. Gibson was known in particular for tinting his sculptures, as the ancient Greeks did.

pleased (hiding it carefully from that grave side of you which bestows devout little books and carbolic acid upon the indigent) that your *protégée* should be a witch than a serving-maid, a maker of philters rather than a knitter of stockings and sewer of shirts.

A maker of philters. Roughly speaking, that is Dionea's profession. She lives upon the money which I dole out to her (with many useless objurgations) on behalf of your Excellency, and her ostensible employment is mending nets, collecting olives, carrying bricks, and other miscellaneous jobs; but her real status is that of village sorceress. You think our peasants are skeptical? Perhaps they do not believe in thought-reading, mesmerism, and ghosts, like you, dear Lady Evelyn. But they believe very firmly in the evil eye, in magic, and in love-potions. Every one has his little story of this or that which happened to his brother or cousin or neighbor. My stable-boy and male factotum's brother-in-law, living some years ago in Corsica, was seized with a longing for a dance with his beloved at one of those balls which our peasants give in the winter, when the snow makes leisure in the mountains. A wizard anointed him for money, and straightway he turned into a black cat, and in three bounds was over the seas, at the door of his uncle's cottage, and among the dancers. He caught his beloved by the skirt to draw her attention; but she replied with a kick which sent him squealing back to Corsica. When he returned in summer he refused to marry the lady, and carried his left arm in a sling. "You broke it when I came to the Veglia!" he said, and all seemed explained. Another lad, returning from working in the vineyards near Marseilles, was walking up to his native village, high in our hills, one moonlight night. He heard sounds of fiddle and fife from a roadside barn, and saw yellow light from its chinks; and then entering, he found many women dancing, old and young, and among them his affianced. He tried to snatch her round the waist for a waltz (they play *Mme. Angot*[25] at our rustic balls), but the girl was unclutchable, and whispered, "Go; for these are witches, who will kill thee; and I am a witch also. Alas! I shall go to hell when I die."

I could tell your Excellency dozens of such stories. But love-philters are among the commonest things to sell and buy. Do you remember the sad little story of Cervantes' Licentiate,[26] who, instead of a love-potion, drank a philter which made him think he was made of glass, fit emblem of a poor mad poet?... It is love-philters that Dionea prepares. No; do not misunderstand; they do not give love of her, still less her love.

Your seller of love-charms is as cold as ice, as pure as snow. The priest has crusaded against her, and stones have flown at her as she went by from dissatisfied lovers; and the very children, paddling in the sea and making mud-pies in the sand, have put out forefinger and little finger and screamed, "Witch, witch! ugly witch!" as she passed with basket or brick load; but Dionea has only smiled, that snake-like, amused smile, but more ominous than of yore. The other day I determined to seek her and argue with her on the subject of her evil trade.

---

25 *La Fille de Madame Angot* (*Madame Angot's Daughter*) was a popular French comic opera that premiered in 1872. Presumably the narrator is referring to music from the opera.
26 In *"The Licentiate Vidriera"* ("The Lawyer of Glass") by the Spanish writer Miguel de Cervantes (1547–1616), a young woman gives a lawyer what she believes to be a love potion. Instead, it causes him to hallucinate that he is made of glass.

Dionea has a certain regard for me; not, I fancy, a result of gratitude, but rather the recognition of a certain admiration and awe which she inspires in your Excellency's foolish old servant. She has taken up her abode in a deserted hut, built of dried reeds and thatch, such as they keep cows in, among the olives on the cliffs. She was not there, but about the hut pecked some white pigeons, and from it, startling me foolishly with its unexpected sound, came the eerie bleat of her pet goat.... Among the olives it was twilight already, with streakings of faded rose in the sky, and faded rose, like long trails of petals, on the distant sea. I clambered down among the myrtle-bushes and came to a little semicircle of yellow sand, between two high and jagged rocks, the place where the sea had deposited Dionea after the wreck. She was seated there on the sand, her bare foot dabbling in the waves; she had twisted a wreath of myrtle and wild roses on her black, crisp hair. Near her was one of our prettiest girls, the Lena of Sor Tullio the blacksmith, with ashy, terrified face under her flowered kerchief. I determined to speak to the child, but without startling her now, for she is a nervous, hysteric little thing. So I sat on the rocks, screened by the myrtle-bushes, waiting till the girl had gone. Dionea, seated listless on the sands, leaned over the sea and took some of its water in the hollow of her hand. "Here," she said to the Lena of Sor Tullio, "fill your bottle with this and give it to drink to Tommasino the Rosebud." Then she set to singing:—

"Love is salt, like sea-water—I drink and I die of thirst.... Water! water! Yet the more I drink, the more I burn. Love! thou art bitter as the seaweed."

* * *

APRIL 20, 1887.

Your friends are settled here, dear Lady Evelyn. The house is built in what was once a Genoese fort, growing like a grey spiked aloes out of the marble rocks of our bay; rock and wall (the walls existed long before Genoa was ever heard of) grown almost into a homogeneous mass, delicate grey, stained with black and yellow lichen, and dotted here and there with myrtle-shoots and crimson snapdragon. In what was once the highest enclosure of the fort, where your friend Gertrude watches the maids hanging out the fine white sheets and pillow-cases to dry (a bit of the North, of Hermann and Dorothea[27] transferred to the South), a great twisted fig-tree juts out like an eccentric gargoyle over the sea, and drops its ripe fruit into the deep blue pools. There is but scant furniture in the house, but a great oleander overhangs it, presently to burst into pink splendor; and on all the window-sills, even that of the kitchen (such a background of shining brass saucepans Waldemar's wife has made of it!) are pipkins and tubs full of trailing carnations, and tufts of sweet basil and thyme and mignonette. She pleases me most, your Gertrude, although you foretold I should prefer the husband; with her thin white face, a Memling Madonna[28] finished by some Tuscan sculptor, and her long, delicate white hands ever busy, like those of a mediaeval lady, with some delicate piece of work; and the strange blue, more limpid than the sky and deeper than the sea, of her rarely lifted glance.

It is in her company that I like Waldemar best; I prefer to

27 The hero and heroine of *Hermann and Dorothea*, an epic poem by the German writer Johann Wolfgang von Goethe (1749–1832).
28 The German artist Hans Memling (c. 1430–94) was known for his religious paintings, including a number of Madonnas.

the genius that infinitely tender and respectful, I would not say *lover*—yet I have no other word—of his pale wife. He seems to me, when with her, like some fierce, generous, wild thing from the woods, like the lion of Una,[29] tame and submissive to this saint.... This tenderness is really very beautiful on the part of that big lion Waldemar, with his odd eyes, as of some wild animal—odd, and, your Excellency remarks, not without a gleam of latent ferocity. I think that hereby hangs the explanation of his never doing any but male figures: the female figure, he says (and your Excellency must hold him responsible, not me, for such profanity), is almost inevitably inferior in strength and beauty; woman is not form, but expression, and therefore suits painting, but not sculpture. The point of a woman is not her body, but (and here his eyes rested very tenderly upon the thin white profile of his wife) her soul. "Still," I answered, "the ancients, who understood such matters, did manufacture some tolerable female statues: the Fates of the Parthenon, the Phidian Pallas, the Venus of Milo."...

"Ah! yes," exclaimed Waldemar, smiling, with that savage gleam of his eyes; "but those are not women, and the people who made them have left us the tales of Endymion, Adonis, Anchises: a goddess might sit for them."...

MAY 5, 1887.

Has it ever struck your Excellency in one of your La Rochefoucauld[30] fits (in Lent say, after too many balls) that

---

29 The story of Una and the lion is told in the epic poem *The Faerie Queene* by the English poet Edmund Spenser (1552/53–1599). The fierce lion is tamed by Una's beauty and goodness.

30 After an active youth, the French aristocrat François, Duc de La

not merely maternal but conjugal unselfishness may be a very selfish thing? There! you toss your little head at my words; yet I wager I have heard you say that *other* women may think it right to humor their husbands, but as to you, the Prince must learn that a wife's duty is as much to chasten her husband's whims as to satisfy them. I really do feel indignant that such a snow-white saint should wish another woman to part with all instincts of modesty merely because that other woman would be a good model for her husband; really it is intolerable. "Leave the girl alone," Waldemar said, laughing. "What do I want with the unaesthetic sex, as Schopenhauer[31] calls it?" But Gertrude has set her heart on his doing a female figure; it seems that folk have twitted him with never having produced one. She has long been on the look-out for a model for him. It is odd to see this pale, demure, diaphanous creature, not the more earthly for approaching motherhood, scanning the girls of our village with the eyes of a slave-dealer.

"If you insist on speaking to Dionea," I said, "I shall insist on speaking to her at the same time, to urge her to refuse your proposal." But Waldemar's pale wife was indifferent to all my speeches about modesty being a poor girl's only dowry. "She will do for a Venus," she merely answered.

We went up to the cliffs together, after some sharp words, Waldemar's wife hanging on my arm as we slowly clambered up

Rochefoucauld (1613–80) retired to his country estate, where he wrote his memoirs and a book of maxims on conducting a virtuous life.

31 In his misogynistic essay "On Women," the German philosopher Arthur Schopenhauer (1788–1860) claims that women are unaesthetic in two ways: they are not physically appealing, and they are incapable of aesthetic appreciation. In other words, they cannot understand or value art, music, and literature. This essay must have particularly rankled a writer like Vernon Lee, who was deeply interested in aesthetic theory and experience.

the stony path among the olives. We found Dionea at the door of her hut, making faggots of myrtle-branches. She listened sullenly to Gertrude's offer and explanations; indifferently to my admonitions not to accept. The thought of stripping for the view of a man, which would send a shudder through our most brazen village girls, seemed not to startle her, immaculate and savage as she is accounted. She did not answer, but sat under the olives, looking vaguely across the sea. At that moment Waldemar came up to us; he had followed with the intention of putting an end to these wranglings.

"Gertrude," he said, "do leave her alone. I have found a model—a fisher-boy, whom I much prefer to any woman."

Dionea raised her head with that serpentine smile. "I will come," she said.

Waldemar stood silent; his eyes were fixed on her, where she stood under the olives, her white shift loose about her splendid throat, her shining feet bare in the grass. Vaguely, as if not knowing what he said, he asked her name. She answered that her name was Dionea; for the rest, she was an Innocentina, that is to say, a foundling; then she began to sing:—

"Flower of the myrtle!
My father is the starry sky,
The mother that made me is the sea."

JUNE 22, 1887.

I confess I was an old fool to have grudged Waldemar his model. As I watch him gradually building up his statue, watch the goddess gradually emerging from the clay heap, I ask myself—and the case might trouble a more subtle moralist than me—whether a village girl, an obscure, useless life within the bounds of what we choose to call right and wrong, can be weighed against the possession by mankind of a great work of art, a Venus immortally beautiful? Still, I am glad that the two alternatives need not be weighed against each other. Nothing can equal the kindness of Gertrude, now that Dionea has consented to sit to her husband; the girl is ostensibly merely a servant like any other; and, lest any report of her real functions should get abroad and discredit her at San Massimo or Montemirto, she is to be taken to Rome, where no one will be the wiser, and where, by the way, your Excellency will have an opportunity of comparing Waldemar's goddess of love with our little orphan of the Convent of the Stigmata. What reassures me still more is the curious attitude of Waldemar towards the girl. I could never have believed that an artist could regard a woman so utterly as a mere inanimate thing, a form to copy, like a tree or flower. Truly he carries out his theory that sculpture knows only the body, and the body scarcely considered as human. The way in which he speaks to Dionea after hours of the most rapt contemplation of her is almost brutal in its coldness. And yet to hear him exclaim, "How beautiful she is! Good God, how beautiful!" No love of mere woman was ever so violent as this love of woman's mere shape.

JUNE 27, 1887.

You asked me once, dearest Excellency, whether there survived among our people (you had evidently added a volume on folklore to that heap of half-cut, dog's-eared books that litter about among the Chineseries and mediaeval brocades of your rooms) any trace of Pagan myths. I explained to you then that all our fairy mythology, classic gods, and demons and heroes, teemed with fairies, ogres, and princes. Last night I had a curious proof of this. Going to see Waldemar, I found Dionea seated under the oleander at the top of the old Genoese fort, telling stories to the two little blonde children who were making the falling pink blossoms into necklaces at her feet; the pigeons, Dionea's white pigeons, which never leave her, strutting and pecking among the basil pots, and the white gulls flying round the rocks overhead. This is what I heard... "And the three fairies said to the youngest son of the King, to the one who had been brought up as a shepherd, 'Take this apple, and give it to her among us who is most beautiful.' And the first fairy said, 'If thou give it to me thou shalt be Emperor of Rome, and have purple clothes, and have a gold crown and gold armor, and horses and courtiers;' and the second said, 'If thou give it to me thou shalt be Pope, and wear a miter, and have the keys of heaven and hell;' and the third fairy said, 'Give the apple to me, for I will give thee the most beautiful lady to wife.' And the youngest son of the King sat in the green meadow and thought about it a little, and then said, 'What use is there in being Emperor or Pope? Give me the beautiful lady to wife, since I am young myself.' And he gave the apple to the third of the three fairies."[32]...

Dionea droned out the story in her half-Genoese dialect, her eyes looking far away across the blue sea, dotted with sails like white sea-gulls, that strange serpentine smile on her lips.

"Who told thee that fable?" I asked.

---

32 This story is a fairytale version of the Judgment of Paris, in which the Trojan prince Paris is asked to award a golden apple between Hera, Athena, and Aphrodite. He awards the apple to Aphrodite, who has promised him the

She took a handful of oleander-blossoms from the ground, and throwing them in the air, answered listlessly, as she watched the little shower of rosy petals descend on her black hair and pale breast—

"Who knows?"

JULY 6, 1887.

How strange is the power of art! Has Waldemar's statue shown me the real Dionea, or has Dionea really grown more strangely beautiful than before? Your Excellency will laugh; but when I meet her I cast down my eyes after the first glimpse of her loveliness; not with the shyness of a ridiculous old pursuer of the Eternal Feminine, but with a sort of religious awe—the feeling with which, as a child kneeling by my mother's side, I looked down on the church flags when the Mass bell told the elevation of the Host.... Do you remember the story of Zeuxis and the ladies of Crotona,[33] five of the fairest not being too much for his Juno? Do you remember—you, who have read everything—all the bosh of our writers about the Ideal in Art? Why, here is a girl who disproves all this nonsense in a minute; she is far, far more beautiful than Waldemar's statue of her. He said so angrily, only yesterday, when his wife took me into his studio (he has made a studio of the long-desecrated chapel of the old

---

most beautiful woman in the world: Helen of Sparta. The consequence of this decision is the Trojan War.

33 The Greek painter Zeuxis could not find a model beautiful enough for his painting of Helen of Troy, so he asked five women to model for him. He painted the most beautiful body parts of each woman to form his Helen. The narrator may be misremembering the subject of the painting as the goddess Hera (or Juno).

Genoese fort, itself, they say, occupying the site of the temple of Venus).

As he spoke that odd spark of ferocity dilated in his eyes, and seizing the largest of his modeling tools, he obliterated at one swoop the whole exquisite face. Poor Gertrude turned ashy white, and a convulsion passed over her face....

JULY 15.

I wish I could make Gertrude understand, and yet I could never, never bring myself to say a word. As a matter of fact, what is there to be said? Surely she knows best that her husband will never love any woman but herself. Yet ill, nervous as she is, I quite understand that she must loathe this unceasing talk of Dionea, of the superiority of the model over the statue. Cursed statue! I wish it were finished, or else that it had never been begun.

JULY 20.

This morning Waldemar came to me. He seemed strangely agitated: I guessed he had something to tell me, and yet I could never ask. Was it cowardice on my part? He sat in my shuttered room, the sunshine making pools on the red bricks and tremulous stars on the ceiling, talking of many things at random, and mechanically turning over the manuscript, the heap of notes of my poor, never-finished book on the Exiled Gods. Then he rose, and walking nervously round my study, talking disconnectedly about his work, his eye suddenly fell upon a little altar, one of my few antiquities, a little block of marble with a carved garland and rams' heads, and a half-effaced inscription dedicating it to Venus, the mother of Love.

"It was found," I explained, "in the ruins of the temple, somewhere on the site of your studio: so, at least, the man said from whom I bought it."

Waldemar looked at it long. "So," he said, "this little cavity was to burn the incense in; or rather, I suppose, since it has two little gutters running into it, for collecting the blood of the victim? Well, well! they were wiser in that day, to wring the neck of a pigeon or burn a pinch of incense than to eat their own hearts out, as we do, all along of Dame Venus;" and he laughed, and left me with that odd ferocious lighting-up of his face. Presently there came a knock at my door. It was Waldemar. "Doctor," he said very quietly, "will you do me a favor? Lend me your little Venus altar—only for a few days, only till the day after tomorrow. I want to copy the design of it for the pedestal of my statue: it is appropriate." I sent the altar to him: the lad who carried it told me that Waldemar had set it up in the studio, and calling for a flask of wine, poured out two glasses. One he had given to my messenger for his pains; of the other he had drunk a mouthful, and thrown the rest over the altar, saying some unknown words. "It must be some German habit," said my servant. What odd fancies this man has!

JULY 25.

You ask me, dearest Excellency, to send you some sheets of my book: you want to know what I have discovered. Alas! dear Donna Evelina, I have discovered, I fear, that there is nothing to discover; that Apollo was never in Styria; that

Chaucer, when he called the Queen of the Fairies Proserpine, meant nothing more than an eighteenth century poet when he called Dolly or Betty Cynthia or Amaryllis; that the lady who damned poor Tannhäuser[34] was not Venus, but a mere little Suabian mountain sprite; in fact, that poetry is only the invention of poets, and that that rogue, Heinrich Heine, is entirely responsible for the existence of *Dieux en Exil*.... My poor manuscript can only tell you what St. Augustine, Tertullian, and sundry morose old Bishops thought about the loves of Father Zeus and the miracles of the Lady Isis, none of which is much worth your attention.... Reality, my dear Lady Evelyn, is always prosaic: at least when investigated into by bald old gentlemen like me.

And yet, it does not look so. The world, at times, seems to be playing at being poetic, mysterious, full of wonder and romance. I am writing, as usual, by my window, the moonlight brighter in its whiteness than my mean little yellow-shining lamp. From the mysterious greyness, the olive groves and lanes beneath my terrace, rises a confused quaver of frogs, and buzz and whirr of insects: something, in sound, like the vague trails of countless stars, the galaxies on galaxies blurred into mere blue shimmer by the moon, which rides slowly across the highest heaven. The olive twigs glisten in the rays: the flowers of the pomegranate and oleander are only veiled as with bluish mist in their scarlet and rose. In the sea is another sea, of molten, rippled silver, or a magic causeway leading to the shining vague offing, the luminous pale sky-line, where the islands of Palmaria and Tino float like unsubstantial, shadowy dolphins.

---

34 Tannhäuser and Heine's *"Dieux en Exil"* (French for "Gods in Exile") are explained in previous footnotes.

The roofs of Montemirto glimmer among the black, pointing cypresses: farther below, at the end of that half-moon of land, is San Massimo: the Genoese fort inhabited by our friends is profiled black against the sky. All is dark: our fisher-folk go to bed early; Gertrude and the little ones are asleep: they at least are, for I can imagine Gertrude lying awake, the moon-beams on her thin Madonna face, smiling as she thinks of the little ones around her, of the other tiny thing that will soon lie on her breast.... There is a light in the old desecrated chapel, the thing that was once the temple of Venus, they say, and is now Waldemar's workshop, its broken roof mended with reeds and thatch. Waldemar has stolen in, no doubt to see his statue again. But he will return, more peaceful for the peacefulness of the night, to his sleeping wife and children. God bless and watch over them! Good-night, dearest Excellency.

JULY 26.

I have your Excellency's telegram in answer to mine. Many thanks for sending the Prince. I await his coming with feverish longing; it is still something to look forward to. All does not seem over. And yet what can he do?

The children are safe: we fetched them out of their bed and brought them up here. They are still a little shaken by the fire, the bustle, and by finding themselves in a strange house; also, they want to know where their mother is; but they have found a tame cat, and I hear them chirping on the stairs.

It was only the roof of the studio, the reeds and thatch, that burned, and a few old pieces of timber. Waldemar must have set fire to it with great care; he had brought armfuls of faggots of dry myrtle and heather from the bakehouse close by, and thrown into the blaze quantities of pine-cones, and of some resin, I know not what, that smelt like incense. When we made our way, early this morning, through the smoldering studio, we were stifled with a hot church-like perfume: my brain swam, and I suddenly remembered going into St. Peter's on Easter Day as a child.

It happened last night, while I was writing to you. Gertrude had gone to bed, leaving her husband in the studio. About eleven the maids heard him come out and call to Dionea to get up and come and sit to him. He had had this craze once before, of seeing her and his statue by an artificial light: you remember he had theories about the way in which the ancients lit up the statues in their temples. Gertrude, the servants say, was heard creeping downstairs a little later.

Do you see it? I have seen nothing else these hours, which have seemed weeks and months. He had placed Dionea on the big marble block behind the altar, a great curtain of dull red brocade—you know that Venetian brocade with the gold pomegranate pattern—behind her, like a Madonna of Van Eyck's.[35] He showed her to me once before like this, the whiteness of her neck and breast, the whiteness of the drapery round her flanks, toned to the color of old marble by the light of the resin burning in pans all round.... Before Dionea was the altar—the altar of Venus which he had borrowed from me. He must have collected all the roses about it, and thrown the incense upon the embers when Gertrude suddenly entered. And then, and then...

35 The Flemish painter Jan van Eyck (c.1390–1441) painted a number of Madonnas, often with brocade hangings in the background.

We found her lying across the altar, her pale hair among the ashes of the incense, her blood—she had but little to give, poor white ghost!—trickling among the carved garlands and rams' heads, blackening the heaped-up roses. The body of Waldemar was found at the foot of the castle cliff. Had he hoped, by setting the place on fire, to bury himself among its ruins, or had he not rather wished to complete in this way the sacrifice, to make the whole temple an immense votive pyre? It looked like one, as we hurried down the hills to San Massimo: the whole hillside, dry grass, myrtle, and heather, all burning, the pale short flames waving against the blue moonlit sky, and the old fortress outlined black against the blaze.

AUGUST 30.

Of Dionea I can tell you nothing certain. We speak of her as little as we can. Some say they have seen her, on stormy nights, wandering among the cliffs: but a sailor-boy assures me, by all the holy things, that the day after the burning of the Castle Chapel—we never call it anything else—he met at dawn, off the island of Palmaria, beyond the Strait of Porto Venere, a Greek boat, with eyes painted on the prow, going full sail to sea, the men singing as she went. And against the mast, a robe of purple and gold about her, and a myrtle-wreath on her head, leaned Dionea, singing words in an unknown tongue, the white pigeons circling around her.

A. Mary F. Robinson

THE DRYADS

The Dryads dwell in Easter woods,
    Though mortals may not see them there;
They haunt our rustling solitudes,
    And love the solemn valleys where
    The bracken mocks their tawny hair.

And where the rushes make a hedge
    With flowering lilies round the lake,
They come to shelter in the sedge;
    They dip their shining feet and slake
    Their thirst where shallow waters break.

But through the sultry noon their home
    Surrounds some smooth old beechen stem.
Behold how thick the empty dome
    Is heaped with russet leaves for them,
    Where burr or thistle never came!

And there they lie in languid flocks,
    A drift of sweetness unespied;
They dream among their tawny locks
    Until the welcome eventide
    Breathe freshly through the woods outside.

And then a gleam of white is seen
  Among the huge old ilex-boughs;
The Dryads love its sombre green;
  They make the tree their summer-house,
  And there they swing and there carouse.

But, if the tender moon by chance
  Come up the skies with silver feet,
They spring upon the ground and dance
  Where most the turf is thick and sweet,—
  And would that we were there to see't!

Nay! Nay! For should the woodman find
  A Dryad in a hollow tree,
He drops his hatchet, stricken blind—
  I know not why, unless it be
  The maid's Immortal, and not he!

For none may see the nymph uncursed.
  And things unchristian haunt the woods...
They stoop above our wells athirst,
  They love our rustling solitudes
  Where olden magic ever broods;

The Dryads dwell in Easter woods!

***Two poems by
Olive Custance***

The White Witch

Her body is a dancing joy, a delicate delight,
Her hair a silver glamour in a net of golden light.

Her face is like the faces that a dreamer sometimes meets,
A face that Leonardo would have followed in the streets.

Her eyelids are like clouds that spread white wings across blue
        skies,
Like shadows in still water are the sorrow in her eyes.

How flower-like are the smiling lips so many have desired,
Curled lips that love's long kisses have left a little tired.

The Changeling

My father was a golden king,
        My mother was a shining queen;
I heard the magic blue-bird sing...
        They wrapped me in a mantle green.

They led their winged white horses out,
    We rode and rode till dawn was grey;
We rode with many a song and shout,
    "Over the hills and far away."

They stole the crying human child,
    And left me laughing by the fire;
And that is why my heart is wild,
    And all my life a long desire...

The old enchantments hold me still...
    And sometimes in a waking trance
I seek again the Fairy Hill,
    The midnight feast, the glittering dance!

The wizard harpers play for me,
    I wear a crown upon my head,
A princess in eternity,
    I dance and revel with the dead...

"Vain lies!" I hear the people cry,
    I listen to their weary truth;
Then turn again to fantasy,
    And the untroubled Land of Youth.

I hear the laughter of the kings,
    I see their jewelled flagons gleam...
O wine of Life!... immortal things
    Move in the splendour of my dream...

My spirit is a homing dove...
    I drain a crystal cup, and fall
Softly into the arms of Love...
    And then the darkness covers all.

MAN-SIZE IN MARBLE

E. NESBIT

Although every word of this story is as true as despair, I do not expect people to believe it. Nowadays a "rational explanation" is required before belief is possible. Let me then, at once, offer the "rational explanation" which finds most favour among those who have heard the tale of my life's tragedy. It is held that we were "under a delusion," Laura and I, on that 31st of October; and that this supposition places the whole matter on a satisfactory and believable basis. The reader can judge, when he, too, has heard my story, how far this is an "explanation," and in what sense it is "rational." There were three who took part in this: Laura and I and another man. The other man still lives, and can speak to the truth of the least credible part of my story.

I never in my life knew what it was to have as much money as I required to supply the most ordinary needs—good colours, books, and cab-fares—and when we were married we knew quite well that we should only be able to live at all by "strict punctuality and attention to business." I used to paint in those days, and Laura used to write, and we felt sure we could keep the pot at least simmering. Living in town was out of the question, so we went to look for a cottage in the country, which should be at once sanitary and picturesque. So rarely do these two qualities meet in one cottage that our search was for some time quite fruitless. We tried advertisements, but most of the desirable rural residences which we did look at proved to be lacking in both essentials, and when a cottage chanced to have drains it always had stucco as well and was shaped like a teacaddy. And if we found a vine or rose-covered porch, corruption invariably lurked within. Our minds got so befogged by the eloquence of house-agents and the rival disadvantages of the fever-traps and outrages to beauty which we had seen and scorned, that I very much doubt whether either of us, on our wedding morning, knew the difference between a house and a haystack. But when we got away from friends and house-agents, on our honeymoon, our wits grew clear again, and we knew a pretty cottage when at last we saw one. It was at Brenzett—a little village set on a hill over against the southern marshes. We had gone there, from the seaside village where we were staying, to see the church, and two fields from the church we found this cottage. It stood quite by itself, about two miles from the village. It was a long, low building, with rooms sticking out in unexpected places. There was a bit of stone-work—ivy-covered and moss-grown, just two old rooms, all that was left of a big house that had once stood there—and round this stonework the house had grown up. Stripped of its roses and jasmine it would have been hideous. As it stood it was charming, and after a brief examination we took it. It was absurdly cheap. The rest of our honeymoon we spent in grubbing about in second-hand shops in the county town, picking up bits of old oak and Chippendale chairs for our furnishing. We wound up with a run up to town and a visit to Liberty's, and soon the low oak-beamed lattice-windowed rooms began to be home. There was a jolly old-fashioned garden, with grass paths, and no end of hollyhocks and sunflowers, and big lilies. From the window you could see the marsh-pastures, and beyond them the blue, thin line of the sea. We were as happy as the summer was glorious, and settled down into work sooner than we ourselves expected. I was never tired of sketching the view and the wonderful cloud effects from the open lattice, and Laura would sit at the table and write verses about them, in which I mostly played the part of foreground.

We got a tall old peasant woman to do for us. Her face and figure were good, though her cooking was of the homeliest; but she understood all about gardening, and told us all the old names of the coppices and cornfields, and the stories of the smugglers and highwaymen, and, better still, of the "things that walked," and of the "sights" which met one in lonely glens of a starlight night. She was a great comfort to us, because Laura hated housekeeping as much as I loved folklore, and we soon came to leave all the domestic business to Mrs. Dorman, and to use her legends in little magazine stories which brought in the jingling guinea.

We had three months of married happiness, and did not have a single quarrel. One October evening I had been down to smoke a pipe with the doctor—our only neighbour—a pleasant young Irishman. Laura had stayed at home to finish a comic sketch of a village episode for the *Monthly Marplot*. I left her laughing over her own jokes, and came in to find her a crumpled heap of pale muslin weeping on the window seat.

"Good heavens, my darling, what's the matter?" I cried, taking her in my arms. She leaned her little dark head against my shoulder and went on crying. I had never seen her cry before—we had always been so happy, you see—and I felt sure some frightful misfortune had happened.

"What is the matter? Do speak."

"It's Mrs. Dorman," she sobbed.

"What has she done?" I inquired, immensely relieved.

"She says she must go before the end of the month, and she says her niece is ill; she's gone down to see her now, but I don't believe that's the reason, because her niece is always ill. I believe someone has been setting her against us. Her manner was so queer—"

"Never mind, Pussy," I said; "whatever you do, don't cry, or I shall have to cry too, to keep you in countenance, and then you'll never respect your man again!"

She dried her eyes obediently on my handkerchief, and even smiled faintly.

"But you see," she went on, "it is really serious, because these village people are so sheepy, and if one won't do a thing you may be quite sure none of the others will. And I shall have to cook the dinners, and wash up the hateful greasy plates; and you'll have to carry cans of water about, and clean the boots and knives—and we shall never have any time for work, or earn any money, or anything. We shall have to work all day, and only be able to rest when we are waiting for the kettle to boil!"

I represented to her that even if we had to perform these duties, the day would still present some margin for other toils and recreations. But she refused to see the matter in any but the greyest light. She was very unreasonable, my Laura, but I could not have loved her any more if she had been as reasonable as Whately.[1]

"I'll speak to Mrs. Dorman when she comes back, and see if I can't come to terms with her," I said. "Perhaps she wants a rise in her screw. It will be all right. Let's walk up to the church."

The church was a large and lonely one, and we loved to go there, especially upon bright nights. The path skirted a wood, cut through it once, and ran along the crest of the hill through two meadows, and round the churchyard wall, over which the old yews loomed in black masses of shadow. This path, which was partly paved, was called "the bier-balk," for it had long been the way by which the corpses had been carried to burial. The churchyard was richly treed, and was shaded by great elms which stood just outside and stretched their majestic arms in benediction over the happy dead. A large, low porch let one into the building by a Norman doorway and a heavy oak door studded with iron. Inside, the arches rose into darkness, and between them the reticulated windows, which stood out white in the moonlight. In the chancel, the windows were of rich glass, which showed in faint light their noble colouring, and made the black oak of the choir pews hardly more solid than the shadows. But on each side of the altar lay a grey marble figure of

---

1 Archbishop Richard Whately (1787–1863), author of *Elements of Logic* (1826) and *Elements of Rhetoric* (1826) as well as a number of texts on political economy, believed that rational scientific inquiry was compatible with religious faith and emphasized a scholarly, intellectual approach to the Bible.

a knight in full plate armour lying upon a low slab, with hands held up in everlasting prayer, and these figures, oddly enough, were always to be seen if there was any glimmer of light in the church. Their names were lost, but the peasants told of them that they had been fierce and wicked men, marauders by land and sea, who had been the scourge of their time, and had been guilty of deeds so foul that the house they had lived in—the big house, by the way, that had stood on the site of our cottage—had been stricken by lightning and the vengeance of Heaven. But for all that, the gold of their heirs had bought them a place in the church. Looking at the bad hard faces reproduced in the marble, this story was easily believed.

The church looked at its best and weirdest on that night, for the shadows of the yew trees fell through the windows upon the floor of the nave and touched the pillars with tattered shade. We sat down together without speaking, and watched the solemn beauty of the old church, with some of that awe which inspired its early builders. We walked to the chancel and looked at the sleeping warriors. Then we rested some time on the stone seat in the porch, looking out over the stretch of quiet moonlit meadows, feeling in every fibre of our being the peace of the night and of our happy love; and came away at last with a sense that even scrubbing and blackleading were but small troubles at their worst.

Mrs. Dorman had come back from the village, and I at once invited her to a *tête-à-tête*.

"Now, Mrs. Dorman," I said, when I had got her into my painting room, "what's all this about your not staying with us?"

"I should be glad to get away, sir, before the end of the month," she answered, with her usual placid dignity.

"Have you any fault to find, Mrs. Dorman?"

"None at all, sir; you and your lady have always been most kind, I'm sure—"

"Well, what is it? Are your wages not high enough?"

"No, sir, I gets quite enough."

"Then why not stay?"

"I'd rather not"—with some hesitation—"my niece is ill."

"But your niece has been ill ever since we came."

No answer. There was a long and awkward silence. I broke it.

"Can't you stay for another month?" I asked.

"No, sir. I'm bound to go by Thursday."

And this was Monday!

"Well, I must say, I think you might have let us know before. There's no time now to get anyone else, and your mistress is not fit to do heavy housework. Can't you stay till next week?"

"I might be able to come back next week."

I was now convinced that all she wanted was a brief holiday, which we should have been willing enough to let her have, as soon as we could get a substitute.

"But why must you go this week?" I persisted. "Come, out with it."

Mrs. Dorman drew the little shawl, which she always wore, tightly across her bosom, as though she were cold. Then she said, with a sort of effort—

"They say, sir, as this was a big house in Catholic times, and there was a many deeds done here."

The nature of the "deeds" might be vaguely inferred from the inflection of Mrs. Dorman's voice—which was enough to make one's blood run cold. I was glad that Laura was not in the room. She was always nervous, as highly-strung natures are, and I felt that these tales about our house, told by this old peasant woman, with her impressive manner and contagious credulity, might have made our home less dear to my wife.

"Tell me all about it, Mrs. Dorman," I said; "you needn't mind about telling me. I'm not like the young people who make fun of such things."

Which was partly true.

"Well, sir"—she sank her voice—"you may have seen in the church, beside the altar, two shapes."

"You mean the effigies of the knights in armour," I said cheerfully.

"I mean them two bodies, drawed out man-size in marble," she returned, and I had to admit that her description was a thousand times more graphic than mine, to say nothing of a certain weird force and uncanniness about the phrase "drawed out man-size in marble."

"They do say, as on All Saints' Eve them two bodies sits up on their slabs, and gets off of them, and then walks down the aisle, *in their marble*"—(another good phrase, Mrs. Dorman)—"and as the church clock strikes eleven they walks out of the church door, and over the graves, and along the bier-balk, and if it's a wet night there's the marks of their feet in the morning."

"And where do they go?" I asked, rather fascinated.

"They comes back here to their home, sir, and if any one meets them—"

"Well, what then?" I asked.

But no—not another word could I get from her, save that her niece was ill and she must go. After what I had heard I scorned to discuss the niece, and tried to get from Mrs. Dorman more details of the legend. I could get nothing but warnings.

"Whatever you do, sir, lock the door early on All Saints' Eve, and make the cross-sign over the doorstep and on the windows."

"But has any one ever seen these things?" I persisted.

"That's not for me to say. I know what I know, sir."

"Well, who was here last year?"

"No one, sir; the lady as owned the house only stayed here in summer, and she always went to London a full month afore the night. And I'm sorry to inconvenience you and your lady, but my niece is ill and I must go on Thursday."

I could have shaken her for her absurd reiteration of that obvious fiction, after she had told me her real reasons.

She was determined to go, nor could our united entreaties move her in the least.

I did not tell Laura the legend of the shapes that "walked in their marble," partly because a legend concerning our house might perhaps trouble my wife, and partly, I think, from some more occult reason. This was not quite the same to me as any other story, and I did not want to talk about it till the day was over. I had very soon ceased to think of the legend, however. I was painting a portrait of Laura, against the lattice window, and I could not think of much else. I had got a splendid background of yellow and grey sunset, and was working away with enthusiasm at her lace. On Thursday Mrs. Dorman went. She relented, at parting, so far as to say—

"Don't you put yourself about too much, ma'am, and if there's any little thing I can do next week, I'm sure I shan't mind."

From which I inferred that she wished to come back to us after Hallowe'en. Up to the last she adhered to the fiction of the niece with touching fidelity.

Thursday passed off pretty well. Laura showed marked ability in the matter of steak and potatoes, and I confess that my knives, and the plates, which I insisted upon washing, were better done than I had dared to expect.

Friday came. It is about what happened on that Friday that this is written. I wonder if I should have believed it, if anyone had told it to me. I will write the story of it as quickly and plainly as I can. Everything that happened on that day is burnt into my brain. I shall not forget anything, nor leave anything out.

I got up early, I remember, and lighted the kitchen fire, and had just achieved a smoky success, when my little wife came running down, as sunny and sweet as the clear October morning itself. We prepared breakfast together, and found it very good fun. The housework was soon done, and when brushes and brooms and pails were quiet again, the house was still indeed. It is wonderful what a difference one makes in a house. We really missed Mrs. Dorman, quite apart from considerations concerning pots and pans. We spent the day in dusting our books and putting them straight, and dined gaily on cold steak and coffee. Laura was, if possible, brighter and gayer and sweeter than usual, and I began to think that a little domestic toil was really good for her. We had never been so merry since we were married, and the walk we had that after-noon was, I think, the happiest time of all my life. When we had watched the deep scarlet clouds slowly pale into leaden grey against a pale-green sky, and saw the white mists curl up along the hedgerows in the distant marsh, we came back to the house, silently, hand in hand.

"You are sad, my darling," I said, half-jestingly, as we sat down together in our little parlour. I expected a disclaimer, for my own silence had been the silence of complete happiness. To my surprise she said—

"Yes. I think I am sad, or rather I am uneasy. I don't think I'm very well. I have shivered three or four times since we came in, and it is not cold, is it?"

"No," I said, and hoped it was not a chill caught from the treacherous mists that roll up from the marshes in the dying light. No—she said, she did not think so. Then, after a silence, she spoke suddenly—

"Do you ever have presentiments of evil?"

"No," I said, smiling, "and I shouldn't believe in them if I had."

"I do," she went on; "the night my father died I knew it, though he was right away in the north of Scotland." I did not answer in words.

She sat looking at the fire for some time in silence, gently stroking my hand. At last she sprang up, came behind me, and, drawing my head back, kissed me.

"There, it's over now," she said. "What a baby I am! Come, light the candles, and we'll have some of these new Rubinstein[2] duets."

And we spent a happy hour or two at the piano.

---

2 Anton Rubinstein (1829–94) was a popular Russian pianist and composer who wrote operas, symphonies, and concertos as well as solo works for the piano. The duet mentioned here would be a vocal duet set to one of his piano compositions, with words by a lyricist, sold as sheet music for home entertainment.

At about half-past ten I began to long for the good-night pipe, but Laura looked so white that I felt it would be brutal of me to fill our sitting-room with the fumes of strong cavendish.

"I'll take my pipe outside," I said.

"Let me come, too."

"No, sweetheart, not to-night; you're much too tired. I shan't be long. Get to bed, or I shall have an invalid to nurse tomorrow as well as the boots to clean."

I kissed her and was turning to go, when she flung her arms round my neck, and held me as if she would never let me go again. I stroked her hair.

"Come, Pussy, you're over-tired. The housework has been too much for you."

She loosened her clasp a little and drew a deep breath.

"No. We've been very happy today, Jack, haven't we? Don't stay out too long."

"I won't, my dearie."

I strolled out of the front door, leaving it unlatched. What a night it was! The jagged masses of heavy dark cloud were rolling at intervals from horizon to horizon, and thin white wreaths covered the stars. Through all the rush of the cloud river, the moon swam, breasting the waves and disappearing again in the darkness. When now and again her light reached the woodlands they seemed to be slowly and noiselessly waving in time to the swing of the clouds above them. There was a strange grey light over all the earth; the fields had that shadowy bloom over them which only comes from the marriage of dew and moonshine, or frost and starlight.

I walked up and down, drinking in the beauty of the quiet earth and the changing sky. The night was absolutely silent.

Nothing seemed to be abroad. There was no skurrying of rabbits, or twitter of the half-asleep birds. And though the clouds went sailing across the sky, the wind that drove them never came low enough to rustle the dead leaves in the woodland paths. Across the meadows I could see the church tower standing out black and grey against the sky. I walked there thinking over our three months of happiness—and of my wife, her dear eyes, her loving ways. Oh, my little girl! my own little girl; what a vision came then of a long, glad life for you and me together!

I heard a bell-beat from the church. Eleven already! I turned to go in, but the night held me. I could not go back into our little warm rooms yet. I would go up to the church. I felt vaguely that it would be good to carry my love and thankfulness to the sanctuary whither so many loads of sorrow and gladness had been borne by the men and women of the dead years.

I looked in at the low window as I went by. Laura was half lying on her chair in front of the fire. I could not see her face; only her little head showed dark against the pale blue wall. She was quite still. Asleep, no doubt. My heart reached out to her, as I went on. There must be a God, I thought, and a God who was good. How otherwise could anything so sweet and dear as she have ever been imagined?

I walked slowly along the edge of the wood. A sound broke the stillness of the night; it was a rustling in the wood. I stopped and listened. The sound stopped too. I went on, and now distinctly heard another step than mine answer mine like an echo. It was a poacher or a wood-stealer, most likely, for these were not unknown in our Arcadian neighbourhood. But whoever it was, he was a fool not to step more lightly. I turned into the wood, and now the footstep seemed to come from the path I had just left. It must be an echo, I thought. The wood looked perfect in the moonlight. The large dying ferns and the brushwood showed where through thinning foliage the pale light came down. The tree trunks stood up like Gothic columns all around me. They reminded me of the church, and I turned into the bier-balk, and passed through the corpse-gate between the graves to the low porch. I paused for a moment on the stone seat where Laura and I had watched the fading landscape. Then I noticed that the door of the church was open, and I blamed myself for having left it unlatched the other night. We were the only people who ever cared to come to the church except on Sundays, and I was vexed to think that through our carelessness the damp autumn airs had had a chance of getting in and injuring the old fabric. I went in. It will seem strange, perhaps, that I should have gone halfway up the aisle before I remembered—with a sudden chill, followed by as sudden a rush of self-contempt—that this was the very day and hour when, according to tradition, the "shapes drawed out man-size in marble" began to walk.

Having thus remembered the legend, and remembered it with a shiver, of which I was ashamed, I could not do otherwise than walk up towards the altar, just to look at the figures—as I said to myself; really what I wanted was to assure myself, first, that I did not believe the legend, and, secondly, that it was not true. I was rather glad that I had come. I thought now I could tell Mrs. Dorman how vain her fancies were, and how peacefully the marble figures slept on through the ghastly hour. With my hands in my pockets I passed up the aisle. In the grey dim light the eastern end of the church looked larger than usual, and the arches above the two tombs looked larger too. The moon came out and showed me the reason. I stopped short; my heart gave a leap that nearly choked me, and then sank sickeningly.

The "bodies drawed out man-size" *were gone*, and their marble slabs lay wide and bare in the vague moonlight that slanted through the east window.

Were they really gone? or was I mad? Clenching my nerves, I stooped and passed my hand over the smooth slabs, and felt their flat unbroken surface. Had someone taken the things away? Was it some vile practical joke? I would make sure, anyway. In an instant I had made a torch of a newspaper, which happened to be in my pocket, and lighting it held it high above my head. Its yellow glare illumined the dark arches and those slabs. The figures were gone. And I was alone in the church; or was I alone?

And then a horror seized me, a horror indefinable and indescribable—an overwhelming certainty of supreme and accomplished calamity. I flung down the torch and tore along the aisle and out through the porch, biting my lips as I ran to keep myself from shrieking aloud. Oh, was I mad—or what was this that possessed me? I leaped the churchyard wall and took the straight cut across the fields, led by the light from our windows. Just as I got over the first stile, a dark figure seemed to spring out of the ground. Mad still with that certainty of misfortune, I made for the thing that stood in my path, shouting, "Get out of the way, can't you!"

But my push met with a more vigorous resistance than I had expected. My arms were caught just above the elbow and held as in a vice, and the raw-boned Irish doctor actually shook me.

"Would ye?" he cried, in his own unmistakable accents— "would ye, then?"

"Let me go, you fool," I gasped. "The marble figures have gone from the church; I tell you they've gone."

He broke into a ringing laugh. "I'll have to give ye a draught tomorrow, I see. Ye've bin smoking too much and listening to old wives' tales."

"I tell you, I've seen the bare slabs."

"Well, come back with me. I'm going up to old Palmer's— his daughter's ill; we'll look in at the church and let me see the bare slabs."

"You go, if you like," I said, a little less frantic for his laughter; "I'm going home to my wife."

"Rubbish, man," said he; "d'ye think I'll permit of that? Are ye to go saying all yer life that ye've seen solid marble endowed with vitality, and me to go all me life saying ye were a coward? No, sir—ye shan't do ut."

The night air—a human voice—and I think also the physical contact with this six feet of solid common sense, brought me back a little to my ordinary self, and the word "coward" was a mental shower-bath.

"Come on, then," I said sullenly; "perhaps you're right."

He still held my arm tightly. We got over the stile and back to the church. All was still as death. The place smelt very damp and earthy. We walked up the aisle. I am not ashamed to confess that I shut my eyes: I knew the figures would not be there. I heard Kelly strike a match.

"Here they are, ye see, right enough; ye've been dreaming or drinking, asking yer pardon for the imputation."

I opened my eyes. By Kelly's expiring vesta[3] I saw two shapes lying "in their marble" on their slabs. I drew a deep breath, and caught his hand.

"I'm awfully indebted to you," I said. "It must have been some trick of light, or I have been working rather hard, perhaps that's it. Do you know, I was quite convinced they were gone."

"I'm aware of that," he answered rather grimly; "ye'll have to be careful of that brain of yours, my friend, I assure ye."

He was leaning over and looking at the right-hand figure, whose stony face was the most villainous and deadly in expression.

"By Jove," he said, "something has been afoot here—this hand is broken."

And so it was. I was certain that it had been perfect the last time Laura and I had been there.

"Perhaps someone has *tried* to remove them," said the young doctor.

"That won't account for my impression," I objected.

"Too much painting and tobacco will account for that, well enough."

"Come along," I said, "or my wife will be getting anxious. You'll come in and have a drop of whisky and drink confusion to ghosts and better sense to me."

"I ought to go up to Palmer's, but it's so late now I'd best leave it till the morning," he replied. "I was kept late at the Union, and I've had to see a lot of people since. All right, I'll come back with ye."

I think he fancied I needed him more than did Palmer's girl, so, discussing how such an illusion could have been

_____
3 A wooden match.

possible, and deducing from this experience large generalities concerning ghostly apparitions, we walked up to our cottage. We saw, as we walked up the garden-path, that bright light streamed out of the front door, and presently saw that the parlour door was open too. Had she gone out?

"Come in," I said, and Dr. Kelly followed me into the parlour. It was all ablaze with candles, not only the wax ones, but at least a dozen guttering, glaring tallow dips, stuck in vases and ornaments in unlikely places. Light, I knew, was Laura's remedy for nervousness. Poor child! Why had I left her? Brute that I was.

We glanced round the room, and at first we did not see her. The window was open, and the draught set all the candles flaring one way. Her chair was empty and her handkerchief and book lay on the floor. I turned to the window. There, in the recess of the window, I saw her. Oh, my child, my love, had she gone to that window to watch for me? And what had come into the room behind her? To what had she turned with that look of frantic fear and horror? Oh, my little one, had she thought that it was I whose step she heard, and turned to meet—what?

She had fallen back across a table in the window, and her body lay half on it and half on the window-seat, and her head hung down over the table, the brown hair loosened and fallen to the carpet. Her lips were drawn back, and her eyes wide, wide open. They saw nothing now. What had they seen last?

The doctor moved towards her, but I pushed him aside and sprang to her; caught her in my arms and cried—

"It's all right, Laura! I've got you safe, wifie."

She fell into my arms in a heap. I clasped her and kissed her, and called her by all her pet names, but I think I knew all the time that she was dead. Her hands were tightly clenched. In one of them she held something fast. When I was quite sure that she was dead, and that nothing mattered at all any more, I let him open her hand to see what she held.

It was a grey marble finger.

Two poems by
Ethna Carbery (Anna MacManus)

THE LOVE-TALKER

I met the Love-Talker one eve in the glen,
He was handsomer than any of our handsome young
    men,
His eyes were blacker than the sloe, his voice sweeter
    far
Than the crooning of old Kevin's pipes beyond in
    Coolnagar.

I was bound for the milking with a heart fair and
    free—
My grief! my grief! that bitter hour drained the life
    from me;
I thought him human lover, though his lips on mine
    were cold,
And the breath of death blew keen on me within his
    hold.

I know not what way he came, no shadow fell behind,
But all the sighing rushes swayed beneath a fairy
    wind;
The thrush ceased its singing, a mist crept about,
We two clung together—with the world shut out.

Beyond the ghostly mist I could hear my cattle low,
The little cow from Ballina, clean as driven snow,
The dun cow from Kerry, the roan from Inisheer,
Oh, pitiful their calling—and his whispers in my ear!

His eyes were a fire; his words were a snare;
I cried my mother's name, but no help was there;
I made the blessed Sign: then he gave a dreary moan,
A wisp of cloud went floating by, and I stood alone.

Running ever thro' my head is an old-time rune—
"Who meets the Love-Talker must weave her shroud
    soon."
My mother's face is furrowed with the salt tears that
    fall,
But the kind eyes of my father are the saddest sight
    of all.

I have spun the fleecy lint and now my wheel is still,
The linen length is woven for my shroud fine and
    chill,
I shall stretch me on the bed where a happy maid I
    lay—
Pray for the soul of Máire Og at dawning of the day!

NIAMH[1]

Oh, who is she, and what is she?
A beauty born eternally
Of shimmering moonshine, sunset flame,
And rose-red heart of dawn;
None knows the secret ways she came—
Whither she journeys on.

I follow her, I follow her
By haunted pools with dreams astir,
And over blue unwearied tides
Of shadow-waves, where sleep
Old loves; old hates, whose doom derides
Vows we forget to keep.

I send my cry, I send my cry
Adown the arches of the sky,
Along the pathway of the stars,
Through quiet and through stress;
I beat against the saffron bars
That guard her loveliness.

---

1 In the Irish Fenian cycle, Niamh of the Golden Hair carries away Oisín, son of Fionn mac Cumhaill, to live with her in Tír na nÓg, the land of eternal youth. After he has lived with her for some time, he asks to return to Ireland so he can visit his father and the band of warriors he leads, the Fianna. She allows him to go but warns him that he must stay on the horse she has given him; his foot must not touch the ground. However, when he returns to Ireland, he finds that hundreds of years have passed—his father and the Fianna are only a memory. On his way back to Tír na nÓg, he tries to help some men move a stone, falls from his horse, and suddenly discovers that he has grown old. He will never find his way back to Niamh or Tír na nÓg again.

And low I hear, oh, low I hear,
Her cruel laughter, fluting clear,
I see far-off the drifted gold
Of wind-blown flying hair;
I stand without in dark and cold
And she is—Where? Where? Where?

THE PRINCESS BALADINA— HER ADVENTURE

WILLA CATHER

The Princess Baladina sat sullenly gazing out of her nursery window. There was no use in crying any more for there was no one there to see and pity her tears, and who ever cries unless there is some one to pity them? She had kicked at the golden door until it became evident that she was much more discomforted than the door, and then she gave it up and sat sullenly down and did nothing but watch the big bumble-bees buzzing about the honeysuckles outside the window. The Princess Baladina had been shut up in her nursery for being naughty. Indeed, she had been unusually naughty that day. In the first place she had scratched and bitten the nurse who had combed her golden hair in the morning. Later, while she was playing about the palace grounds, she had lost in the moat one of the three beautiful golden balls which her father had bought for her of an old Jewish magician from Bagdad who was staying at the court, and who bought up the queen's old dresses and loaned the courtiers money on their diamonds. Then she had been so rude to her fairy godmother who came to luncheon with them that her mother had reprimanded her twice. Finally, when she poured custard in her fairy godmother's ear-trumpet, she was sent up to her nursery. Now she sat locked up there and thinking how cruelly her family had used her. She wondered what she could do to make them repent of their harsh behavior and wish they had been kinder to their little Princess Baladina. Perhaps if she should die they would realize how brutal they had been. O yes, if she were to die, then they would grieve and mourn and put flowers on her grave every day, and cry for their little Baladina who would never gather flowers any more. Baladina wept a little herself at the pathetic picture she had conjured up. But she decided not to die, that was such a very decisive thing to do; besides, then she could not see the remorse of her family, and what good is it to have your family repent if you cannot have the satisfaction of seeing them reduced to sackcloth and ashes? So the Princess cast about for another plan. She might cut off her beautiful golden hair, but then she had no scissors; besides, if a young Prince should happen to come that way it would be awkward not to have any golden hair. Princesses are taught to think of these things early. She began thinking over all the stories she had read about Princesses and their adventures, until suddenly she thought of the story of the Princess Alice, who had been enchanted by a wizard. Yes, that was it, that would be the best revenge of all, she would be enchanted by a wizard, and her family would be in despair; her father would offer his kingdom to the knight who should free her, and some young Prince would come and break the spell and bear her triumphantly off to his own realm, on his saddle bow. Then her unfeeling parents would never see her any more, and her sisters and brothers would have no dear sweet little Princess to wait on.

But the next question was where to find a wizard. The Princess went over all the gentlemen of her acquaintance, but could not think of one who belonged to that somewhat complicated profession. Never mind, she would find one, she had heard of Princesses wandering away from their palaces on strange missions before. She waited through all the hot afternoon, and when the nurse brought her tea she took two of the buns and a piece of raisin cake and did them up carefully in a handkerchief, and said her prayers and let them put her to bed. She lay awake for a time, half hoping that her mother would come up to see her and relieve her from the obvious necessity of running away. But there was a court ball that night and no one came, so listening to the tempting strains of music and feeling more aggrieved and forgotten than ever, the little Princess fell asleep.

As soon as she had breakfasted in the morning, she took the buns tied up in the handkerchief and went down into the yard.

She waited awhile until there was no one looking and then slipped out through one of the rear gates. Once fairly outside, she drew a long breath and looked about her; yes, there was the green meadow and the blue sky, just as they always were in the Princess books. She started off across the meadow, keeping a little under the shadow of the wild crab hedge to better screen herself from the palace windows. She saw some little peasant children down by the pool watching some white things that must be sheep. O yes, they were sheep and the boys were shepherds' sons, thought Baladina. She approached them and greeted them politely.

"Kind shepherds, why keep ye your sheep so near the town?"

"These are not sheep, but geese, Silly," replied the biggest boy surlily.

"That is not the way to speak to a Princess," said Baladina angrily.

"Princess, so that's what you call yourself, Miss Stuck Up?" cried the big boy, and with that he set the geese on her.

The Princess fled in the wildest alarm, with the squawking geese after her, while the little peasant children rolled over and over on the grass, screaming with merriment. The chase did not continue long, for the Princess's long silk gown tripped her and she fell, covering her eyes with her hands and screaming with fright, expecting to feel the sharp beaks of the geese in her face at any moment. But just then a chubby curly-headed boy rode up on a donkey. He chased the geese away with his staff, and sliding down from his beast picked up the little Princess and brushed the dust from her hair.

"Who are you, little girl?" he asked.

"I am the Princess Baladina, and those naughty boys set their geese on me because I corrected them for being rude. They don't believe I'm a Princess; you believe it, don't you?"

"If you say so, of course I do," returned the boy, looking wonderingly at her with his big blue eyes and then doubtfully at his bare feet and rough clothes. "But what are you doing out here?"

"I want to find a wizard; do you know of one?"

"O yes, there's Lean Jack, he lives back of the mill. If you'll get on my donkey I'll walk and lead him and we'll get there in no time."

The Princess accepted this homage as her due and was soon on the donkey, while the boy trotted along beside her.

"What do you want of a wizard anyway, a spell to cure something?" he asked curiously.

"No," said Baladina. "I wish to become enchanted because my family have been unkind to me. And then I want some Prince to come and free me. You are not a Prince in disguise, I suppose?" she added hopefully.

The boy shook his head regretfully. "No, I am only the miller's son."

When they came to Lean Jack's house, they found the old man out in his garden hoeing melon vines. They approached slowly and stood still for some time, Baladina expecting him to at once perceive her and cast his spell. But the old man worked on until the braying of the donkey attracted his attention.

"Well, youngsters, what is it?" he asked, leaning on his spade and wiping his brow.

"I believe you are a wizard, sir?" inquired Baladina politely.

He nodded. "So they say; what can I do for you?"

"I have come," said Baladina, "to allow you to cast a spell upon me, as my family are very unkind to me and if I am enchanted some Prince will come and free me from your power and carry me off to his own country."

The wizard smiled grimly and returned to his hoeing. "Sorry I can't accommodate you, but I can't leave my melons. There is a fat wizard who lives in a little red house over the hill yonder; he may be able to give you what you want."

"Dear me," sighed Baladina as they turned away, "how very rude everyone is. Most wizards would be glad enough to get a chance to enchant a Princess."

"I wish you wouldn't be enchanted at all. It must be very uncomfortable, and I shouldn't like to see you changed into an owl or a fox or anything," said the miller's boy as he trotted beside her.

"It must be," said Baladina firmly; "all Princesses should be enchanted at least once."

When they reached the red house behind the hill they had considerable trouble in finding the wizard, and the miller's boy pounded on the door until his knuckles were quite blue. At last a big, jolly-looking man with a red cap on his head came to the window. The Princess rode her donkey up quite close to the window and told him what she wanted. The fat wizard leaned up against the window sill and laughed until the tears came to his eyes, and the Princess again felt that her dignity was hurt.

"So you want to be enchanted, do you, so a Prince can come and release you? Who sent you here? It was that lean rascal of a Jack, I'll warrant; he's always putting up jokes on me. This is the best yet. Has it occurred to you that when your Prince comes he will certainly kill me? That's the way they always do, you know; they slay the cruel enchanter and then bear off the maiden."

The Princess looked puzzled. "Well," she said thoughtfully, "in this case, if you leave me the power of speech, I will request him not to. It's unusual, but I should hate to have him kill you."

"Thank you, my dear, now I call that considerate. But there is another point. Suppose your Prince should not hear of you, and should never come?"

"But they always do come," objected Baladina.

"Not always, I've known them to tarry a good many years. No, I positively cannot enchant you until you find your Prince."

Baladina turned her donkey and went slowly down to the road, leaving the fat wizard still laughing in the window.

"How disobliging these wizards seem to be, but this one seems to mean well. I believe they are afraid to undertake it with a Princess. Do you know where we can find a Prince?"

The miller's boy shook his head. "No, I don't know of any at all."

"Then I suppose we must just hunt for one," said Baladina.

They asked several carters whom they met if they knew where a Prince was to be found, but they all laughed so that Baladina grew quite discouraged. She stopped one boy on horseback and asked if he were a Prince in disguise, but he indignantly denied the charge.

So they went up the road and down a country lane that ran under the willow trees, and when they were both very tired and hungry Baladina opened her handkerchief and gave the miller's boy a bun. He refused the raisin cake, although he looked longingly at it, for he saw there was scarcely enough for two. Baladina sat down and ate it in the shade while he pulled some grass for the donkey. After their lunch they went on again. Just at the top of a hill they met a young man riding a black horse with a pack of hounds running beside him. "I know he is a Prince out hunting. You must stop him," whispered Baladina. So the miller's boy ran on ahead and shouted to the horseman.

"Are you a Prince, sir?" asked Baladina as she approached.

"Yes, miss, I am," he replied curtly.

Nothing daunted, Baladina told her story. The young man laughed and said impatiently, "You foolish child, have you stopped me all this time to tell me a fairy tale? Go home to your parents and let me follow my dogs, I have no time to be playing with silly little girls," and rode away.

"How unkind of him to talk so," said the Princess. "Besides, he is very little older than I."

"If he were here, I'd thrash him!" declared the miller's boy stoutly, clenching his fist.

They went on for a little while in a spiritless sort of way, but the boy hurt his toe on a stone until it bled and the Princess was hot and dusty and ached in every bone of her body. Suddenly she stopped the donkey and began to cry.

"There, there," said the miller's boy kindly, "don't do that. I'll find a Prince for you. You go home and rest and I'll hunt until I find one, if it takes forever."

Baladina dried her tears and spoke with sudden determination.

"You shall be my Prince yourself. I know you are one, really. You must be a changeling left at the mill by some wicked fairy who stole you from your palace."

The boy shook his head stubbornly. "No, I wish I were, but I am only a miller's boy."

"Well, you are the only nice person I have met all day; you have walked till your feet are sore and have let me ride your donkey, and your face is all scratched by the briars and you have had no dinner, and if you are not a Prince, you ought to be one. You are Prince enough for me, anyway. But I am so tired and hungry now, we will go home to the palace tonight and I will be enchanted in the morning. Come, get on the donkey and take me in front of you."

In vain he protested that the donkey could not carry them both; the Princess said that a Prince could not walk.

"I wish you had on shoes and stockings, though," she said. "I think a Prince should always have those."

"I have some for Sunday," said the miller's boy; "if I had only known I would have brought them."

As they turned slowly out of the lane they met a party of horsemen who were hunting for the Princess, and the king himself was among them.

"Ha there, you precious runaway, so here you are, and who is this you have with you?"

"He is my Prince," said the Princess, "and he is to have half the kingdom."

"Oh-h, he is, is he? Who are you, my man?"

"Please, sir, I am only the miller's son, but the Princess was hunting for a Prince and couldn't find one, so she asked me to be one."

"Hear, gentlemen, the Princess is out Prince-hunting early. Come here you little baggage." He lifted her on the saddle in front of him.

"He must come too, for he is my Prince!" cried the willful Princess.

But the king only laughed and gave the boy a gold piece, and rode away followed by his gentlemen, who were all laughing too. The miller's boy stood by his donkey, looking wistfully after them, and the Princess Baladina wept bitterly at the dearth of Princes.

Two poems by
Dora Sigerson Shorter

THE WATCHER IN THE WOOD

Deep in the wood's recesses cool
I see the fairy dancers glide,
In cloth of gold, in gown of green,
My lord and lady side by side.

But who has hung from leaf to leaf,
From flower to flower, a silken twine—
A cloud of grey that holds the dew
In globes of clear enchanted wine?

Or stretches far from branch to branch.
From thorn to thorn, in diamond rain,
Who caught the cup of crystal pure
And hung so fair the shining chain?

'Tis death, the spider, in his net,
Who lures the dancers as they glide,
In cloth of gold, in gown of green,
My lord and lady side by side.

THE WHITE WITCH

Heaven help your home tonight,
M'Cormac, for I know
A white witch woman is your bride:
You married for your woe.

You thought her but a simple maid
That roamed the mountainside;
She put the witch's glance on you,
And so became your bride.

But I have watched her close and long
And know her all too well;
I never churned before her glance
But evil luck befell.

Last week the cow beneath my hand
Gave out no milk at all;
I turned, and saw the pale-haired girl
Lean laughing by the wall.

"A little sup," she cried, "for me;
The day is hot and dry."
"Begone!" I said, "you witch's child,"
She laughed a loud goodbye.

And when the butter in the churn
Will never rise, I see
Beside the door the white witch girl
Has got her eyes on me.

At dawn today I met her out
Upon the mountainside,
And all her slender fingertips
Were each a crimson dyed.

Now I had gone to seek a lamb
The darkness sent astray:
Sore for a lamb the dawning winds
And sharp-beaked birds of prey.

But when I saw the white witch maid
With blood upon her gown,
I said, "I'm poorer by a lamb;
The witch has dragged it down."

And, "Why is this, your hands so red
All in the early day?"
I seized her by the shoulder fair.
She pulled herself away.

"It is the raddle on my hands,
The raddle all so red.
For I have marked M'Cormac's sheep
And little lambs," she said.

"And what is this upon your mouth
And on your cheek so white?"
"Oh, it is but the berries' stain";
She trembled in her fright.

"I swear it is no berries' stain.
Nor raddle all so red";
I laid my hands about her throat.
She shook me off, and fled.

I had not gone to follow her
A step upon the way,
When came I to my own lost lamb,
That dead and bloody lay.

"Come back," I cried, "you witch's child,
Come back and answer me";
But no maid on the mountainside
Could ever my eyes see.

I looked into the glowing east,
I looked into the south,
But did not see the slim young witch,
With crimson on her mouth.

Now, though I looked both well and long,
And saw no woman there,
Out from the bushes by my side
There crept a snow-white hare.

With knife in hand I followed it
By ditch, by bog, by hill:
I said, "Your luck be in your feet.
For I shall do you ill."

I said, "Come, be you fox or hare.
Or be you mountain maid,
I'll cut the witch's heart from you,
For mischief you have made."

She laid her spells upon my path,
The brambles held and tore,
The pebbles slipped beneath my feet,
The briars wounded sore.

And then she vanished from my eyes
Beside M'Cormac's farm,
I ran to catch her in the house
And keep the man from harm.

She stood with him beside the fire,
And when she saw my knife,
She flung herself upon his breast
And prayed he'd save her life.

"The woman is a witch," I cried,
"So cast her off from you";
"She'll be my wife today," he said,
"Be careful what you do!"

"The woman is a witch," I said;
He laughed both loud and long:
She laid her arms about his neck,
Her laugh was like a song.

"The woman is a witch," he mocked,
And laughed both long and loud;
She bent her head upon his breast,
Her hair was like a cloud.

I said, "See blood upon her mouth
And on each fingertip!"
He said, "I see a pretty maid,
A rose upon her lip."

He took her slender hand in his
To kiss the stain away—
Oh, well she cast her spell on him,
What could I do but pray?

"May Heaven guard your house tonight!"
I whisper as I go,
"For you have won a witch for bride,
And married for your woe."

BEWITCHED

Edith Wharton

I.

The snow was still falling thickly when Orrin Bosworth, who farmed the land south of Lonetop, drove up in his cutter to Saul Rutledge's gate. He was surprised to see two other cutters ahead of him. From them descended two muffled figures. Bosworth, with increasing surprise, recognized Deacon Hibben, from North Ashmore, and Sylvester Brand, the widower, from the old Bearcliff farm on the way to Lonetop.

It was not often that anybody in Hemlock County entered Saul Rutledge's gate; least of all in the dead of winter, and summoned (as Bosworth, at any rate, had been) by Mrs. Rutledge, who passed, even in that unsocial region, for a woman of cold manners and solitary character. The situation was enough to excite the curiosity of a less imaginative man than Orrin Bosworth.

As he drove in between the broken-down white gateposts topped by fluted urns, the two men ahead of him were leading their horses to the adjoining shed. Bosworth followed, and hitched his horse to a post. Then the three tossed off the snow from their shoulders, clapped their numb hands together, and greeted each other.

"Hallo, Deacon."

"Well, well, Orrin—." They shook hands.

"'Day, Bosworth," said Sylvester Brand, with a brief nod. He seldom put any cordiality into his manner, and on this occasion he was still busy about his horse's bridle and blanket.

Orrin Bosworth, the youngest and most communicative of the three, turned back to Deacon Hibben, whose long face, queerly blotched and mouldy-looking, with blinking peering eyes, was yet less forbidding than Brand's heavily-hewn countenance.

"Queer, our all meeting here this way. Mrs. Rutledge sent me a message to come," Bosworth volunteered.

The Deacon nodded. "I got a word from her too—Andy Pond come with it yesterday noon. I hope there's no trouble here—"

He glanced through the thickening fall of snow at the desolate front of the Rutledge house, the more melancholy in its present neglected state because, like the gateposts, it kept traces of former elegance. Bosworth had often wondered how such a house had come to be built in that lonely stretch between North Ashmore and Cold Corners. People said there had once been other houses like it, forming a little township called Ashmore, a sort of mountain colony created by the caprice of an English Royalist officer, one Colonel

Ashmore, who had been murdered by the Indians, with all his family, long before the Revolution. This tale was confirmed by the fact that the ruined cellars of several smaller houses were still to be discovered under the wild growth of the adjoining slopes, and that the Communion plate of the moribund Episcopal church of Cold Corners was engraved with the name of Colonel Ashmore, who had given it to the church of Ashmore in the year 1723. Of the church itself no traces remained. Doubtless it had been a modest wooden edifice, built on piles, and the conflagration which had burnt the other houses to the ground's edge had reduced it utterly to ashes. The whole place, even in summer, wore a mournful solitary air, and people wondered why Saul Rutledge's father had gone there to settle.

"I never knew a place," Deacon Hibben said, "as seemed as far away from humanity. And yet it ain't so in miles."

"Miles ain't the only distance," Orrin Bosworth answered; and the two men, followed by Sylvester Brand, walked across the drive to the front door. People in Hemlock County did not usually come and go by their front doors, but all three men seemed to feel that, on an occasion which appeared to be so exceptional, the usual and more familiar approach by the kitchen would not be suitable.

They had judged rightly; the Deacon had hardly lifted the knocker when the door opened and Mrs. Rutledge stood before them.

"Walk right in," she said in her usual dead-level tone; and Bosworth, as he followed the others, thought to himself: "Whatever's happened, she's not going to let it show in her face."

It was doubtful, indeed, if anything unwonted could be made to show in Prudence Rutledge's face, so limited was its scope, so fixed were its features. She was dressed for the occasion in a black calico with white spots, a collar of crochet-lace fastened by a gold brooch, and a gray woollen shawl crossed under her arms and tied at the back. In her small narrow head the only marked prominence was that of the brow projecting roundly over pale spectacled eyes. Her dark hair, parted above this prominence, passed tight and flat over the tips of her ears into a small braided coil at the nape; and her contracted head looked still narrower from being perched on a long hollow neck with cord-like throat muscles. Her eyes were of a pale cold gray, her complexion was an even white. Her age might have been anywhere from thirty-five to sixty.

The room into which she led the three men had probably been the dining-room of the Ashmore house. It was now used as a front parlour, and a black stove planted on a sheet of zinc stuck out from the delicately fluted panels of an old wooden mantel. A newly-lit fire smouldered reluctantly, and the room was at once close and bitterly cold.

"Andy Pond," Mrs. Rutledge cried to someone at the back of the house, "step out and call Mr. Rutledge. You'll likely find him in the woodshed, or round the barn somewheres." She rejoined her visitors. "Please suit yourselves to seats," she said.

The three men, with an increasing air of constraint, took the chairs she pointed out, and Mrs. Rutledge sat stiffly down upon a fourth, behind a rickety bead-work table. She glanced from one to the other of her visitors.

"I presume you folks are wondering what it is I asked you to come here for," she said in her dead-level voice. Orrin Bosworth and Deacon Hibben murmured an assent; Sylvester

Brand sat silent, his eyes, under their great thicket of eyebrows, fixed on the huge boot-tip swinging before him.

"Well, I allow you didn't expect it was for a party," continued Mrs. Rutledge.

No one ventured to respond to this chill pleasantry, and she continued: "We're in trouble here, and that's the fact. And we need advice—Mr. Rutledge and myself do." She cleared her throat, and added in a lower tone, her pitilessly clear eyes looking straight before her: "There's a spell been cast over Mr. Rutledge."

The Deacon looked up sharply, an incredulous smile pinching his thin lips. "A spell?"

"That's what I said: he's bewitched."

Again the three visitors were silent; then Bosworth, more at ease or less tongue-tied than the others, asked with an attempt at humour: "Do you use the word in the strict Scripture sense, Mrs. Rutledge?"

She glanced at him before replying: "That's how he uses it."

The Deacon coughed and cleared his long rattling throat. "Do you care to give us more particulars before your husband joins us?"

Mrs. Rutledge looked down at her clasped hands, as if considering the question. Bosworth noticed that the inner fold of her lids was of the same uniform white as the rest of her skin, so that when she dropped them her rather prominent eyes looked like the sightless orbs of a marble statue. The impression was unpleasing, and he glanced away at the text over the mantelpiece, which read:

The Soul That Sinneth It Shall Die.

"No," she said at length, "I'll wait."

At this moment Sylvester Brand suddenly stood up and pushed back his chair. "I don't know," he said, in his rough bass voice, "as I've got any particular lights on Bible mysteries; and this happens to be the day I was to go down to Starkfield to close a deal with a man."

Mrs. Rutledge lifted one of her long thin hands. Withered and wrinkled by hard work and cold, it was nevertheless of the same leaden white as her face. "You won't be kept long," she said. "Won't you be seated?"

Farmer Brand stood irresolute, his purplish underlip twitching. "The Deacon here—such things is more in his line..."

"I want you should stay," said Mrs. Rutledge quietly; and Brand sat down again.

A silence fell, during which the four persons present seemed all to be listening for the sound of a step; but none was heard, and after a minute or two Mrs. Rutledge began to speak again.

"It's down by that old shack on Lamer's pond; that's where they meet," she said suddenly.

Bosworth, whose eyes were on Sylvester Brand's face, fancied he saw a sort of inner flush darken the farmer's heavy leathern skin. Deacon Hibben leaned forward, a glitter of curiosity in his eyes.

"They—*who*, Mrs. Rutledge?"

"My husband, Saul Rutledge...and her..."

Sylvester Brand again stirred in his seat. "Who do you mean by her?" he asked abruptly, as if roused out of some far-off musing.

Mrs. Rutledge's body did not move; she simply revolved her head on her long neck and looked at him.

"Your daughter, Sylvester Brand."

The man staggered to his feet with an explosion of inarticulate sounds. "M—my daughter? What the hell are you talking about? My daughter? It's a damned lie...it's...it's..."

"Your daughter *Ora*, Mr. Brand," said Mrs. Rutledge slowly.

Bosworth felt an icy chill down his spine. Instinctively he turned his eyes away from Brand, and they rested on the mildewed countenance of Deacon Hibben. Between the blotches it had become as white as Mrs. Rutledge's, and the Deacon's eyes burned in the whiteness like live embers among ashes.

Brand gave a laugh: the rusty creaking laugh of one whose springs of mirth are never moved by gaiety. "My daughter *Ora*?" he repeated.

"Yes."

"My *dead* daughter?"

"That's what he says."

"Your husband?"

"That's what Mr. Rutledge says."

Orrin Bosworth listened with a sense of suffocation; he felt as if he were wrestling with long-armed horrors in a dream. He could no longer resist letting his eyes return to Sylvester Brand's face. To his surprise it had resumed a natural imperturbable expression. Brand rose to his feet. "Is that all?" he queried contemptuously.

"All? Ain't it enough? How long is it since you folks seen Saul Rutledge, any of you?" Mrs. Rutledge flew out at them.

Bosworth, it appeared, had not seen him for nearly a

year; the Deacon had only run across him once, for a minute, at the North Ashmore post office, the previous autumn, and acknowledged that he wasn't looking any too good then. Brand said nothing, but stood irresolute.

"Well, if you wait a minute you'll see with your own eyes; and he'll tell you with his own words. That's what I've got you here for—to see for yourselves what's come over him. Then you'll talk different," she added, twisting her head abruptly toward Sylvester Brand.

The Deacon raised a lean hand of interrogation.

"Does your husband know we've been sent for on this business, Mrs. Rutledge?" Mrs. Rutledge signed assent.

"It was with his consent, then—?"

She looked coldly at her questioner. "I guess it had to be," she said. Again Bosworth felt the chill down his spine. He tried to dissipate the sensation by speaking with an affectation of energy.

"Can you tell us, Mrs. Rutledge, how this trouble you speak of shows itself...what makes you think...?"

She looked at him for a moment; then she leaned forward across the rickety bead-work table. A thin smile of disdain narrowed her colourless lips. "I don't think—I know."

"Well—but how?"

She leaned closer, both elbows on the table, her voice dropping. "I seen 'em."

In the ashen light from the veiling of snow beyond the windows the Deacon's little screwed-up eyes seemed to give out red sparks. "Him and the dead?"

"Him and the dead."

"Saul Rutledge and—and Ora Brand?"

"That's so."

Sylvester Brand's chair fell backward with a crash. He was on his feet again, crimson and cursing. "It's a God-damned fiend-begotten lie..."

"Friend Brand...friend Brand..." the Deacon protested.

"Here, let me get out of this. I want to see Saul Rutledge himself, and tell him—"

"Well, here he is," said Mrs. Rutledge.

The outer door had opened; they heard the familiar stamping and shaking of a man who rids his garments of their last snowflakes before penetrating to the sacred precincts of the best parlour. Then Saul Rutledge entered.

II.

As he came in he faced the light from the north window, and Bosworth's first thought was that he looked like a drowned man fished out from under the ice—"self-drowned," he added. But the snow-light plays cruel tricks with a man's colour, and even with the shape of his features; it must have been partly that, Bosworth reflected, which transformed Saul Rutledge from the straight muscular fellow he had been a year before into the haggard wretch now before them.

The Deacon sought for a word to ease the horror. "Well, now, Saul—you look's if you'd ought to set right up to the stove. Had a touch of ague, maybe?"

The feeble attempt was unavailing. Rutledge neither moved nor answered. He stood among them silent, incommunicable, like one risen from the dead.

Brand grasped him roughly by the shoulder. "See here, Saul Rutledge, what's this dirty lie your wife tells us you've been putting about?"

Still Rutledge did not move. "It's no lie," he said.

Brand's hand dropped from his shoulder. In spite of the man's rough bullying power he seemed to be undefinably awed by Rutledge's look and tone.

"No lie? You've gone plumb crazy, then, have you?"

Mrs. Rutledge spoke. "My husband's not lying, nor he ain't gone crazy. Don't I tell you I seen 'em?"

Brand laughed again. "Him and the dead?"

"Yes."

"Down by the Lamer pond, you say?"

"Yes."

"And when was that, if I might ask?"

"Day before yesterday."

A silence fell on the strangely assembled group. The Deacon at length broke it to say to Mr. Brand: "Brand, in my opinion we've got to see this thing through."

Brand stood for a moment in speechless contemplation: there was something animal and primitive about him, Bosworth thought, as he hung thus, lowering and dumb, a little foam beading the corners of that heavy purplish underlip. He let himself slowly down into his chair. "I'll see it through."

The two other men and Mrs. Rutledge had remained seated. Saul Rutledge stood before them, like a prisoner at the bar, or rather like a sick man before the physicians who were to heal him. As Bosworth scrutinized that hollow face, so wan under the dark sunburn, so sucked inward and consumed by some hidden fever, there stole over the sound healthy man the thought that perhaps, after all, husband and wife spoke the truth, and that they were all at that moment really standing on the edge of some forbidden mystery. Things that the rational mind would reject without a thought seemed no longer so easy to dispose of as one looked at the actual Saul Rutledge and remembered the man he had been a year before. Yes; as the Deacon said, they would have to see it through...

"Sit down then, Saul; draw up to us, won't you?" the Deacon suggested, trying again for a natural tone.

Mrs. Rutledge pushed a chair forward, and her husband sat down on it. He stretched out his arms and grasped his knees in his brown bony fingers; in that attitude he remained, turning neither his head nor his eyes.

"Well, Saul," the Deacon continued, "your wife says you thought mebbe we could do something to help you through this trouble, whatever it is."

Rutledge's gray eyes widened a little. "No; I didn't think that. It was her idea to try what could be done."

"I presume, though, since you've agreed to our coming, that you don't object to our putting a few questions?"

Rutledge was silent for a moment; then he said with a visible effort: "No; I don't object."

"Well—you've heard what your wife says?"

Rutledge made a slight motion of assent. "And—what have you got to answer? How do you explain...?"

Mrs. Rutledge intervened. "How can he explain? I seen 'em."

There was a silence; then Bosworth, trying to speak in an easy reassuring tone, queried: "That so, Saul?"

"That's so."

Brand lifted up his brooding head. "You mean to say you... you sit here before us all and say..."

The Deacon's hand again checked him. "Hold on, friend Brand. We're all of us trying for the facts, ain't we?" He turned to Rutledge. "We've heard what Mrs. Rutledge says. What's your answer?"

"I don't know as there's any answer. She found us."

"And you mean to tell me the person with you was...was what you took to be..." the Deacon's thin voice grew thinner: "Ora Brand?"

Saul Rutledge nodded.

"You knew...or thought you knew...you were meeting with the dead?"

Rutledge bent his head again. The snow continued to fall in a steady unwavering sheet against the window, and Bosworth felt as if a winding-sheet were descending from the sky to envelop them all in a common grave.

"Think what you're saying! It's against our religion! Ora... poor child!...died over a year ago. I saw you at her funeral, Saul. How can you make such a statement?"

"What else can he do?" thrust in Mrs. Rutledge.

There was another pause. Bosworth's resources had failed him, and Brand once more sat plunged in dark meditation. The Deacon laid his quivering fingertips together, and moistened his lips.

"Was the day before yesterday the first time?" he asked.

The movement of Rutledge's head was negative.

"Not the first? Then when..."

"Nigh on a year ago, I reckon."

"God! And you mean to tell us that ever since—?"

"Well...look at him," said his wife. The three men lowered their eyes.

After a moment Bosworth, trying to collect himself, glanced at the Deacon. "Why not ask Saul to make his own statement, if that's what we're here for?"

"That's so," the Deacon assented. He turned to Rutledge. "Will you try and give us your idea...of...of how it began?"

There was another silence. Then Rutledge tightened his grasp on his gaunt knees, and still looking straight ahead, with his curiously clear unseeing gaze: "Well," he said, "I guess it begun away back, afore even I was married to Mrs. Rutledge..." He spoke in a low automatic tone, as if some invisible agent were dictating his words, or even uttering them for him. "You know," he added, "Ora and me was to have been married."

Sylvester Brand lifted his head. "Straighten that statement out first, please," he interjected.

"What I mean is, we kept company. But Ora she was very young. Mr. Brand here he sent her away. She was gone nigh to three years, I guess. When she come back I was married."

"That's right," Brand said, relapsing once more into his sunken attitude.

"And after she came back did you meet her again?" the Deacon continued.

"Alive?" Rutledge questioned.

A perceptible shudder ran through the room.

"Well—of course," said the Deacon nervously.

Rutledge seemed to consider. "Once I did—only once. There was a lot of other people round. At Cold Corners fair it was."

"Did you talk with her then?"

"Only a minute."

"What did she say?"

His voice dropped. "She said she was sick and knew she was going to die, and when she was dead she'd come back to me."

"And what did you answer?"

"Nothing."

"Did you think anything of it at the time?"

"Well, no. Not till I heard she was dead I didn't. After that I thought of it—and I guess she drew me." He moistened his lips.

"Drew you down to that abandoned house by the pond?"

Rutledge made a faint motion of assent, and the Deacon added: "How did you know it was there she wanted you to come?"

"She...just drew me..."

There was a long pause. Bosworth felt, on himself and the other two men, the oppressive weight of the next question to be asked. Mrs. Rutledge opened and closed her narrow lips once or twice, like some beached shellfish gasping for the tide. Rutledge waited.

"Well, now, Saul, won't you go on with what you was telling us?" the Deacon at length suggested.

"That's all. There's nothing else."

The Deacon lowered his voice. "She just draws you?"

"Yes."

"Often?"

"That's as it happens..."

"But if it's always there she draws you, man, haven't you the strength to keep away from the place?"

For the first time, Rutledge wearily turned his head toward his questioner. A spectral smile narrowed his colourless lips. "Ain't any use. She follers after me..."

There was another silence. What more could they ask, then and there? Mrs. Rutledge's presence checked the next question. The Deacon seemed hopelessly to revolve the matter. At length he spoke in a more authoritative tone. "These are forbidden things. You know that, Saul. Have you tried prayer?"

Rutledge shook his head.

"Will you pray with us now?"

Rutledge cast a glance of freezing indifference on his spiritual adviser. "If you folks want to pray, I'm agreeable," he said. But Mrs. Rutledge intervened.

"Prayer ain't any good. In this kind of thing it ain't no manner of use; you know it ain't. I called you here, Deacon, because you remember the last case in this parish. Thirty years ago it was, I guess; but you remember. Lefferts Nash—did praying help him? I was a little girl then, but I used to hear my folks talk of it winter nights. Lefferts Nash and Hannah Cory. They drove a stake through her breast. That's what cured him."

"Oh—" Orrin Bosworth exclaimed.

Sylvester Brand raised his head. "You're speaking of that old story as if this was the same sort of thing?"

"Ain't it? Ain't my husband pining away the same as Lefferts Nash did? The Deacon here knows—"

The Deacon stirred anxiously in his chair. "These are forbidden things," he repeated. "Supposing your husband is quite sincere in thinking himself haunted, as you might say. Well, even then, what proof have we that the...the dead woman...is the spectre of that poor girl?"

"Proof? Don't he say so? Didn't she tell him? Ain't I seen 'em?" Mrs. Rutledge almost screamed.

The three men sat silent, and suddenly the wife burst out: "A stake through the breast! That's the old way; and it's the only way. The Deacon knows it!"

"It's against our religion to disturb the dead."

"Ain't it against your religion to let the living perish as my husband is perishing?" She sprang up with one of her abrupt movements and took the family Bible from the what-not[1] in a corner of the parlour. Putting the book on the table, and moistening a livid fingertip, she turned the pages rapidly, till she came to one on which she laid her hand like a stony paper-weight. "See here," she said, and read out in her level chanting voice:

"'Thou shalt not suffer a witch to live.'

"That's in Exodus, that's where it is," she added, leaving the book open as if to confirm the statement.

Bosworth continued to glance anxiously from one to the other of the four people about the table. He was younger than any of them, and had had more contact with the modern world; down in Starkfield, in the bar of the Fielding House, he could hear himself laughing with the rest of the men at such old wives' tales. But it was not for nothing that he had been born under the icy shadow of Lonetop, and had shivered and hungered as a lad through the bitter Hemlock County winters. After his parents died, and he had taken hold of the farm himself, he had got more out of it by using improved methods, and by supplying

---

1 A piece of furniture with open shelves specifically to display ornaments and curios.

the increasing throng of summer-boarders over Stotesbury way with milk and vegetables. He had been made a selectman of North Ashmore; for so young a man he had a standing in the county. But the roots of the old life were still in him. He could remember, as a little boy, going twice a year with his mother to that bleak hill-farm out beyond Sylvester Brand's, where Mrs. Bosworth's aunt, Cressidora Cheney, had been shut up for years in a cold clean room with iron bars in the windows. When little Orrin first saw Aunt Cressidora she was a small white old woman, whom her sisters used to "make decent" for visitors the day that Orrin and his mother were expected. The child wondered why there were bars to the window. "Like a canary-bird," he said to his mother. The phrase made Mrs. Bosworth reflect. "I do believe they keep Aunt Cressidora too lonesome," she said; and the next time she went up the mountain with the little boy he carried to his great-aunt a canary in a little wooden cage. It was a great excitement; he knew it would make her happy.

The old woman's motionless face lit up when she saw the bird, and her eyes began to glitter. "It belongs to me," she said instantly, stretching her soft bony hand over the cage.

"Of course it does, Aunt Cressy," said Mrs. Bosworth, her eyes filling.

But the bird, startled by the shadow of the old woman's hand, began to flutter and beat its wings distractedly. At the sight, Aunt Cressidora's calm face suddenly became a coil of twitching features. "You she-devil, you!" she cried in a high squealing voice; and thrusting her hand into the cage she dragged out the terrified bird and wrung its neck. She was plucking the hot body, and squealing "she-devil, she-devil!" as they drew little Orrin from the room. On the way down the mountain his mother wept a great deal, and said: "You must never tell anybody that poor Auntie's crazy, or the men would come and take her down to the asylum at Starkfield, and the shame of it would kill us all. Now promise." The child promised.

He remembered the scene now, with its deep fringe of mystery, secrecy and rumour. It seemed related to a great many other things below the surface of his thoughts, things which stole up anew, making him feel that all the old people he had known, and who "believed in these things," might after all be right. Hadn't a witch been burned at North Ashmore? Didn't the summer folk still drive over in jolly buckboard loads to see the meeting-house where the trial had been held, the pond where they had ducked her and she had floated?...Deacon Hibben believed; Bosworth was sure of it. If he didn't, why did people from all over the place come to him when their animals had queer sicknesses, or when there was a child in the family that had to be kept shut up because it fell down flat and foamed? Yes, in spite of his religion, Deacon Hibben *knew*...

And Brand? Well, it came to Bosworth in a flash: that North Ashmore woman who was burned had the name of Brand. The same stock, no doubt; there had been Brands in Hemlock County ever since the white men had come there. And Orrin, when he was a child, remembered hearing his parents say that Sylvester Brand hadn't ever oughter married his own cousin, because of the blood. Yet the couple had had two healthy girls, and when Mrs. Brand pined away and died nobody suggested that anything had been wrong with her mind. And Vanessa and Ora were the handsomest girls anywhere round. Brand knew it, and scrimped and saved all he could to send Ora, the eldest, down to Starkfield to learn book-keeping. "When she's married I'll send you," he used to say to little Venny, who was his favourite. But Ora never married. She was away three years, during which Venny ran wild on the slopes of Lonetop; and when Ora came back she sickened and died—poor girl! Since then Brand had grown more savage and morose. He was a hard-working farmer, but there wasn't much to be got out of those barren Bearcliff acres. He was said to have taken to drink since his wife's death; now and then men ran across him in the "dives" of Stotesbury. But not often. And between times he laboured hard on his stony acres and did his best for his daughters. In the neglected graveyard of Cold Corners there was a slanting head-stone marked with his wife's name; near it, a year since, he had laid his eldest daughter. And sometimes, at dusk, in the autumn, the village people saw him walk slowly by, turn in between the graves, and stand looking down on the two stones. But he never brought a flower there, or planted a bush; nor Venny either. She was too wild and ignorant...

Mrs. Rutledge repeated: "That's in Exodus."

The three visitors remained silent, turning about their hats in reluctant hands. Rutledge faced them, still with that empty pellucid gaze which frightened Bosworth. What was he seeing?

"Ain't any of you folks got the grit——?" his wife burst out again, half hysterically.

Deacon Hibben held up his hand. "That's no way, Mrs. Rutledge. This ain't a question of having grit. What we want first of all is...proof..."

"That's so," said Bosworth, with an explosion of relief, as if the words had lifted something black and crouching from his breast. Involuntarily the eyes of both men had turned to Brand. He stood there smiling grimly, but did not speak.

"Ain't it so, Brand?" the Deacon prompted him.

"Proof that spooks walk?" the other sneered.

"Well—I presume you want this business settled too?"

The old farmer squared his shoulders. "Yes—I do. But I ain't a sperritualist. How the hell are you going to settle it?"

Deacon Hibben hesitated; then he said, in a low incisive tone: "I don't see but one way—Mrs. Rutledge's."

There was a silence.

"What?" Brand sneered again. "Spying?"

The Deacon's voice sank lower. "If the poor girl does walk...her that's your child...wouldn't you be the first to want her laid quiet? We all know there've been such cases...mysterious visitations...Can any one of us here deny it?"

"I seen 'em," Mrs. Rutledge interjected.

There was another heavy pause. Suddenly Brand fixed his gaze on Rutledge. "See here, Saul Rutledge, you've got to clear up this damned calumny, or I'll know why. You say my dead girl comes to you." He laboured with his breath, and then jerked out: "When? You tell me that, and I'll be there."

Rutledge's head drooped a little, and his eyes wandered to the window. "Round about sunset, mostly."

"You know beforehand?"

Rutledge made a sign of assent.

"Well, then—tomorrow, will it be?" Rutledge made the same sign.

Brand turned to the door. "I'll be there." That was all he said. He strode out between them without another glance or word. Deacon Hibben looked at Mrs. Rutledge. "We'll be there too," he said, as if she had asked him; but she had not spoken, and Bosworth saw that her thin body was trembling all over. He was glad when he and Hibben were out again in the snow.

III.

They thought that Brand wanted to be left to himself, and to give him time to unhitch his horse they made a pretense of hanging about in the doorway while Bosworth searched his pockets for a pipe he had no mind to light.

But Brand turned back to them as they lingered. "You'll meet me down by Lamer's pond tomorrow?" he suggested. "I want witnesses. Round about sunset."

They nodded their acquiescence, and he got into his sleigh, gave the horse a cut across the flanks, and drove off under the snow-smothered hemlocks. The other two men went to the shed.

"What do you make of this business, Deacon?" Bosworth asked, to break the silence.

The Deacon shook his head. "The man's a sick man—that's sure. Something's sucking the life clean out of him."

But already, in the biting outer air, Bosworth was getting himself under better control. "Looks to me like a bad case of the ague, as you said."

"Well—ague of the mind, then. It's his brain that's sick."

Bosworth shrugged. "He ain't the first in Hemlock County."

"That's so," the Deacon agreed. "It's a worm in the brain, solitude is."

"Well, we'll know this time tomorrow, maybe," said Bosworth. He scrambled into his sleigh, and was driving off in his turn when he heard his companion calling after him. The Deacon explained that his horse had cast a shoe; would Bosworth drive him down to the forge near North Ashmore, if it wasn't too much out of his way? He didn't want the mare slipping about on the freezing snow, and he could probably get the blacksmith to drive him back and shoe her in Rutledge's shed. Bosworth made room for him under the bearskin, and the two men drove off, pursued by a puzzled whinny from the Deacon's old mare.

The road they took was not the one that Bosworth would have followed to reach his own home. But he did not mind that. The shortest way to the forge passed close by Lamer's pond, and Bosworth, since he was in for the business, was not sorry to look the ground over. They drove on in silence.

The snow had ceased, and a green sunset was spreading upward into the crystal sky. A stinging wind barbed with ice-flakes caught them in the face on the open ridges, but when they dropped down into the hollow by Lamer's pond the air was as soundless and empty as an unswung bell. They jogged along slowly, each thinking his own thoughts.

"That's the house...that tumble-down shack over there, I suppose?" the Deacon said, as the road drew near the edge of the frozen pond.

"Yes: that's the house. A queer hermit-fellow built it years ago, my father used to tell me. Since then I don't believe it's ever been used but by the gipsies."

Bosworth had reined in his horse, and sat looking through pine-trunks purpled by the sunset at the crumbling structure.

Twilight already lay under the trees, though day lingered in the open. Between two sharply-patterned pine-boughs he saw the evening star, like a white boat in a sea of green.

His gaze dropped from that fathomless sky and followed the blue-white undulations of the snow. It gave him a curious agitated feeling to think that here, in this icy solitude, in the tumble-down house he had so often passed without heeding it, a dark mystery, too deep for thought, was being enacted. Down that very slope, coming from the graveyard at Cold Corners, the being they called "Ora" must pass toward the pond. His heart began to beat stiflingly. Suddenly he gave an exclamation: "Look!"

He had jumped out of the cutter and was stumbling up the bank toward the slope of snow. On it, turned in the direction of the house by the pond, he had detected a woman's footprints; two; then three; then more. The Deacon scrambled out after him, and they stood and stared.

"God—barefoot!" Hibben gasped. "Then it is...the dead..."

Bosworth said nothing. But he knew that no live woman would travel with naked feet across that freezing wilderness. Here, then, was the proof the Deacon had asked for—they held it. What should they do with it?

"Supposing we was to drive up nearer—round the turn of the pond, till we get close to the house," the Deacon proposed in a colourless voice. "Mebbe then..."

Postponement was a relief. They got into the sleigh and drove on. Two or three hundred yards farther the road, a mere lane under steep bushy banks, turned sharply to the right, following the bend of the pond. As they rounded the turn they saw Brand's cutter ahead of them. It was empty, the horse tied to a tree-trunk. The two men looked at each other again. This was not Brand's nearest way home.

Evidently he had been actuated by the same impulse which had made them rein in their horse by the pond-side, and then hasten on to the deserted hovel. Had he too discovered those spectral footprints? Perhaps it was for that very reason that he had left his cutter and vanished in the direction of the house. Bosworth found himself shivering all over under his bearskin. "I wish to God the dark wasn't coming on," he muttered. He tethered his own horse near Brand's, and without a word he and the Deacon ploughed through the snow, in the track of Brand's huge feet. They had only a few yards to walk to overtake him. He did not hear them following him, and when Bosworth spoke his name, and he stopped short and turned, his heavy face was dim and confused, like a darker blot on the dusk. He looked at them dully, but without surprise.

"I wanted to see the place," he merely said.

The Deacon cleared his throat. "Just take a look...yes...We thought so...But I guess there won't be anything to see..." He attempted a chuckle.

The other did not seem to hear him, but laboured on ahead through the pines. The three men came out together in the cleared space before the house. As they emerged from beneath the trees they seemed to have left night behind. The evening star shed a lustre on the speckless snow, and Brand, in that lucid circle, stopped with a jerk, and pointed to the same light foot-prints turned toward the house—the track of a woman in the snow. He stood still, his face working. "Bare feet..." he said.

The Deacon piped up in a quavering voice: "The feet of the dead."

Brand remained motionless. "The feet of the dead," he echoed.

Deacon Hibben laid a frightened hand on his arm. "Come away now, Brand; for the love of God come away."

The father hung there, gazing down at those light tracks on the snow—light as fox or squirrel trails they seemed, on the white immensity. Bosworth thought to himself, *The living couldn't walk so light—not even Ora Brand couldn't have, when she lived...* The cold seemed to have entered into his very marrow. His teeth were chattering.

Brand swung about on them abruptly. "Now!" he said, moving on as if to an assault, his head bowed forward on his bull neck.

"Now—now? Not in there?" gasped the Deacon. "What's the use? It was tomorrow he said—." He shook like a leaf.

"It's now," said Brand. He went up to the door of the crazy house, pushed it inward, and meeting with an unexpected resistance, thrust his heavy shoulder against the panel. The door collapsed like a playing-card, and Brand stumbled after it into the darkness of the hut. The others, after a moment's hesitation, followed.

Bosworth was never quite sure in what order the events that succeeded took place. Coming in out of the snow-dazzle, he seemed to be plunging into total blackness. He groped his way across the threshold, caught a sharp splinter of the fallen door in his palm, seemed to see something white and wraith-like surge up out of the darkest corner of the hut, and then heard a revolver shot at his elbow, and a cry—

Brand had turned back, and was staggering past him out into the lingering daylight. The sunset, suddenly flushing through the trees, crimsoned his face like blood. He held a revolver in his hand and looked about him in his stupid way.

"They do walk, then," he said and began to laugh. He bent his head to examine his weapon. "Better here than in the churchyard. They shan't dig her up now," he shouted out. The two men caught him by the arms, and Bosworth got the revolver away from him.

IV.

The next day Bosworth's sister Loretta, who kept house for him, asked him, when he came in for his midday dinner, if he had heard the news.

Bosworth had been sawing wood all the morning, and in spite of the cold and the driving snow, which had begun again in the night, he was covered with an icy sweat, like a man getting over a fever.

"What news?"

"Venny Brand's down sick with pneumonia. The Deacon's been there. I guess she's dying."

Bosworth looked at her with listless eyes. She seemed far off from him, miles away. "Venny Brand?" he echoed.

"You never liked her, Orrin."

"She's a child. I never knew much about her."

"Well," repeated his sister, with the guileless relish of the unimaginative for bad news, "I guess she's dying." After a pause she added: "It'll kill Sylvester Brand, all alone up there."

Bosworth got up and said: "I've got to see to poulticing the gray's fetlock." He walked out into the steadily falling snow.

Venny Brand was buried three days later. The Deacon read

the service; Bosworth was one of the pall-bearers. The whole countryside turned out, for the snow had stopped falling, and at any season a funeral offered an opportunity for an outing that was not to be missed. Besides, Venny Brand was young and handsome—at least some people thought her handsome, though she was so swarthy—and her dying like that, so suddenly, had the fascination of tragedy.

"They say her lungs filled right up...Seems she'd had bronchial troubles before...I always said both them girls was frail... Look at Ora, how she took and wasted away. And it's colder'n all outdoors up there to Brand's...Their mother, too, she pined away just the same. They don't ever make old bones on the mother's side of the family...There's that young Bedlow over there; they say Venny was engaged to him...Oh, Mrs. Rutledge, excuse me...Step right into the pew; there's a seat for you alongside of grandma..."

Mrs. Rutledge was advancing with deliberate step down the narrow aisle of the bleak wooden church. She had on her best bonnet, a monumental structure which no one had seen out of her trunk since old Mrs. Silsee's funeral, three years before. All the women remembered it. Under its perpendicular pile her narrow face, swaying on the long thin neck, seemed whiter than ever; but her air of fretfulness had been composed into a suitable expression of mournful immobility.

"Looks as if the stonemason had carved her to put atop of Venny's grave," Bosworth thought as she glided past him; and then shivered at his own sepulchral fancy. When she bent over her hymn book her lowered lids reminded him again of marble eyeballs; the bony hands clasping the book were bloodless. Bosworth had never seen such hands since he had seen old Aunt Cressidora Cheney strangle the canary-bird because it fluttered.

The service was over, the coffin of Venny Brand had been low-ered into her sister's grave, and the neighbours were slowly dispersing. Bosworth, as pall-bearer, felt obliged to linger and say a word to the stricken father. He waited till Brand had turned from the grave with the Deacon at his side. The three men stood together for a moment; but not one of them spoke. Brand's face was the closed door of a vault, barred with wrin-kles like bands of iron.

Finally the Deacon took his hand and said: "The Lord gave—"

Brand nodded and turned away toward the shed where the horses were hitched. Bosworth followed him. "Let me drive along home with you," he suggested.

Brand did not so much as turn his head. "Home? What home?" he said; and the other fell back.

Loretta Bosworth was talking with the other women while the men unblanketed their horses and backed the cutters out into the heavy snow. As Bosworth waited for her, a few feet off, he saw Mrs. Rutledge's tall bonnet lording it above the group. Andy Pond, the Rutledge farmhand, was backing out the sleigh.

"Saul ain't here today, Mrs. Rutledge, is he?" one of the vil-lage elders piped, turning a benevolent old tortoise-head about on a loose neck, and blinking up into Mrs. Rutledge's marble face.

Bosworth heard her measure out her answer in slow inci-sive words. "No. Mr. Rutledge he ain't here. He would 'a' come for certain, but his aunt Minorca Cummins is being buried down to Stotesbury this very day and he had to go down there. Don't it sometimes seem zif we was all walking right in the Shadow of Death?"

As she walked toward the cutter, in which Andy Pond was already seated, the Deacon went up to her with visible hesitation. Involuntarily Bosworth also moved nearer. He heard the Deacon say: "I'm glad to hear that Saul is able to be up and around."

She turned her small head on her rigid neck, and lifted the lids of marble.

"Yes, I guess he'll sleep quieter now.—And her too, maybe, now she don't lay there alone any longer," she added in a low voice, with a sudden twist of her chin toward the fresh black stain in the graveyard snow. She got into the cutter, and said in a clear tone to Andy Pond: "'S long as we're down here I don't know but what I'll just call round and get a box of soap at Hiram Pringle's."

Two poems by Charlotte Mew

THE FARMER'S BRIDE

Three Summers since I chose a maid,
Too young maybe—but more's to do
At harvest-time than bide and woo.
  When us was wed she turned afraid
Of love and me and all things human;
Like the shut of a winter's day
Her smile went out, and 'twadn't a woman—
  More like a little frightened fay.
    One night, in the Fall, she runned away.

"Out 'mong the sheep, her be," they said,
'Should properly have been abed;
But sure enough she wadn't there
Lying awake with her wide brown stare.
So over seven-acre field and up-along across the down
  We chased her, flying like a hare
  Before our lanterns. To Church-Town
    All in a shiver and a scare
  We caught her, fetched her home at last
    And turned the key upon her, fast.

She does the work about the house
As well as most, but like a mouse:
    Happy enough to chat and play
    With birds and rabbits and such as they,
    So long as men-folk keep away.
"Not near, not near!" her eyes beseech
When one of us comes within reach.
    The women say that beasts in stall
    Look round like children at her call.
    I've hardly heard her speak at all.

Shy as a leveret, swift as he,
Straight and slight as a young larch tree,
Sweet as the first wild violets, she,
To her wild self. But what to me?

The short days shorten and the oaks are brown,
    The blue smoke rises to the low grey sky,
One leaf in the still air falls slowly down,
    A magpie's spotted feathers lie
On the black earth spread white with rime,
The berries redden up to Christmas-time.
    What's Christmas-time without there be
    Some other in the house than we!

    She sleeps up in the attic there
    Alone, poor maid. 'Tis but a stair
Betwixt us. Oh! my God! the down,
The soft young down of her, the brown,
The brown of her—her eyes, her hair, her hair!

THE CHANGELING

Toll no bell for me, dear Father, dear Mother,
    Waste no sighs;
There are my sisters, there is my little brother
    Who plays in the place called Paradise,
Your children all, your children for ever;
    But I, so wild,
Your disgrace, with the queer brown face, was never,
    Never, I know, but half your child!

In the garden at play, all day, last summer,
    Far and away I heard
The sweet "tweet-tweet" of a strange new-comer,
    The dearest, clearest call of a bird.
It lived down there in the deep green hollow,
    My own old home, and the fairies say
The word of a bird is a thing to follow,
    So I was away a night and a day.

One evening, too, by the nursery fire,
    We snuggled close and sat round so still,
When suddenly as the wind blew higher,
    Something scratched on the window-sill.
A pinched brown face peered in—I shivered;
    No one listened or seemed to see;
The arms of it waved and the wings of it quivered,
    Whoo—I knew it had come for me;
    Some are as bad as bad can be!

All night long they danced in the rain,
Round and round in a dripping chain,
Threw their caps at the window-pane,
    Tried to make me scream and shout
    And fling the bedclothes all about:
I meant to stay in bed that night,
And if only you had left a light
    They would never have got me out.

    Sometimes I wouldn't speak, you see,
    Or answer when you spoke to me,
Because in the long, still dusks of Spring
You can hear the whole world whispering:
    The shy green grasses making love,
    The feathers grow on the dear, grey dove,
    The tiny heart of the redstart beat,
    The patter of the squirrel's feet,
The pebbles pushing in the silver streams,
The rushes talking in their dreams,
    The swish-swish of the bat's black wings,
    The wild-wood bluebell's sweet ting-tings,
        Humming and hammering at your ear,
        Everything there is to hear
In the heart of hidden things,
    But not in the midst of the nursery riot.
    That's why I wanted to be quiet,
        Couldn't do my sums, or sing,
        Or settle down to anything.
    And when, for that, I was sent upstairs
    I did kneel down to say my prayers;

But the King who sits on your high church steeple
Has nothing to do with us fairy people!

'Times I pleased you, dear Father, dear Mother,
    Learned all my lessons and liked to play,
And dearly I loved the little pale brother
    Whom some other bird must have called away.
Why did They bring me here to make me
    Not quite bad and not quite good,
Why, unless They're wicked, do They want, in spite, to take me
      Back to their wet, wild wood?

Now, every night I shall see the windows shining,
    The gold lamp's glow, and the fire's red gleam,
While the best of us are twining twigs and the rest of
      us are whining
    In the hollow by the stream.
Black and chill are Their nights on the wold;
    And They live so long and They feel no pain:
I shall grow up, but never grow old,
I shall always, always be very cold,
    I shall never come back again!

THE YELLOW WALLPAPER

CHARLOTTE PERKINS GILMAN

It is very seldom that mere ordinary people like John and myself secure ancestral halls for the summer.

A colonial mansion, a hereditary estate, I would say a haunted house, and reach the height of romantic felicity—but that would be asking too much of fate!

Still I will proudly declare that there is something queer about it.

Else, why should it be let so cheaply? And why have stood so long untenanted?

John laughs at me, of course, but one expects that in marriage.

John is practical in the extreme. He has no patience with faith, an intense horror of superstition, and he scoffs openly at any talk of things not to be felt and seen and put down in figures.

John is a physician, and *perhaps*—(I would not say it to a living soul, of course, but this is dead paper and a great relief to my mind)—*perhaps* that is one reason I do not get well faster.

You see, he does not believe I am sick!

And what can one do?

If a physician of high standing, and one's own husband, assures friends and relatives that there is really nothing the matter with one but temporary nervous depression—a slight hysterical tendency—what is one to do?

My brother is also a physician, and also of high standing, and he says the same thing.

So I take phosphates or phosphites—whichever it is, and tonics, and journeys, and air, and exercise, and am absolutely forbidden to "work" until I am well again.

Personally, I disagree with their ideas.

Personally, I believe that congenial work, with excitement and change, would do me good.

But what is one to do?

I did write for a while in spite of them; but it *does* exhaust me a good deal—having to be so sly about it, or else meet with heavy opposition.

I sometimes fancy that in my condition if I had less opposition and more society and stimulus—but John says the very worst thing I can do is to think about my condition, and I confess it always makes me feel bad.

So I will let it alone and talk about the house.

The most beautiful place! It is quite alone, standing well back from the road, quite three miles from the village. It makes me think of English places that you read about, for there are hedges and walls and gates that lock, and lots of separate little houses for the gardeners and people.

There is a *delicious* garden! I never saw such a garden—large and shady, full of box-bordered paths, and lined with long grape-covered arbors with seats under them.

There were greenhouses, too, but they are all broken now.

There was some legal trouble, I believe, something about the heirs and co-heirs; anyhow, the place has been empty for years.

That spoils my ghostliness, I am afraid, but I don't care—there is something strange about the house—I can feel it.

I even said so to John one moonlight evening, but he said what I felt was a *draught*, and shut the window.

I get unreasonably angry with John sometimes. I'm sure I never used to be so sensitive. I think it is due to this nervous condition.

But John says if I feel so I shall neglect proper self-control; so I take pains to control myself—before him, at least, and that makes me very tired.

I don't like our room a bit. I wanted one downstairs that opened on the piazza and had roses all over the window, and such pretty old-fashioned chintz hangings! but John would not hear of it.

He said there was only one window and not room for two beds, and no near room for him if he took another.

He is very careful and loving, and hardly lets me stir without special direction.

I have a schedule prescription for each hour in the day; he takes all care from me, and so I feel basely ungrateful not to value it more.

He said we came here solely on my account, that I was to have perfect rest and all the air I could get. "Your exercise depends on your strength, my dear," said he, "and your food somewhat on your appetite; but air you can absorb all the time." So we took the nursery at the top of the house.

It is a big, airy room, the whole floor nearly, with windows that look all ways, and air and sunshine galore. It was nursery first and then playground and gymnasium, I should judge; for the windows are barred for little children, and there are rings and things in the walls.

The paint and paper look as if a boys' school had used it. It is stripped off—the paper—in great patches all around the head of my bed, about as far as I can reach, and in a great place on the other side of the room low down. I never saw a worse paper in my life.

One of those sprawling flamboyant patterns committing every artistic sin.

It is dull enough to confuse the eye in following, pronounced enough to constantly irritate and provoke study, and when you follow the lame uncertain curves for a little distance they suddenly commit suicide—plunge off at outrageous angles, destroy themselves in unheard-of contradictions.

The color is repellant, almost revolting; a smouldering, unclean yellow, strangely faded by the slow-turning sunlight.

It is a dull yet lurid orange in some places, a sickly sulphur tint in others.

No wonder the children hated it! I should hate it myself if I had to live in this room long.

There comes John, and I must put this away,—he hates to have me write a word.

* * *

We have been here two weeks, and I haven't felt like writing before, since that first day.

I am sitting by the window now, up in this atrocious nursery, and there is nothing to hinder my writing as much as I please, save lack of strength.

John is away all day, and even some nights when his cases are serious.

I am glad my case is not serious!

But these nervous troubles are dreadfully depressing.

John does not know how much I really suffer. He knows there is no *reason* to suffer, and that satisfies him.

Of course it is only nervousness. It does weigh on me so not to do my duty in any way!

I meant to be such a help to John, such a real rest and comfort, and here I am a comparative burden already!

Nobody would believe what an effort it is to do what little I am able,—to dress and entertain, and order things.

It is fortunate Mary is so good with the baby. Such a dear baby!

And yet I *cannot* be with him, it makes me so nervous.

I suppose John never was nervous in his life. He laughs at me so about this wallpaper!

At first he meant to repaper the room, but afterwards he said that I was letting it get the better of me, and that nothing was worse for a nervous patient than to give way to such fancies.

He said that after the wallpaper was changed it would be the heavy bedstead, and then the barred windows, and then that gate at the head of the stairs, and so on.

"You know the place is doing you good," he said, "and really, dear, I don't care to renovate the house just for a three months' rental."

"Then do let us go downstairs," I said, "there are such pretty rooms there."

Then he took me in his arms and called me a blessed little goose, and said he would go down cellar, if I wished, and have it whitewashed into the bargain.

But he is right enough about the beds and windows and things.

It is as airy and comfortable a room as any one need wish, and, of course, I would not be so silly as to make him uncomfortable just for a whim.

I'm really getting quite fond of the big room, all but that horrid paper.

Out of one window I can see the garden, those mysterious deep-shaded arbors, the riotous old-fashioned flowers, and bushes and gnarly trees.

Out of another I get a lovely view of the bay and a little private wharf belonging to the estate. There is a beautiful shaded lane that runs down there from the house. I always fancy I see people walking in these numerous paths and arbors, but John has cautioned me not to give way to fancy in the least. He says that with my imaginative power and habit of story-making, a nervous weakness like mine is sure to lead to all manner of excited fancies, and that I ought to use my will and good sense to check the tendency. So I try.

I think sometimes that if I were only well enough to write a little it would relieve the press of ideas and rest me.

But I find I get pretty tired when I try.

It is so discouraging not to have any advice and companionship about my work. When I get really well, John says we will ask Cousin Henry and Julia down for a long visit; but he says he would as soon put fire-works in my pillow-case as to let me have those stimulating people about now.

I wish I could get well faster.

But I must not think about that. This paper looks to me as if it knew what a vicious influence it had!

There is a recurrent spot where the pattern lolls like a broken neck and two bulbous eyes stare at you upside down.

I get positively angry with the impertinence of it and the everlastingness. Up and down and sideways they crawl, and those absurd, unblinking eyes are everywhere. There is one place where two breadths didn't match, and the eyes go all up and down the line, one a little higher than the other.

I never saw so much expression in an inanimate thing before, and we all know how much expression they have! I used to lie awake as a child and get more entertainment and terror out of blank walls and plain furniture than most children could find in a toy-store.

I remember what a kindly wink the knobs of our big old bureau used to have, and there was one chair that always seemed like a strong friend.

I used to feel that if any of the other things looked too fierce I could always hop into that chair and be safe.

The furniture in this room is no worse than inharmonious, however, for we had to bring it all from downstairs. I suppose when this was used as a playroom they had to take the nursery things out, and no wonder! I never saw such ravages as the children have made here.

The wallpaper, as I said before, is torn off in spots, and it sticketh closer than a brother—they must have had persever-ance as well as hatred.

Then the floor is scratched and gouged and splintered, the plaster itself is dug out here and there, and this great heavy bed, which is all we found in the room, looks as if it had been through the wars.

But I don't mind it a bit—only the paper.

There comes John's sister. Such a dear girl as she is, and so careful of me! I must not let her find me writing.

She is a perfect and enthusiastic housekeeper, and hopes for no better profession. I verily believe she thinks it is the writing which made me sick!

But I can write when she is out, and see her a long way off from these windows.

There is one that commands the road, a lovely, shaded, winding road, and one that just looks off over the country. A lovely country, too, full of great elms and velvet meadows.

This wallpaper has a kind of sub-pattern in a different shade, a particularly irritating one, for you can only see it in certain lights, and not clearly then.

But in the places where it isn't faded and where the sun is just so, I can see a strange, provoking, formless sort of fig-ure, that seems to sulk about behind that silly and conspicuous front design.

There's sister on the stairs!

Well, the Fourth of July is over! The people are all gone and I am tired out. John thought it might do me good to see a little company, so we just had mother and Nellie and the children down for a week.

Of course I didn't do a thing. Jennie sees to everything now.

But it tired me all the same.

John says if I don't pick up faster he shall send me to Weir Mitchell[1] in the fall.

But I don't want to go there at all. I had a friend who was in his hands once, and she says he is just like John and my brother, only more so!

Besides, it is such an undertaking to go so far.

I don't feel as if it was worth while to turn my hand over for anything, and I'm getting dreadfully fretful and querulous.

I cry at nothing, and cry most of the time.

Of course I don't when John is here, or anybody else, but when I am alone.

And I am alone a good deal just now. John is kept in town very often by serious cases, and Jennie is good and lets me alone when I want her to.

So I walk a little in the garden or down that lovely lane, sit on the porch under the roses, and lie down up here a good deal.

I'm getting really fond of the room in spite of the wallpaper. Perhaps *because* of the wallpaper.

It dwells in my mind so!

---

1 Silas Weir Mitchell (1829–1914) was an American physician and specialist in neurology who developed the "rest cure" for what were then called hysteria and neurasthenia. Patients undergoing the rest cure were isolated and forbidden to work. They were largely confined to bed, fed a high-fat diet, and given electroconvulsive therapy to maintain their muscles. Both Charlotte Perkins Gilman and Virginia Woolf underwent the rest cure and spoke out against its use. In a 1913 article in *The Forerunner*, Gilman stated that she wrote "The Yellow Wallpaper" specifically as a commentary on the rest cure and sent a copy of it to Weir Mitchell. Although he never replied, he did change his treatment of nervous illnesses as a result.

I lie here on this great immovable bed—it is nailed down, I believe—and follow that pattern about by the hour. It is as good as gymnastics, I assure you. I start, we'll say, at the bottom, down in the corner over there where it has not been touched, and I determine for the thousandth time that I *will* follow that pointless pattern to some sort of a conclusion.

I know a little of the principle of design, and I know this thing was not arranged on any laws of radiation, or alternation, or repetition, or symmetry, or anything else that I ever heard of.

It is repeated, of course, by the breadths, but not otherwise.

Looked at in one way each breadth stands alone, the bloated curves and flourishes—a kind of "debased Romanesque" with *delirium tremens*[2]—go waddling up and down in isolated columns of fatuity.

But, on the other hand, they connect diagonally, and the sprawling outlines run off in great slanting waves of optic horror, like a lot of wallowing seaweeds in full chase.

The whole thing goes horizontally, too, at least it seems so, and I exhaust myself in trying to distinguish the order of its going in that direction.

They have used a horizontal breadth for a frieze, and that adds wonderfully to the confusion.

There is one end of the room where it is almost intact, and there, when the cross lights fade and the low sun shines directly upon it, I can almost fancy radiation after all,—the interminable grotesques seem to form around a common centre and rush off in headlong plunges of equal distraction.

It makes me tired to follow it. I will take a nap, I guess.

---

2 A severe form of alcohol withdrawal that can result in symptoms such as nausea, confusion, and hallucinations.

* * *

I don't know why I should write this.

I don't want to.

I don't feel able.

And I know John would think it absurd. But I *must* say what I feel and think in some way—it is such a relief!

But the effort is getting to be greater than the relief.

Half the time now I am awfully lazy, and lie down ever so much.

John says I mustn't lose my strength, and has me take cod liver oil and lots of tonics and things, to say nothing of ale and wine and rare meat.

Dear John! He loves me very dearly, and hates to have me sick. I tried to have a real earnest reasonable talk with him the other day, and tell him how I wish he would let me go and make a visit to Cousin Henry and Julia.

But he said I wasn't able to go, nor able to stand it after I got there; and I did not make out a very good case for myself, for I was crying before I had finished.

It is getting to be a great effort for me to think straight. Just this nervous weakness, I suppose.

And dear John gathered me up in his arms, and just carried me upstairs and laid me on the bed, and sat by me and read to me till it tired my head.

He said I was his darling and his comfort and all he had, and that I must take care of myself for his sake, and keep well.

He says no one but myself can help me out of it, that I must use my will and self-control and not let any silly fancies run away with me.

There's one comfort, the baby is well and happy, and does not have to occupy this nursery with the horrid wallpaper.

If we had not used it that blessed child would have! What a fortunate escape! Why, I wouldn't have a child of mine, an impressionable little thing, live in such a room for worlds.

I never thought of it before, but it is lucky that John kept me here after all. I can stand it so much easier than a baby, you see.

Of course I never mention it to them any more—I am too wise,—but I keep watch of it all the same.

There are things in that paper that nobody knows but me, or ever will.

Behind that outside pattern the dim shapes get clearer every day.

It is always the same shape, only very numerous.

And it is like a woman stooping down and creeping about behind that pattern. I don't like it a bit. I wonder—I begin to think—I wish John would take me away from here!

It is so hard to talk with John about my case, because he is so wise, and because he loves me so.

But I tried it last night.

It was moonlight. The moon shines in all around, just as the sun does.

I hate to see it sometimes, it creeps so slowly, and always comes in by one window or another.

John was asleep and I hated to waken him, so I kept still and watched the moonlight on that undulating wallpaper till I felt creepy.

The faint figure behind seemed to shake the pattern, just as if she wanted to get out.

I got up softly and went to feel and see if the paper *did* move, and when I came back John was awake.

"What is it, little girl?" he said. "Don't go walking about like that—you'll get cold."

I though it was a good time to talk, so I told him that I really was not gaining here, and that I wished he would take me away.

"Why darling!" said he, "our lease will be up in three weeks, and I can't see how to leave before.

"The repairs are not done at home, and I cannot possibly leave town just now. Of course if you were in any danger, I could and would, but you really are better, dear, whether you can see it or not. I am a doctor, dear, and I know. You are gaining flesh and color, your appetite is better, I feel really much easier about you."

"I don't weigh a bit more," said I, "nor as much; and my appetite may be better in the evening when you are here, but it is worse in the morning when you are away!"

"Bless her little heart!" said he with a big hug, "she shall be as sick as she pleases! But now let's improve the shining hours by going to sleep, and talk about it in the morning!"

"And you won't go away?" I asked gloomily.

"Why, how can I, dear? It is only three weeks more and then we will take a nice little trip of a few days while Jennie is getting the house ready. Really, dear, you are better!"

"Better in body perhaps"—I began, and stopped short, for he sat up straight and looked at me with such a stern, reproachful look that I could not say another word.

"My darling," said he, "I beg of you, for my sake and for our child's sake, as well as for your own, that you will never for one instant let that idea enter your mind! There is nothing so dangerous, so fascinating, to a temperament like yours. It is a false and foolish fancy. Can you not trust me as a physician when I tell you so?"

So of course I said no more on that score, and we went to sleep before long. He thought I was asleep first, but I wasn't, and I lay there for hours trying to decide whether that front pattern and the back pattern really did move together or separately.

On a pattern like this, by daylight, there is a lack of sequence, a defiance of law, that is a constant irritant to a normal mind.

The color is hideous enough, and unreliable enough, and infuriating enough, but the pattern is torturing.

You think you have mastered it, but just as you get well under way in following, it turns a back-somersault and there you are. It slaps you in the face, knocks you down, and tramples upon you. It is like a bad dream.

The outside pattern is a florid arabesque, reminding one of a fungus. If you can imagine a toadstool in joints, an interminable string of toadstools, budding and sprouting in endless convolutions,—why, that is something like it.

That is, sometimes!

There is one marked peculiarity about this paper, a thing nobody seems to notice but myself, and that is that it changes as the light changes.

When the sun shoots in through the east window—I

always watch for that first long, straight ray—it changes so quickly that I never can quite believe it.

That is why I watch it always.

By moonlight—the moon shines in all night when there is a moon—I wouldn't know it was the same paper.

At night in any kind of light, in twilight, candlelight, lamplight, and worst of all by moonlight, it becomes bars! The outside pattern I mean, and the woman behind it is as plain as can be.

I didn't realize for a long time what the thing was that showed behind, that dim sub-pattern, but now I am quite sure it is a woman.

By daylight she is subdued, quiet. I fancy it is the pattern that keeps her so still. It is so puzzling. It keeps me quiet by the hour.

I lie down ever so much now. John says it is good for me, and to sleep all I can.

Indeed, he started the habit by making me lie down for an hour after each meal.

It is a very bad habit I am convinced, for you see I don't sleep.

And that cultivates deceit, for I don't tell them I'm awake—O no!

The fact is, I am getting a little afraid of John.

He seems very queer sometimes, and even Jennie has an inexplicable look.

It strikes me occasionally, just as a scientific hypothesis,— that perhaps it is the paper!

I have watched John when he did not know I was looking,

and come into the room suddenly on the most innocent excuses, and I've caught him several times *looking at the paper!* And Jennie too. I caught Jennie with her hand on it once.

She didn't know I was in the room, and when I asked her in a quiet, a very quiet voice, with the most restrained manner possible, what she was doing with the paper—she turned around as if she had been caught stealing, and looked quite angry—asked me why I should frighten her so!

Then she said that the paper stained everything it touched, that she had found yellow smooches on all my clothes and John's, and she wished we would be more careful!

Did not that sound innocent? But I know she was studying that pattern, and I am determined that nobody shall find it out but myself!

Life is very much more exciting now than it used to be. You see I have something more to expect, to look forward to, to watch. I really do eat better, and am more quiet than I was.

John is so pleased to see me improve! He laughed a little the other day, and said I seemed to be flourishing in spite of my wallpaper.

I turned it off with a laugh. I had no intention of telling him it was *because* of the wallpaper—he would make fun of me. He might even want to take me away.

I don't want to leave now until I have found it out. There is a week more, and I think that will be enough.

I'm feeling ever so much better! I don't sleep much at night, for it is so interesting to watch developments; but I sleep a good deal in the daytime.

In the daytime it is tiresome and perplexing.

There are always new shoots on the fungus, and new shades of yellow all over it. I cannot keep count of them, though I have tried conscientiously.

It is the strangest yellow, that wallpaper! It makes me think of all the yellow things I ever saw—not beautiful ones like buttercups, but old foul, bad yellow things.

But there is something else about that paper—the smell! I noticed it the moment we came into the room, but with so much air and sun it was not bad. Now we have had a week of fog and rain, and whether the windows are open or not, the smell is here.

It creeps all over the house.

I find it hovering in the dining-room, skulking in the parlor, hiding in the hall, lying in wait for me on the stairs.

It gets into my hair.

Even when I go to ride, if I turn my head suddenly and surprise it—there is that smell!

Such a peculiar odor, too! I have spent hours in trying to analyze it, to find what it smelled like.

It is not bad—at first, and very gentle, but quite the subtlest, most enduring odor I ever met.

In this damp weather it is awful, I wake up in the night and find it hanging over me.

It used to disturb me at first. I thought seriously of burning the house—to reach the smell.

But now I am used to it. The only thing I can think of that it is like is the color of the paper! A yellow smell.

There is a very funny mark on this wall, low down, near the mopboard. A streak that runs round the room. It goes behind every piece of furniture, except the bed, a long, straight, even smooch, as if it had been rubbed over and over.

I wonder how it was done and who did it, and what they did it for. Round and round and round—round and round and round—it makes me dizzy!

I really have discovered something at last.

Through watching so much at night, when it changes so, I have finally found out.

The front pattern *does* move—and no wonder! The woman behind shakes it!

Sometimes I think there are a great many women behind, and sometimes only one, and she crawls around fast, and her crawling shakes it all over.

Then in the very bright spots she keeps still, and in the very shady spots she just takes hold of the bars and shakes them hard.

And she is all the time trying to climb through. But nobody could climb through that pattern—it strangles so; I think that is why it has so many heads.

They get through, and then the pattern strangles them off and turns them upside down, and makes their eyes white!

If those heads were covered or taken off it would not be half so bad.

I think that woman gets out in the daytime!

And I'll tell you why—privately—I've seen her!

I can see her out of every one of my windows!

It is the same woman, I know, for she is always creeping, and most women do not creep by daylight.

I see her on that long shaded lane, creeping up and down. I see her in those dark grape arbors, creeping all around the garden.

I see her on that long road under the trees, creeping along, and when a carriage comes she hides under the blackberry vines.

I don't blame her a bit. It must be very humiliating to be caught creeping by daylight!

I always lock the door when I creep by daylight. I can't do it at night, for I know John would suspect something at once.

And John is so queer now, that I don't want to irritate him. I wish he would take another room! Besides, I don't want anybody to get that woman out at night but myself.

I often wonder if I could see her out of all the windows at once.

But, turn as fast as I can, I can only see out of one at one time.

And though I always see her, she *may* be able to creep faster than I can turn!

I have watched her sometimes away off in the open country, creeping as fast as a cloud shadow in a high wind.

If only that top pattern could be gotten off from the under one! I mean to try it, little by little.

I have found out another funny thing, but I shan't tell it this time! It does not do to trust people too much.

There are only two more days to get this paper off, and I believe John is beginning to notice. I don't like the look in his eyes.

And I heard him ask Jennie a lot of professional questions about me. She had a very good report to give.

She said I slept a good deal in the daytime.

John knows I don't sleep very well at night, for all I'm so quiet!

He asked me all sorts of questions, too, and pretended to be very loving and kind.

As if I couldn't see through him!

Still, I don't wonder he acts so, sleeping under this paper for three months.

It only interests me, but I feel sure John and Jennie are secretly affected by it.

Hurrah! This is the last day, but it is enough. John is to stay in town over night, and won't be out until this evening.

Jennie wanted to sleep with me—the sly thing! but I told her I should undoubtedly rest better for a night all alone.

That was clever, for really I wasn't alone a bit! As soon as it was moonlight and that poor thing began to crawl and shake the pattern, I got up and ran to help her.

I pulled and she shook, I shook and she pulled, and before morning we had peeled off yards of that paper.

A strip about as high as my head and half around the room.

And then when the sun came and that awful pattern began to laugh at me, I declared I would finish it today!

We go away tomorrow, and they are moving all my furniture down again to leave things as they were before.

Jennie looked at the wall in amazement, but I told her merrily that I did it out of pure spite at the vicious thing.

She laughed and said she wouldn't mind doing it herself, but I must not get tired.

How she betrayed herself that time!

But I am here, and no person touches this paper but me,—not *alive*!

She tried to get me out of the room—it was too patent! But I said it was so quiet and empty and clean now that I believed I would lie down again and sleep all I could; and not to wake me even for dinner—I would call when I woke.

So now she is gone, and the servants are gone, and the things are gone, and there is nothing left but that great bedstead nailed down, with the canvas mattress we found on it.

We shall sleep downstairs tonight, and take the boat home tomorrow.

I quite enjoy the room, now it is bare again.

How those children did tear about here!

This bedstead is fairly gnawed!

But I must get to work.

I have locked the door and thrown the key down into the front path.

I don't want to go out, and I don't want to have anybody come in, till John comes.

I want to astonish him.

I've got a rope up here that even Jennie did not find. If that woman does get out, and tries to get away, I can tie her!

But I forgot I could not reach far without anything to stand on!

This bed will *not* move!

I tried to lift and push it until I was lame, and then I got so angry I bit off a little piece at one corner—but it hurt my teeth.

Then I peeled off all the paper I could reach standing on the floor. It sticks horribly and the pattern just enjoys it! All

those strangled heads and bulbous eyes and waddling fungus growths just shriek with derision!

I am getting angry enough to do something desperate. To jump out of the window would be admirable exercise, but the bars are too strong even to try.

Besides I wouldn't do it. Of course not. I know well enough that a step like that is improper and might be misconstrued.

I don't like to *look* out of the windows even—there are so many of those creeping women, and they creep so fast.

I wonder if they all come out of that wallpaper as I did?

But I am securely fastened now by my well-hidden rope— you don't get *me* out in the road there!

I suppose I shall have to get back behind the pattern when it comes night, and that is hard!

It is so pleasant to be out in this great room and creep around as I please!

I don't want to go outside. I won't, even if Jennie asks me to.

For outside you have to creep on the ground, and everything is green instead of yellow.

But here I can creep smoothly on the floor, and my shoulder just fits in that long smooch around the wall, so I cannot lose my way.

Why, there's John at the door!

It is no use, young man, you can't open it!

How he does call and pound!

Now he's crying for an axe.

It would be a shame to break down that beautiful door!

"John dear!" said I in the gentlest voice, "the key is down by the front steps, under a plantain leaf!"

That silenced him for a few moments.

Then he said—very quietly indeed, "Open the door, my darling!"

"I can't," said I. "The key is down by the front door under a plantain leaf!"

And then I said it again, several times, very gently and slowly, and said it so often that he had to go and see, and he got it, of course, and came in. He stopped short by the door.

"What is the matter?" he cried. "For God's sake, what are you doing!"

I kept on creeping just the same, but I looked at him over my shoulder.

"I've got out at last," said I, "in spite of you and Jane! And I've pulled off most of the paper, so you can't put me back!"

Now why should that man have fainted? But he did, and right across my path by the wall, so that I had to creep over him every time!

Two poems by Rosamund Marriott Watson

BALLAD OF THE BIRD-BRIDE

They never come back, though I loved them well;
  I watch the South in vain;
The snow-bound skies are blear and grey,
Waste and wide is the wild gull's way,
  And she comes never again.

Years agone, on the flat white strand,
  I won my sweet sea-girl:
Wrapped in my coat of the snow-white fur,
I watched the wild birds settle and stir,
  The grey gulls gather and whirl.

One, the greatest of all the flock,
  Perched on an ice-floe bare,
Called and cried as her heart were broke,
And straight they were changed, that fleet bird-folk,
  To women young and fair.

Swift I sprang from my hiding-place
  And held the fairest fast;
I held her fast, the sweet, strange thing:
Her comrades skirled, but they all took wing,
  And smote me as they passed.

I bore her safe to my warm snow house;
      Full sweetly there she smiled;
And yet, whenever the shrill winds blew,
She would beat her long white arms anew,
      And her eyes glanced quick and wild.

But I took her to wife, and clothed her warm
      With skins of the gleaming seal;
Her wandering glances sank to rest
When she held a babe to her fair, warm breast,
      And she loved me dear and leal.

Together we tracked the fox and the seal,
      And at her behest I swore
That bird and beast my bow might slay
For meat and for raiment, day by day,
      But never a grey gull more.

A weariful watch I keep for aye
      'Mid the snow and the changeless frost:
Woe is me for my broken word!
Woe, woe's me for my bonny bird,
      My bird and the love-time lost!

Have ye forgotten the old keen life?
      The hut with the skin-strewn floor?
O winged white wife, and children three,
Is there no room left in your hearts for me,
      Or our home on the low sea-shore?

Once the quarry was scarce and shy,
   Sharp hunger gnawed us sore,
My spoken oath was clean forgot,
My bow twanged thrice with a swift, straight shot,
   And slew me sea-gulls four.

The sun hung red on the sky's dull breast,
   The snow was wet and red;
Her voice shrilled out in a woeful cry,
She beat her long white arms on high,
   "The hour is here," she said.

She beat her arms, and she cried full fain
   As she swayed and wavered there.
"Fetch me the feathers, my children three,
Feathers and plumes for you and me,
   Bonny grey wings to wear!"

They ran to her side, our children three,
   With the plumage black and grey;
Then she bent her down and drew them near,
She laid the plumes on our children dear,
   'Mid the snow and the salt sea-spray.

"Babes of mine, of the wild wind's kin,
   Feather ye quick, nor stay.
Oh, oho! but the wild winds blow!
Babes of mine, it is time to go:
   Up, dear hearts, and away!"

And lo! the grey plumes covered them all,
     Shoulder and breast and brow.
I felt the wind of their whirling flight:
Was it sea or sky? was it day or night?
     It is always night-time now.

Dear, will you never relent, come back?
     I loved you long and true.
O winged white wife, and our children three,
Of the wild wind's kin though ye surely be,
     Are ye not of my kin too?

Ay, ye once were mine, and, till I forget,
     Ye are mine forever and aye,
Mine, wherever your wild wings go,
While shrill winds whistle across the snow
     And the skies are blear and grey.

THE ORCHARD OF THE MOON

So white with frost my garden flowers,
    The blinking sun seems half afraid
To shine among its sparkling bowers,
    Lest their frail garlands fade.

With dust of silver and of snow,
    From elfin uplands wide and white,
They came, their faërie crops to sow—
    The People of the Night.

The Little People, lithe and slim,
    With filmy wings and golden eyes—
Through the blue twilight cold and dim,
    I heard their mocking cries.

"Sleep sound, O Sun! sleep sound and sweet!
    Sunk in your purple-curtained bed,
The snow draws nigh on feathered feet,
    And all your flowers are dead."

"O Lady Moon!" is all their song,
    "Speed thou our harvest, Lady Moon!
Shine on our orchards all night long,
    So they may ripen soon."

And still they laugh, and still they sing;
    Their rustling voices come and go

Like last year's leaves that fall in Spring,
    Or birds amid the snow.

Nor, till the harvest-time be done
    Of faërie flower, of faërie fruit,
Shall he return, the golden Sun,
    To earthly bud and shoot.

A WHITE NIGHT

CHARLOTTE MEW

"The incident," said Cameron, "is spoiled inevitably in the telling, by its merely accidental quality of melodrama, its sensational machinery, which, to the view of anyone who didn't witness it, is apt to blur the finer outlines of the scene. The subtlety, or call it the significance, is missed, and unavoidably, as one attempts to put the thing before you, in a certain casual crudity, and unessential violence of fact. Make it a mediaeval matter—put it back some centuries—and the affair takes on its proper tone immediately, is tinctured with the sinister solemnity which actually enveloped it. But as it stands, a recollection, an experience, a picture, well, it doesn't reproduce; one must have the original if one is going to hang it on one's wall."

In spite of which I took it down the night he told it and, thanks to a trick of accuracy, I believe you have the story as I heard it, almost word for word.

It was in the spring of 1876, a rainless spring, as I remember it, of white roads and brown crops and steely skies.

Sent out the year before on mining business, I had been then some eighteen months in Spain. My job was finished; I was leaving the Black Country,[1] planning a vague look round, perhaps a little sport among the mountains, when a letter from my sister Ella laid the dust of doubtful schemes.

She was on a discursive honeymoon. They had come on from Florence to Madrid, and disappointed with the rank modernity of their last halt, wished to explore some of the least known towns of the interior: "Something unique, untrodden, and uncivilised," she indicated modestly. Further, if I were free and amiable, and so on, they would join me anywhere in Andalusia. I was in fact to show them round.

I did "my possible"; we roughed it pretty thoroughly, but the young person's passion for the strange bore her robustly through the risks and discomforts of those wilder districts which at best, perhaps, are hardly woman's ground.

King, on occasion nursed anxiety, and mourned his little luxuries; Ella accepted anything that befell, from dirt to danger, with a humorous composure dating back to nursery days—she had the instincts and the physique of a traveller, with a brilliancy of touch and a decision of attack on human

---

1 In the nineteenth century, the "Black Country" of Spain referred to the mining districts of the interior. There was a Black Country in England as well, comprising an area of the West Midlands dominated by the coal industry.

instruments which told. She took our mule-drivers in hand with some success. Later, no doubt, their wretched beasts were made to smart for it, in the reaction from a lull in that habitual brutality which makes the animals of Spain a real blot upon the gay indifferentism of its people.

It pleased her to devise a lurid *Dies Irae*[2] for these affable barbarians, a special process of re-incarnation for the Spaniard generally, whereby the space of one dog's life at least should be ensured to him.

And on the day I'm coming to, a tedious, dislocating journey in a springless cart had brought her to the verge of quite unusual weariness, a weariness of spirit only, she protested, waving a hand toward our man who lashed and sang alternately, fetching at intervals a sunny smile for the poor lady's vain remonstrances before he lashed again.

The details of that day—our setting forth, our ride, and our arrival—all the minor episodes stand out with singular distinctness, forming a background in one's memory to the eventual, central scene.

We left our inn—a rough *posada*[3]—about sunrise, and our road, washed to a track by winter rains, lay first through wide half-cultivated slopes, capped everywhere with orange trees and palm and olive patches, curiously bare of farms or villages, till one recalls the lawless state of those outlying regions and the absence of communication between them and town.

Abruptly, blotted in blue mist, vineyards and olives, with the groups of aloes marking off field boundaries, disappeared.

---

2 "Day of Wrath," the first words of a hymn that formerly began the Requiem Mass.

3 In Spanish, an inn.

We entered on a land of naked rock, peak after peak of it, cutting a jagged line against the clear intensity of the sky.

This passed again; with early afternoon our straight, white road grew featureless, a dusty, stretch, save far ahead the sun-tipped ridge of a sierra, and the silver ribbon of the river twisting among the barren hills. Toward the end we passed one of the wooden crosses set up on these roads to mark some spot of violence or disaster. These are the only sign-posts one encounters, and as we came up with it, our beasts were goaded for the last ascent.

Irregular grey walls came into view; we skirted them and turned in through a Roman gateway and across a bridge into a maze of narrow stone-pitched streets, spanned here and there by Moorish arches, and execrably rough to rattle over.

A strong illusion of the Orient, extreme antiquity and dream-like stillness marked the place.

Crossing the grey arcaded Plaza, just beginning at that hour to be splashed with blots of gaudy colour moving to the tinkling of the mule-bells, we were soon upon the outskirts of the town—the most untouched, remote and, I believe, the most remarkable that we had dropped upon.

In its neglect and singularity, it made a claim to something like supremacy of charm. There was the quality of diffidence belonging to unrecognised abandoned personalities in that appeal.

That's how it's docketed in memory—a city with a claim, which, as it happened, I was not to weigh.

Our inn, a long, one-storeyed building with caged windows, most of them unglazed, had been an old palacio; its broken fortunes hadn't robbed it of its character, its air.

The spacious place was practically empty, and the shuttered rooms, stone-flagged and cool, after our shadeless ride, invited one to a prolonged siesta; but Ella wasn't friendly to a pause. Her buoyancy survived our meal. She seemed even to face the morrow's repetition of that indescribable experience with serenity. We found her in the small paved garden, sipping chocolate and airing Spanish with our host, a man of some distinction, possibly of broken fortunes too.

The conversation, delicately edged with compliment on his side, was on hers a little blunted by a limited vocabulary, and left us both presumably a margin for imagination. *Sí, la Señora*, he explained as we came up, knew absolutely nothing of fatigue, and the impetuosity of the *Señora*, this attractive eagerness to make acquaintance with it, did great honour to his much forgotten, much neglected town. He spoke of it with rather touching ardour, as a place unvisited, but *"digno de renombre illustre,"* worthy of high fame.

It has stood still, it was perhaps too stationary; innovation was repellent to the Spaniard, yet this conservatism, lack of enterprise, the virtue or the failing of his country—as we pleased—had its aesthetic value. Was there not, he would appeal to the *Señora*, *"una belleza de reposo,"* a beauty of quiescence, a dignity above prosperity? *"Muy bien."* Let the *Señora* judge, you had it there!

We struck out from the town, perhaps insensibly toward the landmark of a Calvary, planted a mile or so beyond the walls, its three black shafts above the mass of roofs and pinnacles, in sharp relief against the sky, against which suddenly a flock of vultures threw the first white cloud. With the descending sun, the clear persistence of the blue was losing permanence, a breeze sprang up and birds began to call.

The Spanish evening has unique effects and exquisite exhilarations: this one led us on some distance past the Calvary and the last group of scattered houses—many in complete decay—which straggle, thinning outwards from the city boundaries into the *campo*.[4]

Standing alone, after a stretch of crumbling wall, a wretched little *venta*,[5] like a stop to some meandering sentence, closed the broken line.

The place was windowless, but through the open door an oath or two—the common blend of sacrilege and vileness—with a smell of charcoal, frying oil-cakes and an odour of the stable, drifted out into the freshness of the evening air.

Immediately before us lay a dim expanse of treeless plain: behind, clear cut against a smokeless sky, the flat roof lines and towers of the city, seeming, as we looked back on them, less distant than in fact they were.

We took a road which finally confronted us with a huge block of buildings, an old church and convent, massed in the shadow of a hill and standing at the entrance to three cross-roads.

The convent, one of the few remaining in the south, not fallen into ruin, nor yet put, as far as one could judge, to worldly uses, was exceptionally large. We counted over thirty windows in a line upon the western side below the central tower with its pointed turret; the eastern wing, an evidently older part, was cut irregularly with a few square gratings.

---

4 In Spanish, a grassy field or plain.
5 In Spanish, an inn, smaller than a *posada*.

The big, grey structure was impressive in its loneliness, its blank negation of the outside world, its stark expressionless detachment.

The church, of darker stone, was massive too; its only noticeable feature a small cloister with Romanesque arcades joining the nave on its south-western wall.

A group of peasant women coming out from vespers passed us and went chattering up the road, the last, an aged creature shuffling painfully some yards behind the rest still muttering her

> "*Madre purisima,*
> *Madre castisima.*
> *Ruega por nosostros,*"[6]

in a kind of automatic drone.

We looked in, as one does instinctively: the altar lights which hang like sickly stars in the profound obscurity of Spanish churches were being quickly blotted out.

We didn't enter then, but turned back to the convent gate, which stood half open, showing a side of the uncorniced cloisters, and a crowd of flowers, touched to an intensity or brilliance and fragrance by the twilight. Six or seven dogs, the sandy-coloured lurchers of the country, lean and wolfish-looking hounds, were sprawling round the gateway; save for this dejected crew, the place seemed resolutely lifeless; and this absence of a human note was just. One didn't want its solitude or silence touched, its really fine impersonality destroyed.

---

6 A prayer to the Virgin Mary. "*Nosostros*" is likely a typographical error for "*nosotros.*" Loosely translated, it means "Purest mother, most chaste mother, pray for us."

We hadn't meant—there wasn't light enough—to try the church again, but as we passed it, we turned into the small cloister. King, who had come to his last match, was seeking shelter from the breeze which had considerably freshened, and at the far end we came upon a little door, unlocked. I don't know why we tried it, but mechanically, as the conscientious tourist will, we drifted in and groped round. Only the vaguest outlines were discernible; the lancets of the lantern at the transept crossing, and a large rose window at the western end seemed, at a glance, the only means of light, and this was failing, leaving fast the fading panes.

One half-detected, almost guessed, the blind triforium, but the enormous width of the great building made immediate mark. The darkness, masking as it did distinctive features, emphasised the sense of space, which, like the spirit of a shrouded form, gained force, intensity, from its material disguise.

We stayed not more than a few minutes, but on reaching the small door again we found it fast; bolted or locked undoubtedly in the short interval. Of course we put our backs to it and made a pretty violent outcry, hoping the worthy sacristan was hanging round or somewhere within call. Of course he wasn't. We tried two other doors; both barred, and there was nothing left for it but noise. We shouted, I suppose, for half an hour, intermittently, and King persisted hoarsely after I had given out.

The echo of the vast, dark, empty place caught up our cries, seeming to hold them in suspension for a second in the void invisibility of roof and arches, then to fling them down in hollow repetition with an accent of unearthly mimicry which struck a little grimly on one's ear; and when we paused the silence seemed alert, expectant, ready to repel the first recurrence of unholy clamour. Finally, we gave it up; the hope of a release before the dawn, at earliest, was too forlorn. King, explosive and solicitous, was solemnly perturbed, but Ella faced the situation with an admirable tranquillity. Some chocolate and a muff would certainly, for her, she said, have made it more engaging, but poor dear men, the really tragic element resolved itself into—No matches, no cigar!

Unluckily we hadn't even this poor means of temporary light. Our steps and voices sounded loud, almost aggressive, as we groped about; the darkness then was shutting down and shortly it grew absolute. We camped eventually in one of the side chapels on the south side of the chancel, and kept a conversation going for a time, but gradually it dropped. The temperature, the fixed obscurity, and possibly a curious oppression in the spiritual atmosphere relaxed and forced it down.

The scent of incense clung about; a biting chillness crept up through the aisles; it got intensely cold. The stillness too became insistent; it was literally deathlike, rigid, exclusive, even awfully remote. It shut us out and held aloof; our passive presences, our mere vitality, seemed almost a disturbance of it; quiet as we were, we breathed, but it was breathless, and as time went on, one's impulse was to fight the sort of shapeless personality it presently assumed, to talk, to walk about and make a definite attack on it. Its influence on the others was presumably more soothing; obviously they weren't that way inclined.

Five or six hours must have passed. Nothing had marked them, and they hadn't seemed to move. The darkness seemed to thicken, in a way, to muddle thought and filter through into one's brain, and waiting, cramped and cold for it to lift, the soundlessness again impressed itself unpleasantly—it was intense, unnatural, acute.

And then it stirred.

The break in it was vague but positive; it might have been that, scarcely audible, the wind outside was rising, and yet not precisely that. I barely caught, and couldn't localise the sound.

Ella and King were dosing, they had had some snatches of uncomfortable sleep; I, I suppose, was preternaturally awake. I heard a key turn, and the swing back of a door, rapidly followed by a wave of voices breaking in. I put my hand out and touched King, and in a moment, both of them waked and started up.

I can't say how, but it at once occurred to us that quiet was our cue, that we were in for something singular.

The place was filling slowly with a chant, and then, emerging from the eastern end of the north aisle and travelling down just opposite, across the intervening dark, a line of light came into view, crossing the opening of the arches, out by the massive piers, a moving, flickering line, advancing and advancing with the voices.

The outlines of the figures in the long procession weren't perceptible, the faces, palely lit and level with the tapers they were carrying, one rather felt than saw; but unmistakably the voices were men's voices, and the chant, the measured, reiterated cadences, prevailed over the wavering light.

Heavy and sombre as the stillness which it broke, vaguely akin to it, the chant swept in and gained upon the silence with a motion of the tide. It was a music neither of the senses, nor the spirit, but the mind, as set, as stately, almost as inanimate as the dark aisles through which it echoed; even, colourless and cold.

And then, quite suddenly, against its grave and passionless inflections something clashed, a piercing intermittent note, an awful discord, shrilling out and dying down and shrilling out again—a cry—a scream.

The chant went on; the light, from where we stood, was steadily retreating, and we ventured forward. Judging our whereabouts as best we could, we made towards the choir and stumbled up some steps, placing ourselves eventually behind one of the pillars of the apse. And from this point, the whole proceeding was apparent.

At the west end the line of light was turning; fifty or sixty monks (about—and at a venture) habited in brown and carrying tapers, walking two and two, were moving up the central aisle towards us, headed by three, one with the cross between two others bearing heavy silver candlesticks with tapers, larger than those carried by the rest.

Reaching the chancel steps, they paused; the three bearing the cross and candlesticks stood facing the altar, while those following diverged to right and left and lined the aisle. The first to take up this position were quite young, some almost boys; they were succeeded gradually by older men, those at the tail of the procession being obviously aged and infirm.

And then a figure, white and slight, erect—a woman's figure—struck a startling note at the far end of the brown line, a note as startling as the shrieks which jarred recurrently, were jarring still against the chant.

A pace or two behind her walked two priests in surplices, and after them another, vested in a cope. And on the whole impassive company her presence, her disturbance, made no mark. For them, in fact, she wasn't there.

Neither was she aware of them; I doubt if to her consciousness, or mine, as she approached, grew definite, there was a creature in the place besides herself.

She moved and uttered her successive cries as if both sound and motion were entirely mechanical—more like a person in some trance of terror or of anguish than a voluntary rebel; her cries bespoke a physical revulsion into which her spirit didn't enter; they were not her own—they were outside herself; there was no discomposure in her carriage, nor, when we presently saw it, in her face. Both were distinguished by a certain exquisite hauteur, and this detachment of her personality from her distress impressed one curiously. She wasn't altogether real, she didn't altogether live, and yet her presence there was the supreme reality of the unreal scene, and lent to it, at least as I was viewing it, its only element of life.

She had, one understood, her part to play; she wasn't, for the moment, quite prepared; she played it later with superb effect.

As she came up with the three priests, the monks closed in and formed a semi-circle round them, while the priests advanced and placed themselves behind the monks who bore the cross and candlesticks, immediately below the chancel steps, facing the altar. They left her standing some few paces back, in the half-ring of sickly light shed by the tapers.

Now one saw her face. It was of striking beauty, but its age? One couldn't say. It had the tints, the purity of youth—it might have been extremely young, matured merely by the moment; but for a veil of fine repression which only years, it

seemed, could possibly have woven. And it was itself—this face—a mask, one of the loveliest that spirit ever wore. It kept the spirit's counsel. Though what stirred it then, in that unique emergency, one saw—to what had stirred it, or might stir it gave no clue. It threw one back on vain conjecture.

Put the match of passion to it—would it burn? Touch it with grief and would it cloud, contract? With joy—and could it find, or had it ever found, a smile? Again, one couldn't say.

Only, as she stood there, erect and motionless, it showed the faintest flicker of distaste, disgust, as if she shrank from some repellent contact. She was clad, I think I said, from head to foot in a white linen garment; head and ears were covered too, the oval of the face alone was visible, and this was slightly flushed. Her screams were changing into little cries or moans, like those of a spent animal, from whom the momentary pressure of attack has been removed. They broke from her at intervals, unnoticed, unsuppressed, and now on silence, for the monks had ceased their chanting.

As they did so one realised the presence of these men, who, up to now, had scarcely taken shape as actualities, been more than an accompaniment—a drone. They shifted from a mass of voices to a row of pallid faces, each one lit by its own taper, hung upon the dark, or thrown abruptly, as it were, upon a screen; all different; all, at first distinct, but linked together by a subtle likeness, stamped with that dye which blurs the print of individuality—the signet of the cloister.

Taking them singly, though one did it roughly, rapidly enough, it wasn't difficult at starting to detect varieties of natural and spiritual equipment. There they were, spread out for sorting, nonentities and saints and devils, side by side, and what was queerer, animated by one purpose, governed by one law.

Some of the faces touched upon divinity; some fell below humanity; some were, of course, merely a blotch of book and bell, and all were set impassively toward the woman standing there.

And then one lost the sense of their diversity in their resemblance; the similarity persisted and persisted till the row of faces seemed to merge into one face—the face of nothing human—of a system, of a rule. It framed the woman's, and one felt the force of it: she wasn't in the hands of men.

There was a pause filled only by her cries, a space of silence which they hardly broke; and then one of the monks stepped forward, slid into the chancel and began to light up the high altar. The little yellow tongues of flame struggled and started up, till first one line and then another starred the gloom.

Her glance had followed him; her eyes were fixed upon that point of darkness growing to a blaze. There was for her, in that illumination, some intense significance, and as she gazed intently on the patch of brilliance, her cries were suddenly arrested—quelled. The light had lifted something, given back to her an unimpaired identity. She was at last in full possession of herself. The flicker of distaste had passed and left her face to its inflexible, inscrutable repose.

She drew herself to her full height and turned towards the men behind her with an air of proud surrender, of magnificent disdain. I think she made some sign.

Another monk stepped out, extinguished and laid down his taper, and approached her.

I was prepared for something singular, for something

passably bizarre, but not for what immediately occurred. He touched her eyes and closed them; then her mouth, and made a feint of closing that, while one of the two priests threw over his short surplice a black stole and started audibly with a *Sub venite*. The monks responded. Here and there I caught the words or sense of a response. The prayers for the most part were unintelligible: it was no doubt the usual office for the dead, and if it was, no finer satire for the work in hand could well have been devised.[7] Loudly and unexpectedly above his unctuous monotone a bell clanged out three times. An Ave followed, after which two bells together, this time muffled, sounded out again three times. The priest proceeded with a *Miserere*, during which they rang the bells alternately, and there was something curiously suggestive and determinate about this part of the performance. The real action had, one felt, begun.

At the first stroke of the first bell her eyelids fluttered, but she kept them down; it wasn't until later at one point in the response, "*Non intres in judicium cum ancilla tua Domine*," she yielded to an impulse of her lips, permitted them the shadow of a smile. But for this slip she looked the thing of death they reckoned to have made of her—detached herself, with an inspired touch, from all the living actors in the solemn farce, from all apparent apprehension of the scene. I, too, was quite incredibly outside it all.

I hadn't even asked myself precisely what was going to take place. Possibly I had caught the trick of her quiescence,

---

7 The Office of the Dead is a cycle of psalms and prayers for the souls of those who have died. It could also be read to individuals as a part of Extreme Unction, the final sacrament administered to those about to die, or recited during a funeral. The Latin phrases that follow are from the Office of the Dead.

acquiescence, and I went no further than she went; I waited—
waited with her, as it were, to see it through. And I experienced
a vague, almost resentful sense of interruption, incongruity,
when King broke in to ask me what was up. He brought me
back to Ella's presence, to the consciousness that this, so far
as the spectators were concerned, was not a woman's comedy.

I made it briefly plain to them, as I knew something of
the place and people, that any movement on our side would
probably prove more than rash, and turned again to what was
going forward.

They were clumsily transforming the white figure. Two
monks had robed her in a habit of their colour of her order,
I suppose, and were now putting on the scapular and girdle.
Finally they flung over her the long white-hooded cloak and
awkwardly arranged the veil, leaving her face uncovered; then
they joined her hands and placed between them a small cross.

This change of setting emphasised my first impression of
her face; the mask was lovelier now and more complete.

Two voices started sonorously, "*Libera me, Domine*," the
monks took up the chant, the whole assembly now began to
move, the muffled bells to ring again at intervals, while the procession formed and filed into the choir. The monks proceeded
to their stalls, the younger taking places in the rear. The two
who had assisted at the robing led the passive figure to the
centre of the chancel, where the three who bore the cross and
candlesticks turned round and stood a short way off confronting her. Two others, carrying the censer and *bénitier*,[8] stationed
themselves immediately behind her with the priests and the
officiant, who now, in a loud voice, began his recitations.

---

8 A container for holy water.

They seemed, with variations, to be going through it all again. I caught the "*Non intres in judicium*" and the "*Sub venite*" recurring with the force of a refrain. It was a long elaborate affair. The grave deliberation of its detail heightened its effect. Not to be tedious, I give it you in brief. It lasted altogether possibly two hours.

The priest assisting the officiant, lifting the border of his cope, attended him when he proceeded first to sprinkle, then to incense the presumably dead figure, with the crucifix confronting it, held almost like a challenge to its sightless face. They made the usual inclinations to the image as they passed it, and repeated the performance of the incensing and sprinkling with extreme formality at intervals, in all, I think, three times.

There was no break in the continuous drone proceeding from the choir; they kept it going; none of them looked up—or none at least of whom I had a view—when four young monks slid out, and, kneeling down in the clear space between her and the crucifix, dislodged a stone which must have previously been loosened in the paving of the chancel, and disclosed a cavity, the depth of which I wasn't near enough to see.

For this I wasn't quite prepared, and yet I wasn't discomposed. I can't attempt to make it clear under what pressure I accepted this impossible *dénouement*, but I did accept it. More than that, I was exclusively absorbed in her reception of it. Though she couldn't, wouldn't see, she must have been aware of what was happening. But on the other hand, she was prepared, dispassionately ready, for the end.

All through the dragging length of the long offices, although she hadn't stirred or given any sign (except that one faint shadow of a smile) of consciousness, I felt the force of her

intense vitality, the tension of its absolute impression. The life
of those enclosing presences seemed to have passed into her
presence, to be concentrated there. For to my view it was these
men who held her in death's grip who didn't live, and she alone
who was absorbently alive.

The candles, burning steadily on either side the crucifix,
the soft illumination of innumerable altar lights confronting
her, intensified the darkness which above her and behind her—
everywhere beyond the narrow confines of the feeble light in
which she stood—prevailed.

This setting lent to her the aspect of an unsubstantial,
almost supernatural figure, suddenly arrested in its passage
through the dark.

She stood compliantly and absolutely still. If she had
swayed, or given any hint of wavering, of an appeal to God or
man, I must have answered it magnetically. It was she who had
the key to what I might have done but didn't do. Make what
you will of it—we were inexplicably *en rapport*.

But failing failure I was backing her; it hadn't once
occurred to rue, without her sanction, to step in, to intervene;
that I had anything to do with it beyond my recognition of
her—of her part, her claim to play it as she pleased. And now it
was—a thousand years too late!

They managed the illusion for themselves and me magnifi-
cently. She had come to be a thing of spirit only, not in any sort
of clay. She was already in the world of shades; some power as
sovereign and determinate as Death itself had lodged her there,
past rescue or the profanation of recall.

King was in the act of springing forward; he had got out
his revolver; meant, if possible, to shoot her before closing with

the rest. It was the right and only workable idea. I held him back, using the first deterrent that occurred to me, reminding him of Ella, and the notion of her danger may have hovered on the outskirts of my mind. But it was not for her at all that I was consciously concerned. I was impelled to stand aside, to force him, too, to stand aside and see it through.

What followed, followed as such things occur in dreams; the senses seize, the mind, or what remains of it, accepts mechanically the natural or unnatural sequence of events.

I saw the grave surrounded by the priests and blessed; and then the woman and the grave repeatedly, alternately, incensed and sprinkled with deliberate solemnity; and heard, as if from a great distance, the recitations of the prayers, and chanting of interminable psalms.

At the last moment, with their hands upon her, standing for a second still erect, before she was committed to the darkness, she unclosed her eyes, sent one swift glance towards the light, a glance which caught it, flashed it back, recaptured it and kept it for the lighting of her tomb. And then her face was covered with her veil.

The final act was the supreme illusion of the whole. I watched the lowering of the passive figure as if I had been witnessing the actual entombment of the dead.

The grave was sprinkled and incensed again, the stone replaced and fastened down. A long sequence of prayers said over it succeeded, at the end of which, the monks put out their tapers, only one or two remaining lit with those beside the Crucifix.

The priests and the officiant at length approached the altar, kneeling and prostrating there some minutes and repeating "*Pater Nosters*," followed by the choir.

Finally in rising, the officiant pronounced alone and loudly "*Requiescat in pace.*" The monks responded sonorously, "Amen."

The altar lights were one by one extinguished; at a sign, preceded by the cross, the vague, almost invisible procession formed and travelled down the aisle, reciting quietly the "*De Profundis*," and guided now, by only, here and there, a solitary light. The quiet recitation, growing fainter, was a new and unfamiliar impression; I felt that I was missing something— what? I missed, in fact, the chanting; then quite suddenly and certainly I missed—the scream. In place of it there was this "*De Profundis*" and her silence. Out of her deep I realised it, dreamily, of course she would not call.

The door swung to; the church was dark and still again— immensely dark and still.

There was a pause, in which we didn't move or speak; in which I doubted for a second the reality of the incredibly remote, yet almost present scene, trying to reconstruct it in imagination, pit the dream against the fact, the fact against the dream.

"Good God!" said King at length, "what are we going to do?"

His voice awoke me forcibly to something nearer daylight, to the human and inhuman elements in the remarkable affair, which hitherto had missed my mind; they struck against it now with a tremendous shock, and mentally I rubbed my eyes. I saw what King had all along been looking at, the sheer, unpicturesque barbarity. What *were* we going to do?

She breathed perhaps, perhaps she heard us—something of us—we were standing not more than a yard or so away; and if she did, she waited, that was the most poignant possibility, for our decision, our attack.

Ella was naturally unstrung: we left her crouching by the pillar; later I think she partially lost consciousness. It was as well—it left us free.

Striking, as nearly as we could, the centre of the altar, working from it, we made a guess at the position of the stone, and on our hands and knees felt blindly for some indication of its loosened edge. But everywhere the paving, to our touch, presented an unevenness of surface, and we picked at random, chiefly for the sake of doing something. In that intolerable darkness there was really nothing to be done but wait for dawn or listen for some guidance from below. For that we listened breathless and alert enough, but nothing stirred. The stillness had become again intense, acute, and now a grim significance attached to it.

The minutes, hours, dragged; time wasn't as it had been, stationary, but desperately, murderously slow.

Each moment of inaction counted—counted horribly, as we stood straining ears and eyes for any hint of sound, of light.

At length the darkness lifted, almost imperceptibly at first; the big rose window to the west became a scarcely visible grey blot; the massive piers detached themselves from the dense mass of shadow and stood out, immense and vague; the windows of the lantern just above us showed a ring of slowly lightening panes; and with the dawn, we found the spot and set to work.

The implements we improvised we soon discovered to be practically useless. We loosened, but we couldn't move the stone.

At intervals we stopped and put our ears to the thin crevices. King thought, and still believes, he heard some sound or movement; but I didn't. I was somehow sure, for that, it was too late.

For everything it was too late, and we returned reluctantly to a consideration of our own predicament; we had, if possible, to get away unseen. And this time luck was on our side. The sacristan, who came in early by the cloister door which we had entered by, without perceiving us, proceeded to the sacristy.

We made a rapid and effectual escape.

We sketched out and elaborated, on our way back to the town, the little scheme of explanation to be offered to our host, which was to cover an announcement of abrupt departure. He received it with polite credulity, profound regret. He ventured to believe that the *Señora* was unfortunately missing a unique experience—cities, like men, had elements of beauty, or of greatness which escape the crowd; but the *Señora* was not of the crowd, and he had hoped she would be able to remain.

Nothing, however, would induce her to remain for more than a few hours. We must push on without delay and put the night's occurrences before the nearest British Consul. She made no comments and admitted no fatigue, but on this point she was persistent to perversity. She carried it.

The Consul proved hospitable and amiable. He heard the story and was suitably impressed. It was a truly horrible experience—remarkably dramatic—yes. He added it—we saw him doing it—to his collection of strange tales.

The country was, he said, extremely rich in tragic anecdote; and men in his position earned their reputation for romance.

But as to doing anything in this case, as in others even more remarkable, why, there was absolutely nothing to be done!

The laws of Spain were theoretically admirable, but practically, well—the best that could be said of them was that they had their comic side.

And this was not a civil matter, where the wheels might often, certainly, be oiled. The wheel ecclesiastic was more intractable.

He asked if we were leaving Spain immediately. We said, "Perhaps in a few days." "Take my advice," said he, "and make it a few hours."

We did.

Ella would tell you that the horror of those hours hasn't ever altogether ceased to haunt her, that it visits her in dreams and poisons sleep.

She hasn't ever understood, or quite forgiven me my attitude of temporary detachment. She refuses to admit that, after all, what one is pleased to call reality is merely the intensity of one's illusion. My illusion was intense.

"Oh, for you," she says, and with a touch of bitterness, "it was a spectacle. The woman didn't really count."

For me it was a spectacle, but more than that: it was an acquiescence in a rather splendid crime.

On looking back I see that, at the moment in my mind, the woman didn't really count. She saw herself she didn't. That's precisely what she made me see.

What counted chiefly with her, I suspect, was something infinitely greater to her vision than the terror of men's dreams.

She lies, one must remember, in the very centre of the sanctuary—has a place uniquely sacred to her order, the traditions of her kind. It was this honour, satisfying, as it did, some pride of spirit or of race, which bore her honourably through.

She had, one way or other, clogged the wheels of an inflexible machine. But for the speck of dust she knew herself to be, she was—oh horribly, I grant you!—yet not lightly, not dishonourably, swept away.

Two poems by
Nora Hopper Chesson

A DROWNED GIRL TO HER LOVER

I hear the hill-winds, I hear them calling
The long gray twilights and white morns thro',
The tides are rising, the tides are falling,
And how will I answer or come to you?
For over my head the waves are brawling,
And I shall never come back to you!

Dark water's flowing my dark head over,
And where's the charm that shall bid it back?
Wild merrows sing, and strange fishes hover
Above my bed o' the pale sea-wrack:
And Achill sands have not kept for my lover
The fading print of my footstep's track.

Under the sea all my nights are lonely,
Wanting a song that I used to hear.
I dream and I wake and I listen only
For the sound of your footfall kind and dear,
Avourneen deelish, your Moirin's lonely,
And is the day of our meeting near?

The hill-winds coming, the hill-winds going,
I send my voice on their wings to you,—
To you, mo bouchal, whose boat is blowing

Out where the green sea meets the blue:
Come down to me now, for there's no knowing
But the bed I lie in might yet hold two!

HERTHA

I am the spirit of all that lives,
Labours and loses and forgives;
My breath's the wind among the reeds,
I'm wounded when a birch-tree bleeds.
I am the clay nest 'neath the eaves
And the young life wherewith it brims,
The silver minnow where it swims
Under a roof of lily-leaves
Beats with my pulses; from my eyes
The violet gathered amethyst;
I am the rose of winter skies,
The moonlight conquering the mist.

I am the bird the falcon strikes;
My strength is in the kestrel's wing,
My cruelty is in the shrikes.
My pity bids the dock-leaves grow
Large, that a little child may know
Where he shall heal the nettle's sting.
I am the snowdrop and the snow,
Dead amber, and the living fir—
The corn-sheaf and the harvester.

My craft is breathed into the fox
When, a red cub, he snarls and plays
With his red vixen. Yea, I am
The wolf, the hunter, and the lamb;
I am the slayer and the slain,
The thought new-shapen in the brain.
I am the ageless strength of rocks;
The weakness that is all a grace,
Being the weakness of a flower.
The secret on the dead man's face
Written in his last living hour.
The endless trouble of the seas
That fret and struggle with the shore,
Strive and are striven with evermore—
The changeless beauty that they wear
Through all their changes; all of these
Are mine. The brazen streets of hell
I know, and heaven's gold ways as well.
Mortality, eternity,
Change, death, and life are mine—are me.

THE HERMIT AND THE WILD WOMAN

Edith Wharton

I.

The Hermit lived in a cave in the hollow of a hill. Below him was a glen, with a stream in a coppice of oaks and alders, and across the valley, half a day's journey distant, another hill, steep and bristling, raised against the sky a little walled town with Ghibelline swallow-tails.

When the Hermit was a lad, and lived in the town, the crenellations of the walls had been square-topped, and a Guelf lord had flown his standard from the keep.[1] Then one day a steel-coloured line of men-at-arms rode across the valley, wound up the hill and battered in the gates. Stones and

---

1 The Guelphs and Ghibellines were political factions in medieval Italy. The Guelphs supported the Pope and the Ghibellines supported the Holy Roman Emperor in their battle over whether church or state should possess supreme power.

Greek fire rained from the ramparts, shields clashed in the streets, blade sprang at blade in passages and stairways, pikes and lances dripped above huddled flesh, and all the still familiar place was a stew of dying bodies. The boy fled from it in horror. He had seen his father go forth and not come back, his mother drop dead from an arquebuse shot as she leaned from the platform of the tower, his little sister fall with a slit throat across the altar steps of the chapel—and he ran, ran for his life, through the slippery streets, over warm twitching bodies, between legs of soldiers carousing, out of the gates, past burning farms, trampled wheat-fields, orchards stripped and broken, till the still woods received him and he fell face down on the unmutilated earth.

He had no wish to go back. His longing was to live hidden from life. Up the hillside he found a hollow rock, and built before it a porch of boughs bound with withies. He fed on nuts and roots, and on trout caught with his hands under the stones in the stream. He had always been a quiet boy, liking to sit at his mother's feet and watch the flowers grow under her needle, while the chaplain read aloud the histories of the Desert Fathers from a great silver-clasped volume. He would rather have been bred a clerk and scholar than a knight's son, and his happiest moments were when he served mass for the chaplain in the early morning, and felt his heart flutter up and up like a lark, up and up till it was lost in infinite space and brightness. Almost as happy were the hours when he sat beside the foreign painter who came over the mountains to paint the chapel, and under whose brush celestial faces grew out of the rough wall as if he had sown some magic seed which flowered while you watched it. With the appearing of every gold-rimmed face the boy felt he had won another friend, a friend who would come and bend above him at night, keeping the ugly visions from his pillow—visions of the gnawing monsters about the church-porch, evil-faced bats and dragons, giant worms and winged bristling hogs, a devil's flock who crept down from the stone-work at night and hunted the souls of sinful children through the town. With the growth of the picture the bright mailed angels thronged so close about the boy's bed that between their interwoven wings not a snout or a claw could force itself; and he would turn over sighing on his pillow, which felt as soft and warm as if it had been lined with down from those shelter-ing pinions.

All these thoughts came back to him now in his cave on the cliff-side. The stillness seemed to enclose him with wings, to fold him away from life and evil. He was never restless or discontented. He loved the long silent empty days, each one as like the other as pearls in a well-matched string. Above all he liked to have time to save his soul. He had been greatly troubled about his soul since a band of Flagellants had passed through the town, showing their gaunt scourged bodies and exhorting the people to turn from soft raiment and delicate fare, from marriage and money-getting and dancing and games, and think only how they might escape the devil's talons and the great red blaze of hell. For days that red blaze hung on the edge of the boy's thoughts like the light of a burning city across a plain. There seemed to be so many pitfalls to avoid—so many things were wicked which one might have supposed to be harmless. How could a child of his age tell? He dared not for a moment think of anything else. And the scene of sack and slaughter from which he had fled gave shape and distinctness to that blood-red vision. Hell was like that, only a million million times worse. Now he knew how flesh looked when devils' pincers tore it, how the shrieks of the damned sounded, and how roasting bodies smelled. How could a Christian spare one moment of his days and nights from the long long struggle to keep safe from the wrath to come?

Gradually the horror faded, leaving only a tranquil pleasure in the minute performance of his religious duties. His mind was not naturally given to the contemplation of evil, and in the blessed solitude of his new life his thoughts dwelt more and more on the beauty of holiness. His desire was to be perfectly good, and to live in love and charity with his fellows; and how could one do this without fleeing from them?

At first his life was difficult, for in winter he was put to great straits to feed himself; and there were nights when the sky was like an iron vault, and a hoarse wind rattled the oakwood in the valley, and a fear came on him that was worse than any cold. But in time it became known to his townsfolk and to the peasants in the neighbouring valleys that he had withdrawn to the wilderness to lead a godly life; and after that his worst hardships were over, for pious persons brought him gifts of oil and dried fruit, one good woman gave him seeds from her garden, another spun for him a hodden gown, and others would have brought him all manner of food and clothing, had he not refused to accept anything but for his bare needs. The woman who had given him the seeds showed him also how to build a little garden on the southern ledge of his cliff, and all one summer the Hermit carried up soil from the streamside, and the next he carried up water to keep his garden green. After that the fear of solitude passed from him, for he was so busy all day that at night he had much ado to fight off the demon of sleep, which Saint Arsenius the Abbot has denounced as the chief foe of the solitary. His memory kept good store of prayers and litanies, besides long passages from the Mass and other offices, and he marked the hours of his day by different acts of devotion. On Sundays and feast days, when the wind was set his way, he could hear the church bells from his native town, and these helped him to follow the worship of the faithful, and to bear in mind the seasons of the liturgical year; and what with carrying up water from the river, digging in the garden, gathering fagots for his fire, observing his religious duties, and keeping his thoughts continually upon the salvation of his soul, the Hermit knew not a moment's idleness.

At first, during his night vigils, he had felt a fear of the stars, which seemed to set a cruel watch on him, as though they spied out the frailty of his heart and took the measure of his littleness. But one day a wandering clerk, to whom he chanced to give a night's shelter, explained to him that, in the opinion of the most learned doctors in theology, the stars were inhabited by the spirits of the blessed, and this thought brought great solace to the Hermit. Even on winter nights, when the eagles screamed among the peaks, and he heard the long howl of wolves about the sheep-cotes in the valley, he no longer felt any fear, but thought of those sounds as representing the evil voices of the world, and hugged himself in the seclusion of his cave. Sometimes, to keep himself awake, he composed lauds in honour of Christ and the saints, and they seemed to him so pleasant that he feared to forget them, so after much debate with himself he decided to ask a friendly priest, who sometimes visited him, to write them down; and the priest wrote them on comely sheepskin, which the Hermit dried and prepared with his own hands. When the Hermit saw them written they appeared to him so beautiful that he feared to commit the sin of vanity if he looked at them too often, so he hid them between two smooth stones in his cave, and vowed that he would take them out only once in the year, at Easter, when our Lord has risen and it is meet that Christians should rejoice. And this vow he faithfully kept; but, alas, when Easter drew near, he found he was looking forward to the blessed festival less because of our Lord's rising than because he should then be able to read his pleasant lauds written on fair sheepskin; and thereupon he took a vow that he would not look upon the lauds till he lay dying.

So the Hermit, for many years, lived to the glory of God and in great peace of mind.

II.

One day he resolved to set forth on a visit to the Saint of the Rock, who lived on the other side of the mountains. Travellers had brought the Hermit report of this solitary, how he lived in great holiness and austerity in a desert place among the hills, where snow lay all winter, and in summer the sun beat down cruelly. The Saint, it appeared, had vowed that he would withdraw from the world to a spot where there was neither shade nor water, lest he should be tempted to take his ease and think less continually upon his Maker; but wherever he went he found a spreading tree or a gushing spring, till at last he climbed to the bare heights where nothing grows, and where the only water comes from the melting of the snow in spring. Here he found a tall rock rising from the ground, and in it he scooped a hollow with his own hands, labouring for five years and wearing his fingers to the bone. Then he seated himself in the hollow, which faced the west, so that in winter he should have small warmth of the sun and in summer be consumed by it; and there he had sat without moving for years beyond number.

The Hermit was greatly drawn by the tale of such austerities, which in his humility he did not dream of emulating, but desired, for his soul's good, to contemplate and praise; so one day he bound sandals to his feet, cut an alder staff from the stream, and set out to visit the Saint of the Rock.

It was the pleasant season when seeds are shooting and the bud is on the tree. The Hermit was troubled at the thought of leaving his plants without water, but he could not travel in winter by reason of the snows, and in summer he feared the garden would suffer even more from his absence. So he set out, praying that rain might fall while he was away, and hoping to return again in five days. The peasants in the fields left their work to ask his blessing; and they would even have followed him in great numbers had he not told them that he was bound on a pilgrimage to the Saint of the Rock, and that it behoved him to go alone, as one solitary seeking another. So they respected his wish, and he went on and entered the forest. In the forest he walked for two days and slept for two nights. He heard the wolves crying, and foxes rustling in the covert, and once, at twilight, a shaggy brown man peered at him through the leaves and galloped away with a soft padding of hoofs; but the Hermit feared neither wild beasts nor evil-doers, nor even the fauns and satyrs who linger in unhallowed forest depths where the Cross has not been raised; for he said: "If I die, I die to the glory of God, and if I live, it must be to the same end." Only he felt a secret pang at the thought that he might die without seeing his lauds again. But the third day, without misadventure, he came out on another valley.

Then he began to climb the mountain, first through brown woods of beech and oak, then through pine and broom, and then across red stony ledges where only a pinched growth of lentisk and briar spread over the bald rock. By this time he thought to have reached his goal, but for two more days he fared on through the same scene, the sky close over him and the green earth receding far below. Sometimes for hours he saw only the red glistering slopes tufted with thin bushes, and the hard blue heaven so close that it seemed his hand could touch it; then at a turn of the path the rocks rolled apart, the eye plunged down a long pine-clad defile, and beyond it the forest flowed to a plain shining with cities and another mountain-range many days' journey away. To some eyes this would have been a terrible spectacle, reminding the wayfarer of his remoteness from his kind, and of the perils which lurk in waste places and the weakness of man against them; but the Hermit was so mated to solitude, and felt such love for all things created, that to him the bare rocks sang of their Maker and the vast distance bore witness to His greatness. So His servant journeyed on unafraid.

But one morning, after a long climb over steep and difficult slopes, the wayfarer halted at a bend of the way; for below him was no plain shining with cities, but a bare expanse of shaken silver that reached to the rim of the world; and the Hermit knew it was the sea. Fear seized him then, for it was terrible to see that great plain move like a heaving bosom, and, as he looked on it, the earth seemed also to heave beneath him. But presently he remembered how Christ had walked the waves, and how even Saint Mary of Egypt, a great sinner, had crossed the waters of Jordan dry-shod to receive the Sacrament from the Abbot Zosimus; and then the Hermit's heart grew still, and he sang as he went down the mountain: "The sea shall praise Thee, O Lord."

All day he kept seeing it and then losing it; but toward night he came to a cleft of the hills, and lay down in a pine-wood to sleep. He had now been six days gone, and once and again he thought anxiously of his herbs; but he said to himself: "What though my garden perish, if I see a holy man face to face and praise God in his company?" So he was never long cast down.

Before daylight he was afoot under the stars; and leaving the wood where he had slept, began climbing the face of a tall cliff, where he had to clutch the jutting ledges with his hands, and with every step he gained, a rock seemed thrust forth to hurl him back. So, footsore and bleeding, he reached a high stony plain as the sun dropped to the sea; and in the red light he saw a hollow rock, and the Saint sitting in the hollow.

The Hermit fell on his knees, praising God; then he rose and ran across the plain to the rock. As he drew near he saw that the Saint was a very old man, clad in goatskin, with a long white beard. He sat motionless, his hands on his knees, and two red eye-sockets turned to the sunset. Near him was a young boy in skins who brushed the flies from his face; but they always came back, and settled on the rheum from his eyes.

He did not appear to hear or see the approach of the Hermit, but sat quite still till the boy said: "Father, here is a pilgrim."

Then he lifted up his voice and asked angrily who was there and what the stranger sought.

The Hermit answered: "Father, the report of your holy practices came to me a long way off, and being myself a solitary, though not worthy to be named with you for godliness, it seemed fitting that I should cross the mountains to visit you, that we might sit together and speak in praise of solitude."

The Saint replied: "You fool, how can two sit together and praise solitude, since by so doing they put an end to the thing they praise?"

The Hermit, at that, was sorely abashed, for he had thought his speech out on the way, reciting it many times over; and now it appeared to him vainer than the crackling of thorns under a pot.

Nevertheless he took heart and said: "True, Father; but may not two sinners sit together and praise Christ, who has taught them the blessings of solitude?"

But the other only answered: "If you had really learned the blessings of solitude you would not squander them in idle wandering." And, the Hermit not knowing how to reply, he said again: "If two sinners meet they can best praise Christ by going each his own way in silence."

After that he shut his lips and continued motionless while the boy brushed the flies from his eye-sockets; but the Hermit's heart sank, and for the first time he felt the weariness of the way he had fared, and the great distance dividing him from home.

He had meant to take counsel with the Saint concerning his lauds, and whether he ought to destroy them; but now he had no heart to say more, and turning away he began to go down the mountain. Presently he heard steps running at his back, and the boy came up and pressed a honey-comb on him.

"You have come a long way and must be hungry," he said; but before the Hermit could thank him he hastened back to his task. So the Hermit crept down the mountain till he reached the wood where he had slept before; and there he made his bed again, but he had no mind to eat before sleeping, for his heart hungered more than his body; and his tears made the honey-comb bitter.

III.

On the fourteenth day he came to his own valley and saw the walls of his native town against the sky. He was foot-sore and heavy of heart, for his long pilgrimage had brought him only weariness and humiliation, and as no drop of rain had fallen he knew that his garden must have perished. So he climbed the cliff heavily and reached his cave at the angelus.

But there a great wonder awaited him. For though the scant earth of the hillside was parched and crumbling, his gar-den-soil shone with moisture, and his plants had shot up, fresh and glistening, to a height they had never before attained. More wonderful still, the tendrils of the gourd had been trained about his door; and kneeling down he saw that the earth had been loosened between the rows of sprouting vege-tables, and that every leaf dripped as though the rain had but newly ceased. Then it appeared to the Hermit that he beheld a miracle, but doubting his own deserts he refused to believe himself worthy, and went within doors to ponder on what had befallen him. And on his bed of rushes he saw a young woman sleeping, clad in an outlandish garment, with strange amulets about her neck.

The sight was full of fear to the Hermit, for he recalled how often the demon, in tempting the Desert Fathers, had taken the form of a woman; but he reflected that, since there was nothing pleasing to him in the sight of this female, who was brown as a nut and lean with wayfaring, he ran no great danger in looking at her. At first he took her for a wandering Egyptian,[2] but as he looked he perceived, among the heathen charms, an Agnus Dei[3] in her bosom; and this so surprised him that he bent over and called on her to wake.

She sprang up with a start, but seeing the Hermit's gown and staff, and his face above her, lay quiet and said: "I have watered your garden daily in return for the beans and oil that I took from your store."

"Who are you, and how come you here?" asked the Hermit.

She said: "I am a wild woman and live in the woods."

And when he pressed her again to tell him why she had sought shelter in his cave, she said that the land to the south, whence she came, was full of armed companies and bands of marauders, and that great license and bloodshed prevailed there; and this the Hermit knew to be true, for he had heard of it on his homeward journey. The Wild Woman went on to tell him that she had been hunted through the woods like an animal by a band of drunken men-at-arms, Lansknechts[4] from

---

2 In the nineteenth century, this term, later shortened to "Gypsy," referred to one of the Romani people, who were believed to originate in Egypt.

3 A wax disk impressed with the figure of a lamb, usually worn around the neck. "Agnus Dei," meaning "Lamb of God," is the beginning of a prayer for salvation recited during Mass.

4 Mercenary soldiers who fought for pay rather than out of loyalty to a leader.

the north by their barbarous dress and speech, and at length, starving and spent, had come on his cave and hidden herself from her pursuers. "For," she said, "I fear neither wild beasts nor the woodland people, charcoal burners, Egyptians, wandering minstrels or chapmen; even the highway robbers do not touch me, because I am poor and brown; but these armed men flown with wine are more terrible than wolves and tigers."

And the Hermit's heart melted, for he thought of his little sister lying with her throat slit across the altar, and of the scenes of blood and rapine from which he had fled into the wilderness. So he said to the stranger that it was not fitting he should house her in his cave, but that he would send a messenger to the town, and beg a pious woman there to give her lodging and work in her household. "For," said he, "I perceive by the blessed image about your neck that you are not a heathen wilding, but a child of Christ, though so far astray in the desert."

"Yes," she said, "I am a Christian, and know as many prayers as you; but I will never set foot in city walls again, lest I be caught and put back into the convent."

"What," cried the Hermit with a start, "you are a runagate nun?" And he crossed himself, and again thought of the demon.

She smiled and said: "It is true I was once a cloistered woman, but I will never willingly be one again. Now drive me forth if you like; but I cannot go far, for I have a wounded foot, which I got in climbing the cliff with water for your garden." And she pointed to a cut in her foot.

At that, for all his fear, the Hermit was moved to pity, and washed the cut and bound it up; and as he did so he bethought him that perhaps his strange visitor had been sent to him not for his soul's undoing but for her own salvation. And from that hour he yearned to save her.

But it was not fitting that she should remain in his cave; so, having given her water to drink and a handful of lentils, he raised her up, and putting his staff in her hand guided her to a hollow not far off in the face of the cliff. And while he was doing this he heard the sunset bells ring across the valley, and set about reciting the *Angelus Domini nuntiavit Mariae;*[5] and she joined in piously, her hands folded, not missing a word.

Nevertheless the thought of her wickedness weighed on him, and the next day when he went to carry her food he asked her to tell him how it came about that she had fallen into such abominable sin. And this is the story she told.

IV.

I was born (said she) in the north country, where the winters are long and cold, where snow sometimes falls in the valleys, and the high mountains for months are white with it. My father's castle is in a tall green wood, where the winds always rustle, and a cold river runs down from the ice-gorges. South of us was the wide plain, glowing with heat, but above us were stony passes where eagles nest and the storms howl; in winter fires roared in our chimneys, and even in summer there was always a cool air off the gorges. But when I was a child my mother went southward in the great Empress's train and I went with her. We travelled many days, across plains and mountains,

---

5 This prayer, and the other prayers mentioned in the story, are spoken or sung as part of the daily ritual of priests, monks, and nuns in the Catholic Church.

and saw Rome, where the Pope lives in a golden palace, and many other cities, till we came to the great Emperor's court. There for two years or more we lived in pomp and merriment, for it was a wonderful court, full of mimes, magicians, philosophers and poets; and the Empress's ladies spent their days in mirth and music, dressed in light silken garments, walking in gardens of roses, and bathing in a cool marble tank, while the Emperor's eunuchs guarded the approach to the gardens. Oh, those baths in the marble tank, my Father! I used to lie awake through the whole hot southern night, and think of that plunge at sunrise under the last stars. For we were in a burning country, and I pined for the tall green woods and the cold stream of my father's valley; and when I had cooled my limbs in the tank I lay all day in the scant cypress shade and dreamed of my next bath.

My mother pined for the coolness till she died; then the Empress put me in a convent and I was forgotten. The convent was on the side of a bare yellow hill, where bees made a hot buzzing in the thyme. Below was the sea, blazing with a million shafts of light; and overhead a blinding sky, which reflected the sun's glitter like a huge baldric of steel. Now the convent was built on the site of an old pleasure-house which a holy Princess had given to our Order; and a part of the house was left standing, with its court and garden. The nuns had built all about the garden; but they left the cypresses in the middle, and the long marble tank where the Princess and her ladies had bathed. The tank, however, as you may conceive, was no longer used as a bath, for the washing of the body is an indulgence forbidden to cloistered virgins; and our Abbess, who was famed for her austerities, boasted that, like holy Sylvia the nun, she never touched water save to bathe her fingertips before receiving the Sacrament. With such an example before them, the nuns were obliged to conform to the same pious rule, and many, having been bred in the convent from infancy, regarded all ablutions with horror, and felt no temptation to cleanse the filth from their flesh; but I, who had bathed daily, had the freshness of clear water in my veins, and perished slowly for want of it, like your garden herbs in a drought.

My cell did not look on the garden, but on the steep mule-path leading up the cliff, where all day long the sun beat as with flails of fire, and I saw the sweating peasants toil up and down behind their thirsty asses, and the beggars whining and scraping their sores. Oh, how I hated to look out on that burning world! I used to turn away from it, sick with disgust, and lying on my hard bed, stare up by the hour at the ceiling of my cell. But flies crawled in hundreds on the ceiling, and the hot noise they made was worse than the glare. Sometimes, at an hour when I knew myself unobserved, I tore off my stifling gown, and hung it over the grated window, that I might no longer see the shaft of hot sunlight lying across my cell, and the dust dancing in it like fat in the fire. But the darkness choked me, and I struggled for breath as though I lay at the bottom of a pit; so that at last I would spring up, and dragging down the dress, fling myself on my knees before the Cross, and entreat our Lord to give me the gift of holiness, that I might escape the everlasting fires of hell, of which this heat was a foretaste. For if I could not endure the scorching of a summer's day, with what constancy could I meet the thought of the flame that dieth not?

This longing to escape the heat of hell made me apply myself to a devouter way of living, and I reflected that if my bodily distress were somewhat eased I should be able to throw myself with greater zeal into the practice of vigils and austerities. And at length, having set forth to the Abbess that the sultry air of my cell induced in me a grievous heaviness of sleep, I prevailed on her to lodge me in that part of the building which overlooked the garden.

For a few days I was happy, for instead of the dusty mountainside, and the sight of the sweating peasants and their asses, I looked out on dark cypresses and rows of budding vegetables. But presently I found I had not bettered myself. For with the approach of midsummer the garden, being all enclosed with buildings, grew as stifling as my cell. All the green things in it withered and dried off, leaving trenches of bare red earth, across which the cypresses cast strips of shade too narrow to cool the aching heads of the nuns; and I began to think sorrowfully of my former cell, where now and then there came a sea-breeze, hot and languid, yet alive, and where at least I could look out on the sea. But this was not the worst; for when the dog-days came I found that the sun, at a certain hour, cast on the ceiling of my cell the reflection of the ripples on the garden-tank; and to say how I suffered from this sight is not within the power of speech. It was indeed agony to watch the clear water rippling and washing above my head, yet feel no solace of it on my limbs: as though I had been a senseless brazen image lying at the bottom of a well. But the image, if it felt no refreshment, would have suffered no torture; whereas every vein of my body was a mouth of Dives[6] praying for water. Oh,

---

6 The name "Dives" is often given to the rich man in the parable of the rich man and Lazarus, told by Jesus in Luke 16:19–31. Lazarus begged the rich man for food and drink but was given none. When he died, he went to Heaven,

Father, how shall I tell you the grievous pains that I endured? Sometimes I so feared the sight of the mocking ripples overhead that I hid my eyes from their approach, lying face down on my bed till I knew that they were gone; yet on cloudy days, when they did not come, the heat was even worse to bear.

By day I hardly dared trust myself in the garden, for the nuns walked there, and one fiery noon they found me hanging so close above the tank that they snatched me away, crying out that I had tried to destroy myself. The scandal of this reaching the Abbess, she sent for me to know what demon had beset me; and when I wept and said, the longing to bathe my burning body, she broke into anger and cried out: "Do you not know that this is a sin well-nigh as grave as the other, and condemned by all the greatest saints? For a nun may be tempted to take her life through excess of self-scrutiny and despair of her own worthiness; but this desire to indulge the despicable body is one of the lusts of the flesh, to be classed with concupiscence and adultery." And she ordered me to sleep every night for a month in my heavy gown, with a veil upon my face.

Now, Father, I believe it was this penance that drove me to sin. For we were in the dog-days, and it was more than flesh could bear. And on the third night, after the portress had passed, and the lights were out, I rose and flung off my veil and gown, and knelt in my window fainting.

There was no moon, but the sky was full of stars. At first the garden was all blackness; but as I looked I saw a faint twinkle between the cypress-trunks, and I knew it was the starlight

---

while the rich man burned in Hell. When he asked God for help, he was told that he had not helped Lazarus in life and would get no help in the afterlife. In Latin, *"dives"* means "rich man."

on the tank. The water! The water! It was there close to me—only a few bolts and bars were between us....

The portress was a heavy sleeper, and I knew where she hung her keys. I stole thither, seized the keys and crept barefoot down the corridor. The bolts of the cloister-door were stiff and heavy, and I dragged at them till my wrists were bursting. Then I turned the key and it cried out in the ward. I stood still, my whole body beating with fear lest the hinges too should have a voice—but no one stirred, and I pushed open the door and slipped out. The garden was as airless as a pit, but at least I could stretch my arms in it; and, oh, my Father, the sweetness of the stars! The stones cut my feet as I ran, but I thought of the joy of bathing them in the tank, and that made the wounds sweet to me.... My Father, I have heard of the temptations which assailed the holy Solitaries of the desert, flattering the reluctant flesh beyond resistance; but none, I think, could have surpassed in ecstasy that first touch of the water on my limbs. To prolong the joy I let myself slip in slowly, resting my hands on the edge of the tank, and smiling to see my body, as I lowered it, break up the shining black surface and shatter the star-beams into splinters. And the water, my Father, seemed to crave me as I craved it. Its ripples rose about me, first in furtive touches, then in a long embrace that clung and drew me down; till at length they lay like kisses on my lips. It was no frank comrade like the mountain pools of my childhood, but a secret playmate compassionating my pains and soothing them with noiseless hands. From the first I thought of it as an accomplice—its whisper seemed to promise me secrecy if I would promise it love. And I went back and back to it, my Father; all day I lived in the thought of it; each night I stole to it with fresh thirst....

But at length the old portress died, and a young lay-sister took her place. She was a light sleeper, and keen-eared; and I knew the danger of venturing to her cell. I knew the danger, but when darkness came I felt the water drawing me. The first night I fought and held out; but the second I crept to her door. She made no motion when I entered, but rose up secretly and stole after me; and the second night she warned the Abbess, and the two came on me by the tank.

I was punished with terrible penances: fasting, scourging, imprisonment, and the privation of drinking water; for the Abbess stood amazed at the obduracy of my sin, and was resolved to make me an example. For a month I endured the pains of hell; then one night the Saracen[7] pirates fell on our convent. On a sudden the darkness was full of flames and blood; but while the other nuns ran hither and thither, clinging to the Abbess or shrieking on the steps of the altar, I slipped through an unwatched postern and made my way to the hills. The next day the Emperor's soldiery descended on the carousing heathen, slew them and burned their vessels on the beach; the Abbess and nuns were rescued, the convent walls rebuilt, and peace was restored to the holy precincts. All this I heard from a shepherdess of the hills, who found me in my hiding, and brought me honey-comb and water. In her simplicity she offered to lead me home to the convent; but while she slept I laid off my wimple and scapular, and stealing her cloak fled away. And since then I have wandered alone over the face of the world, living in woods and desert places, often hungry, often cold and sometimes fearful; yet resigned to any hardship, and with a front for any peril, if only I may

---

7 In the Middle Ages, the term "Saracen" usually referred to Muslim Arabs.

sleep under the free heaven and wash the dust from my body in cool water.

V.

The Hermit, as may be supposed, was much perturbed by this story, and dismayed that such sinfulness should cross his path. His first motion was to drive the woman forth, for he knew the heinousness of the craving for water, and how Saint Jerome, Saint Augustine and other holy doctors have taught that they who would purify the soul must not be distraught by the vain cares of bodily cleanliness; yet, remembering the lust that drew him to his lauds, he dared not judge his sister's fault too harshly.

Moreover he was moved by the Wild Woman's story of the hardships she had suffered, and the godless company she had been driven to keep—Egyptians, jugglers, outlaws and even sorcerers, who are masters of the pagan lore of the East, and still practice their rites among the simple folk of the hills. Yet she would not have him think wholly ill of this vagrant people, from whom she had often received food and comfort; and her worst danger, as he learned with shame, had come from the *girovaghi* or wandering monks, who are the scourge and shame of Christendom; carrying their ribald idleness from one monastery to another, and leaving on their way a trail of thieving, revelry and worse. Once or twice the Wild Woman had nearly fallen into their hands; but had been saved by her own quick wit and skill in woodcraft. Once, so she assured the Hermit, she had found refuge with a faun and his female, who fed and sheltered her in their cave, where she slept on a bed of leaves with their shaggy nurslings; and in this cave she had seen a stock or idol of wood, extremely seamed and ancient, before which the wood-creatures, when they thought she slept, laid garlands and the wild bees' honey-comb.

She told him also of a hill-village of weavers, where she lived many weeks, and learned to ply their trade in return for her lodging; and where wayfaring men in the guise of cobblers, charcoal-burners or goatherds came at midnight and taught strange doctrines in the hovels. What they taught she could not clearly tell, save that they believed each soul could commune directly with its Maker, without need of priest or intercessor; and she had heard from some of their disciples that there are two Gods, one of good and one of evil, and that the God of evil has his throne in the Pope's palace in Rome. But in spite of these dark teachings they were a mild and merciful folk, full of loving-kindness toward poor persons and wayfarers; so that she grieved for them when one day a Dominican monk appeared in the village with a company of soldiers, seizing some of the weavers and dragging them to prison, while others, with their wives and babes, fled to the winter woods. She fled with them, fearing to be charged with their heresy, and for months they lay hid in desert places, the older and weaker, when they fell sick from want and exposure, being devoutly ministered to by their brethren, and dying in the sure faith of heaven.

All this she related modestly and simply, not as one who joys in a godless life, but as having been drawn into it through misadventure; and she told the Hermit that when she heard the sound of church bells she never failed to say an Ave or a Pater; and that often, as she lay in the midnight darkness of the

forest, she had hushed her fears by reciting the versicles from
the Evening Hour:

> *Keep us, O Lord, as the apple of the eye,*
> *Protect us under the shadow of Thy wings.*

The wound in her foot healed slowly; and the Hermit, while it
was mending, repaired daily to her cave, reasoning with her in
love and charity, and exhorting her to return to the cloister. But
this she persistently refused to do; and fearing lest she attempt
to fly before her foot was healed, and so expose herself to hunger and ill-usage, he promised not to betray her presence, or to
take any measures toward restoring her to her Order.

He began indeed to doubt whether she had any calling to
the life enclosed; yet her innocency of mind made him feel that
she might be won back to holy living if only her freedom were
assured. So after many inward struggles (since his promise for-
bade his taking counsel with any concerning her) he resolved to
let her stay in the cave till some light should come to him. And
one day, visiting her about the hour of Nones (for it became
his pious habit to say the evening office with her), he found her
engaged with a little goatherd, who in a sudden seizure had
fallen from a rock above her cave, and lay senseless and full of
blood at her feet. And the Hermit saw with wonder how skil-
fully she bound up his cuts and restored his senses, giving him
to drink of a liquor she had distilled from the simples of the
mountain; whereat the boy opened his eyes and praised God,
as one restored by heaven. Now it was known that this lad was
subject to possessions, and had more than once dropped lifeless
while he heeded his flock; and the Hermit, knowing that only

great saints or unclean necromancers can loosen devils, feared that the Wild Woman had exorcised the spirits by means of unholy spells. But she told him that the goatherd's sickness was caused only by the heat of the sun, and that, such seizures being common in the hot countries whence she came, she had learned from a wise woman how to stay them by a decoction of the *carduus benedictus*,[8] made in the third night of the waxing moon, but without the aid of magic.

"But," she continued, "you need not fear my bringing scandal on your holy retreat, for by the arts of the same wise woman my own wound is well-nigh healed, and tonight at sunset I set forth."

The Hermit's heart grew heavy as she spoke, and it seemed to him that her own look was sorrowful. And suddenly his perplexities were lifted from him, and he saw what was God's purpose with the Wild Woman.

"Why," said he, "do you fly from this place, where you are safe from molestation, and can look to the saving of your soul? Is it that your feet weary for the road, and your spirits are heavy for lack of worldly discourse?"

She replied that she had no wish to travel, and felt no repugnance to solitude. "But," said she, "I must go forth to beg my bread, since in this wilderness there is none but yourself to feed me; and moreover, when it is known that I have healed the goatherd, curious folk and scandal-mongers may seek me out, and, learning whence I come, drag me back to the cloister."

Then the Hermit answered her and said: "In the early days, when the faith of Christ was first preached, there were holy

---

8 Also called Blessed Thistle or Holy Thistle. It was used during the Middle Ages to treat the plague, and is still sometimes made into a medicinal tea.

women who fled to the desert and lived there in solitude, to the glory of God and the edification of their sex. If you are minded to embrace so austere a life, contenting you with such sustenance as the wilderness yields, and wearing out your days in prayer and vigil, it may be that you shall make amends for the great sin you have committed, and live and die in the peace of the Lord Jesus."

He spoke thus, knowing that if she left him and returned to her roaming, hunger and fear might drive her to fresh sin; whereas in a life of penance and reclusion her eyes might be opened to her iniquity.

He saw that his words moved her, and she seemed about to consent, and embrace a life of holiness; but suddenly she fell silent, and looked down on the valley at their feet.

"A stream flows in the glen below us," she said. "Do you forbid me to bathe in it in the heat of summer?"

"It is not I that forbid you, my daughter, but the laws of God," said the Hermit; "yet see how miraculously heaven protects you—for in the hot season, when your lust is upon you, our stream runs dry, and temptation will be removed from you. Moreover on these heights there is no excess of heat to madden the body, but always, before dawn and at the angelus, a cool breeze which refreshes it like water."

And after thinking long on this, and again receiving his promise not to betray her, the Wild Woman agreed to embrace a life of reclusion; and the Hermit fell on his knees, worshipping God and rejoicing to think that, if he saved his sister from sin, his own term of probation would be shortened.

* * *

VI.

Thereafter for two years the Hermit and the Wild Woman lived side by side, meeting together to pray on the great feast-days of the year, but on all other days dwelling apart, engaged in pious practices.

At first the Hermit, knowing the weakness of woman, and her little aptitude for the life apart, had feared that he might be disturbed by the nearness of his penitent; but she faithfully held to his commands, abstaining from all sight of him save on the Days of Obligation;[9] and when they met, so modest and devout was her demeanour that she raised his soul to fresh fervency. And gradually it grew sweet to him to think that, near by though unseen, was one who performed the same tasks at the same hours; so that, whether he tended his garden, or recited his chaplet, or rose under the stars to repeat the midnight office, he had a companion in all his labours and devotions.

Meanwhile the report had spread abroad that a holy woman who cast out devils had made her dwelling in the Hermit's cliff; and many sick persons from the valley sought her out, and went away restored by her. These poor pilgrims brought her oil and flour, and with her own hands she made a garden like the Hermit's, and planted it with corn and lentils; but she would never take a trout from the brook, or receive the gift of a snared wild-fowl, for she said that in her vagrant life the wild creatures of the wood had befriended her, and as she had slept in peace among them, so now she would never suffer them to be molested.

9 The days on which faithful Catholics are expected to attend Mass.

In the third year came a plague, and death walked the cities, and many poor peasants fled to the hills to escape it. These the Hermit and his penitent faithfully tended, and so skillful were the Wild Woman's ministrations that the report of them reached the town across the valley, and a deputation of burgesses came with rich offerings, and besought her to descend and comfort their sick. The Hermit, seeing her depart on so dangerous a mission, would have accompanied her, but she bade him remain and tend those who fled to the hills; and for many days his heart was consumed in prayer for her, and he feared lest every fugitive should bring him word of her death.

But at length she returned, wearied-out but whole, and covered with the blessings of the townsfolk; and thereafter her name for holiness spread as wide as the Hermit's.

Seeing how constant she remained in her chosen life, and what advance she had made in the way of perfection, the Hermit now felt that it behoved him to exhort her again to return to the convent; and more than once he resolved to speak with her, but his heart hung back. At length he bethought him that by failing in this duty he imperilled his own soul, and thereupon, on the next feast-day, when they met, he reminded her that in spite of her good works she still lived in sin and excommunicate, and that, now she had once more tasted the sweets of godliness, it was her duty to confess her fault and give herself up to her superiors.

She heard him meekly, but when he had spoken she was silent and her tears ran over; and looking at her he wept also, and said no more. And they prayed together, and returned each to his cave.

It was not till late winter that the plague abated; and the

spring and early summer following were heavy with rains and great heat. When the Hermit visited his penitent at the feast of Pentecost, she appeared to him so weak and wasted that, when they had recited the *Veni, sancte spiritus*, and the proper psalms, he taxed her with too great rigour of penitential practices; but she replied that her weakness was not due to an excess of discipline, but that she had brought back from her labours among the sick a heaviness of body which the intemperance of the season no doubt increased. The evil rains continued, falling chiefly at night, while by day the land reeked with heat and vapours; so that lassitude fell on the Hermit also, and he could hardly drag himself down to the spring whence he drew his drinking-water. Thus he fell into the habit of going down to the glen before cockcrow, after he had recited Matins; for at that hour the rain commonly ceased, and a faint air was stirring. Now because of the wet season the stream had not gone dry, and instead of replenishing his flagon slowly at the trickling spring, the Hermit went down to the waterside to fill it; and once, as he descended the steep slope of the glen, he heard the covert rustle, and saw the leaves stir as though something moved behind them. As the sound ceased the leaves grew still; but his heart was shaken, for it seemed to him that what he had seen in the dusk had a human semblance, such as the wood-people wear. And he was loth to think that such unhallowed beings haunted the glen.

A few days passed, and again, descending to the stream, he saw a figure flit by him through the covert; and this time a deeper fear entered into him; but he put away the thought, and prayed fervently for all souls in temptation. And when he spoke with the Wild Woman again, on the feast of the Seven

Maccabees, which falls on the first day of August, he was smitten with fear to see her wasted looks, and besought her to cease from labouring and let him minister to her. But she denied him gently, and replied that all she asked of him was to keep her steadfastly in his prayers.

Before the feast of the Assumption the rains ceased, and the plague, which had begun to show itself, was stayed; but the ardency of the sun grew greater, and the Hermit's cliff was a fiery furnace. Never had such heat been known in those regions; but the people did not murmur, for with the cessation of the rain their crops were saved and the pestilence banished; and these mercies they ascribed in great part to the prayers and macerations of the two holy anchorets. Therefore on the eve of the Assumption they sent a messenger to the Hermit, saying that at daylight on the morrow the townspeople and all the dwellers in the valley would come forth, led by their Bishop, who bore the Pope's blessing to the two Solitaries, and who was minded to celebrate the Mass of the Assumption in the Hermit's cave in the cliffside. At the word the Hermit was well-nigh distraught with joy, for he felt this to be a sign from heaven that his prayers were heard, and that he had won the Wild Woman's grace as well as his own. And all night he prayed that on the morrow she might confess her fault and receive the Sacrament with him.

Before dawn he recited the psalms of the proper nocturn; then he girded on his gown and sandals, and went forth to meet the Bishop.

As he went downward daylight stood on the mountains, and he thought he had never seen so fair a dawn. It filled the farthest heaven with brightness, and penetrated even to the woody crevices of the glen, as the grace of God had entered into the obscurest folds of his heart. The morning airs were hushed, and he heard only the sound of his own footfall, and the murmur of the stream which, though diminished, still poured a swift current between the rocks; but as he reached the bottom of the glen a sound of chanting came to him, and he knew that the pilgrims were at hand. His heart leapt up and his feet hastened forward; but at the stream's edge they were suddenly stayed, for in a pool where the water was still deep he saw the shining of a woman's body—and on the bank lay the Wild Woman's gown and sandals.

Fear and rage possessed the Hermit's heart, and he stood as one smitten dumb, covering his eyes from the shame. But the song of the approaching pilgrims swelled louder and nearer, and he cried angrily to the Wild Woman to come forth and hide herself from the people.

She made no answer, but in the dusk he saw her limbs sway with the swaying water, and her eyes were turned to him as if in mockery. At the sight fury filled him, and clambering over the rocks to the pool's edge he bent down and caught her by the shoulder. At that moment he could have strangled her with his hands, so abhorrent was the touch of her flesh; but as he cried out, heaping her with cruel names, he saw that her eyes returned his look without wavering; and suddenly it came to him that she was dead. Then through all his anger and fear a great pang smote him; for here was his work undone, and one he had loved in Christ laid low in her sin, in spite of all his labours.

One moment pity possessed him; the next he thought how the people would find him bending above the body of a naked

woman, whom he had held up to them as holy, but whom they might now well take for the secret instrument of his undoing; and seeing how at her touch all the slow edifice of his holiness was demolished, and his soul in mortal jeopardy, he felt the earth reel round him and his eyes grew blind.

Already the head of the procession had appeared, and the glen shook with the great sound of the *Salve Regina*.[10] When the Hermit opened his eyes once more the air shone with thronged candle-flames, which glittered on the gold thread of priestly vestments, and on the blazing monstrance beneath its canopy; and close above him he saw the Bishop's face.

The Hermit struggled to his knees.

"My Father in God," he cried, "behold, for my sins I have been visited by a demon—" But as he spoke he perceived that those about him no longer listened, and that the Bishop and all his clergy had fallen on their knees beside the pool. Then the Hermit, following their gaze, saw that the brown waters of the pool covered the Wild Woman's limbs as with a garment, and that about her floating head a brightness floated; and to the utmost edges of the throng a cry of praise went up, for many were there whom the Wild Woman had healed, and who read God's mercy in this wonder. But fresh fear fell on the Hermit, for he had cursed a dying saint, and denounced her aloud to all the people; and this new anguish, coming so close on the other, smote down his enfeebled frame, so that his limbs failed him and again he sank to the ground.

The earth reeled, and the bending faces grew dim about him; but as he forced his weak voice once more to proclaim his

10 Literally "Hail, Queen," a hymn praising the Virgin Mary.

sins he felt the touch of absolution, and the holy oils of the last voyage on his lips and eyes. Peace returned to him then, and with it a longing to look once more upon his lauds, as he had dreamed of doing at his death; but he was too far gone to make this longing known, and so tried to put it from his mind. Yet in his weakness it held him, and the tears ran down his face.

Then, as he lay there, feeling the earth slip from him, and the everlasting arms replace it, he heard a great peal of voices that seemed to come down from the sky and mingle with the singing of the throng; and the words of the chant were the words of his own lauds, so long hidden in the secret of his breast, and now rejoicing above him through the spheres. And his soul rose on the chant, and soared with it to the seat of mercy.

Two poems by
Katherine Tynan

NYMPHS

Where are ye now, O beautiful girls of the mountain,
    Oreads all?
Nothing at all stirs here save the drip of the fountain;
    Answers our call
Only the heart-glad thrush, in the Vale of Thrushes;
    Stirs in the brake
But the dew-bright ear of the hare in his couch of rushes
    Listening, awake.

THE CHILDREN OF LIR[1]

Out upon the sand-dunes thrive the coarse long grasses;
Herons standing knee-deep in the brackish pool;
Overhead the sunset fire and flame amasses
And the moon to eastward rises pale and cool.
Rose and green around her, silver-gray and pearly,
Chequered with the black rooks flying home to bed;
For, to wake at daybreak, birds must couch them early:
And the day's a long one since the dawn was red.

On the chilly lakelet, in that pleasant gloaming,
See the sad swans sailing: they shall have no rest:
Never a voice to greet them save the bittern's booming
Where the ghostly sallows[2] sway against the West.
"Sister," saith the gray swan, "Sister, I am weary,"
Turning to the white swan wet, despairing eyes;
"O" she saith, "my young one! O" she saith, "my dearie!"
Casts her wings about him with a storm of cries.

---

1 In Irish legend, King Lir's wife died giving birth, and he married her younger
sister, Aoife. But Aoife was jealous of his love for his four children: his sons
Aodh (here called Hugh), Fiachra, and Conn, and his daughter Fionnuala.
She turned them into swans, telling them that they would remain enchanted
for nine hundred years: three hundred on Lake Derravaragh, three hundred
on the Straits of Moyle, and three hundred on the Isle of Inish Glora. They
would be disenchanted only after St. Patrick came to Ireland. However, they
would retain their human voices, which they used to tell their story to any
who would listen. After the nine hundred years were over, they were finally
disenchanted by a holy man, but when they returned to human form, they
were old and close to death. They asked to be baptized by the holy man before
they died.
2 A type of willow that grows in a shrubby clump, rather than into a large
tree.

Woe for Lir's sweet children whom their vile stepmother
Glamoured with her witch-spells for a thousand years;
Died their father raving, on his throne another,
Blind before the end came from the burning tears.
Long the swans have wandered over lake and river;
Gone is all the glory of the race of Lir:
Gone and long forgotten like a dream of fever:
But the swans remember the sweet days that were.

Hugh, the black and white swan with the beauteous feathers,
Fiachra, the black swan with the emerald breast,
Conn, the youngest, dearest, sheltered in all weathers,
Him his snow-white sister loves the tenderest.
These her mother gave her as she lay a-dying;
To her faithful keeping; faithful hath she been,
With her wings spread o'er them when the tempest's crying,
And her songs so hopeful when the sky's serene.

Other swans have nests made 'mid the reeds and rushes,
Lined with downy feathers where the cygnets sleep
Dreaming, if a bird dreams, till the daylight blushes,
Then they sail out swiftly on the current deep.
With the proud swan-father, tall, and strong, and stately,
And the mild swan-mother, grave with household cares,
All well-born and comely, all rejoicing greatly:
Full of honest pleasure is a life like theirs.

But alas! for my swans with the human nature,
Sick with human longings, starved for human ties,

With their hearts all human cramped to a bird's stature.
And the human weeping in the bird's soft eyes.
Never shall my swans build nests in some green river,
Never fly to Southward in the autumn gray,
Rear no tender children, love no mates for ever;
Robbed alike of bird's joys and of man's are they.

Babbles Conn the youngest, "Sister, I remember
At my father's palace how I went in silk,
Ate the juicy deer-flesh roasted from the ember,
Drank from golden goblets my child's draught of milk.
Once I rode a-hunting, laughed to see the hurly,
Shouted at the ball-play, on the lake did row;
You had for your beauty gauds that shone so rarely."
"Peace," saith Fionnuala, "that was long ago."

"Sister," saith Fiachra, "well do I remember
How the flaming torches lit the banquet-hall,
And the fire leapt skyward in the mid-December,
And among the rushes slept our staghounds tall.
By our father's right hand you sat shyly gazing,
Smiling half and sighing, with your eyes a-glow,
As the bards sang loudly all your beauty praising."
"Peace," saith Fionnuala, "that was long ago."

"Sister," then saith Hugh, "most do I remember
One I called my brother, one, earth's goodliest man,
Strong as forest oaks are where the wild vines clamber,
First at feast or hunting, in the battle's van.

Angus, you were handsome, wise, and true, and tender,
Loved by every comrade, feared by every foe:
Low, low, lies your beauty, all forgot your splendour."
"Peace," saith Fionnuala, "that was long ago."

Dews are in the clear air and the roselight paling;
Over sands and sedges shines the evening star;
And the moon's disc lonely high in heaven is sailing;
Silvered all the spear-heads of the rushes are.
Housèd warm are all things as the night grows colder,
Water-fowl and sky-fowl dreamless in the nest;
But the swans go drifting, drooping wing and shoulder
Cleaving the still water where the fishes rest.

THE PRINCESS AND THE HEDGE-PIG

E. Nesbit

"But I don't see what we're to *do*," said the Queen for the twentieth time.

"Whatever we do will end in misfortune," said the King gloomily; "you'll see it will."

They were sitting in the honeysuckle arbour talking things over, while the nurse walked up and down the terrace with the new baby in her arms.

"Yes, dear," said the poor Queen; "I've not the slightest doubt I shall."

Misfortune comes in many ways, and you can't always know beforehand that a certain way is the way misfortune will come by: but there are things misfortune comes after as surely as night comes after day. For instance, if you let all the water boil away, the kettle will have a hole burnt in it. If you leave the bath taps running and the waste-pipe closed, the stairs of your house will, sooner or later, resemble Niagara. If you leave your purse at home, you won't have it with you when you want to pay your tram-fare. And if you throw lighted wax matches at your muslin curtains, your parent will most likely have to pay five pounds to the fire engines for coming round and blowing the fire out with a wet hose. Also if you are a king and do not invite the wicked fairy to your christening parties, she will come all the same. And if you do ask the wicked fairy, she will come, and in either case it will be the worse for the new princess. So what is a poor monarch to do? Of course there is one way out of the difficulty, and that is not to have a christening party at all. But this offends all the good fairies, and then where are you?

All these reflections had presented themselves to the minds of King Ozymandias and his Queen, and neither of them could deny that they were in a most awkward situation. They were "talking it over" for the hundredth time on the palace terrace where the pomegranates and oleanders grew in green tubs and the marble balustrade is overgrown with roses, red and white and pink and yellow. On the lower terrace the royal nurse was walking up and down with the baby princess that all the fuss was about. The Queen's eyes followed the baby admiringly.

"The darling!" she said. "Oh, Ozymandias, don't you some-times wish we'd been poor people?"

"Never!" said the King decidedly.

"Well, I do," said the Queen; "then we could have had just you and me and your sister at the christening, and no fear of— oh! I've thought of something."

The King's patient expression showed that he did not think it likely that she would have thought of anything useful; but at the first five words his expression changed. You would have said that he pricked up his ears, if kings had ears that could be pricked up. What she said was—

"Let's have a secret christening."

"How?" asked the King.

The Queen was gazing in the direction of the baby with what is called a "far away look" in her eyes.

"Wait a minute," she said slowly. "I see it all—yes—we'll have the party in the cellars—you know they're splendid."

"My great-grandfather had them built by Lancashire men, yes," interrupted the King.

"We'll send out the invitations to look like bills. The baker's boy can take them. He's a very nice boy. He made baby laugh yesterday when I was explaining to him about the Standard Bread. We'll just put '1 loaf 3. A remittance at your earliest convenience will oblige.' That'll mean that 1 person is invited for 3 o'clock, and on the back we'll write where and why in invisible ink. Lemon juice, you know. And the baker's boy shall be told to ask to see the people—just as they do when they *really* mean earliest convenience—and then he shall just whisper: 'Deadly secret. Lemon juice. Hold it to the fire,' and come away. Oh, dearest, do say you approve!"

The King laid down his pipe, set his crown straight, and kissed the Queen with great and serious earnestness.

"You are a wonder," he said. "It is the very thing. But the baker's boy is very small. Can we trust him?"

"He is nine," said the Queen, "and I have sometimes thought that he must be a prince in disguise. He is so very intelligent."

The Queen's plan was carried out. The cellars, which were really extraordinarily fine, were secretly decorated by the

King's confidential man and the Queen's confidential maid and a few of *their* confidential friends whom they knew they could really trust. You would never have thought they were cellars when the decorations were finished. The walls were hung with white satin and white velvet, with wreaths of white roses, and the stone floors were covered with freshly cut turf with white daisies, brisk and neat, growing in it.

The invitations were duly delivered by the baker's boy. On them was written in plain blue ink,

> "The Royal Bakeries
> 1 loaf 3d.
> An early remittance will oblige."

And when the people held the letter to the fire, as they were whisperingly instructed to do by the baker's boy, they read in a faint brown writing:—

"King Ozymandias and Queen Eliza invite you to the christening of their daughter Princess Ozyliza at three on Wednesday in the Palace cellars.

"*P.S.*—We are obliged to be very secret and careful because of wicked fairies, so please come disguised as a tradesman with a bill, calling for the last time before it leaves your hands."

You will understand by this that the King and Queen were not as well off as they could wish; so that tradesmen calling at the palace with that sort of message was the last thing likely to excite remark. But as most of the King's subjects were not very well off either, this was merely a bond between the King and his people. They could sympathise with each other, and understand each other's troubles in a way impossible to most kings and most nations.

You can imagine the excitement in the families of the people who were invited to the christening party, and the interest they felt in their costumes. The Lord Chief Justice disguised himself as a shoemaker; he still had his old blue brief-bag by him, and a brief-bag and a boot-bag are very much alike. The Commander-in-Chief dressed as a dog's meat man and wheeled a barrow. The Prime Minister appeared as a tailor; this required no change of dress and only a slight change of expression. And the other courtiers all disguised themselves perfectly. So did the good fairies, who had, of course, been invited first of all. Benevola, Queen of the Good Fairies, disguised herself as a moonbeam, which can go into any palace and no questions asked. Serena, the next in command, dressed as a butterfly, and all the other fairies had disguises equally pretty and tasteful.

The Queen looked most kind and beautiful, the King very handsome and manly, and all the guests agreed that the new princess was the most beautiful baby they had ever seen in all their born days.

Everybody brought the most charming christening presents concealed beneath their disguises. The fairies gave the usual gifts, beauty, grace, intelligence, charm, and so on.

Everything seemed to be going better than well. But of course you know it wasn't. The Lord High Admiral had not been able to get a cook's dress large enough completely to cover his uniform; a bit of an epaulette had peeped out, and the wicked fairy, Malevola, had spotted it as he went past her to the palace back door, near which she had been sitting disguised as a dog without a collar hiding from the police, and enjoying what she took to be the trouble the royal household were having with their tradesmen.

Malevola almost jumped out of her dog-skin when she saw the glitter of that epaulette.

"Hullo?" she said, and sniffed quite like a dog. "I must look into this," said she, and disguising herself as a toad, she crept unseen into the pipe by which the copper[1] emptied itself into the palace moat—for of course there was a copper in one of the palace cellars as there always is in cellars in the North Country.

Now this copper had been a great trial to the decorators. If there is anything you don't like about your house, you can either try to conceal it or "make a feature of it." And as concealment of the copper was impossible, it was decided to "make it a feature" by covering it with green moss and planting a tree in it, a little apple tree all in bloom. It had been very much admired.

Malevola, hastily altering her disguise to that of a mole, dug her way through the earth that the copper was full of, got to the top and put out a sharp nose just as Benevola was saying in that soft voice which Malevola always thought so affected,—

"The Princess shall love and be loved all her life long."

"So she shall," said the wicked fairy, assuming her own shape amid the screams of the audience. "Be quiet, you silly cuckoo," she said to the Lord Chamberlain, whose screams were specially piercing, "or I'll give *you* a christening present too."

Instantly there was a dreadful silence. Only Queen Eliza, who had caught up the baby at Malevola's first word, said feebly,—

"Oh, *don't*, dear Malevola."

And the King said, "It isn't exactly a party, don't you know. Quite informal. Just a few friends dropped in, eh, what?"

---

1 A boiler for heating water.

"So I perceive," said Malevola, laughing that dreadful laugh of hers which makes other people feel as though they would never be able to laugh any more. "Well, I've dropped in too. Let's have a look at the child."

The poor Queen dared not refuse. She tottered forward with the baby in her arms.

"Humph!" said Malevola, "your precious daughter will have beauty and grace and all the rest of the tuppenny half-penny rubbish those niminy-piminy minxes have given her. But she will be turned out of her kingdom. She will have to face her enemies without a single human being to stand by her, and she shall never come to her own again until she finds—" Malevola hesitated. She could not think of anything sufficiently unlikely— "until she finds," she repeated—

"A thousand spears to follow her to battle," said a new voice, "a thousand spears devoted to her and to her alone."

A very young fairy fluttered down from the little apple tree where she had been hiding among the pink and white blossoms.

"I am very young, I know," she said apologetically, "and I've only just finished my last course of Fairy History. So I know that if a fairy stops more than half a second in a curse she can't go on, and some one else may finish it for her. That is so, Your Majesty, isn't it?" she said, appealing to Benevola. And the Queen of the Fairies said Yes, that was the law, only it was such an old one most people had forgotten it.

"You think yourself very clever," said Malevola, "but as a matter of fact you're simply silly. That's the very thing I've provided against. She *can't* have any one to stand by her in battle, so she'll lose her kingdom and every one will be killed, and I shall come to the funeral. It will be enormous," she added rubbing her hands at the joyous thought.

"If you've quite finished," said the King politely, "and if you're sure you won't take any refreshment, may I wish you a very good afternoon?" He held the door open himself, and Malevola went out chuckling. The whole of the party then burst into tears.

"Never mind," said the King at last, wiping his eyes with the tails of his ermine. "It's a long way off and perhaps it won't happen after all."

But of course it did.

The King did what he could to prepare his daughter for the fight in which she was to stand alone against her enemies. He had her taught fencing and riding and shooting, both with the cross bow and the long bow, as well as with pistols, rifles, and artillery. She learned to dive and to swim, to run and to jump, to box and to wrestle, so that she grew up as strong and healthy as any young man, and could, indeed, have got the best of a fight with any prince of her own age. But the few princes who called at the palace did not come to fight the Princess, and when they heard that the Princess had no dowry except the gifts of the fairies, and also what Malevola's gift had been, they all said they had just looked in as they were passing and that they must be going now, thank you. And went.

And then the dreadful thing happened. The tradesmen, who had for years been calling for the last time before, etc., really decided to place the matter in other hands. They called in a neighbouring king who marched his army into Ozymandias's country, conquered the army—the soldiers' wages hadn't been paid for years—turned out the King and Queen, paid the tradesmen's bills, had most of the palace walls papered with the receipts, and set up housekeeping there himself.

Now when this happened the Princess was away on a visit to her aunt, the Empress of Oricalchia, half the world away, and there is no regular post between the two countries, so that when she came home, travelling with a train of fifty-four camels, which is rather slow work, and arrived at her own kingdom, she expected to find all the flags flying and the bells ringing and the streets decked in roses to welcome her home.

Instead of which nothing of the kind. The streets were all as dull as dull, the shops were closed because it was early-closing day, and she did not see a single person she knew.

She left the fifty-four camels laden with the presents her aunt had given her outside the gates, and rode alone on her own pet camel to the palace, wondering whether perhaps her father had not received the letter she had sent on ahead by carrier pigeon the day before.

And when she got to the palace and got off her camel and went in, there was a strange king on her father's throne and a strange queen sat in her mother's place at his side.

"Where's my father?" said the Princess, bold as brass, standing on the steps of the throne. "And what are you doing there?"

"I might ask you that," said the King. "Who are you, anyway?"

"I am the Princess Ozyliza," said she.

"Oh, I've heard of you," said the King. "You've been expected for some time. Your father's been evicted, so now you know. No, I can't give you his address."

Just then some one came and whispered to the Queen that fifty-four camels laden with silks and velvets and monkeys and parakeets and the richest treasures of Oricalchia were outside the city gate. She put two and two together, and whispered to the King, who nodded and said:

"I wish to make a new law."

Every one fell flat on his face. The law is so much respected in that country.

"No one called Ozyliza is allowed to own property in this kingdom," said the King. "Turn out that stranger." So the Princess was turned out of her father's palace, and went out and cried in the palace gardens where she had been so happy when she was little.

And the baker's boy, who was now the baker's young man, came by with the standard bread and saw some one crying among the oleanders, and went to say, "Cheer up!" to whoever it was. And it was the Princess. He knew her at once.

"Oh, Princess," he said, "cheer up! Nothing is ever so bad as it seems."

"Oh, Baker's Boy," said she, for she knew him too, "how can I cheer up? I am turned out of my kingdom. I haven't got my father's address, and I have to face my enemies without a single human being to stand by me."

"That's not true, at any rate," said the baker's boy, whose name was Erinaceus, "you've got me. If you'll let me be your squire, I'll follow you round the world and help you to fight your enemies."

"You won't be let," said the Princess sadly, "but I thank you very much all the same."

She dried her eyes and stood up.

"I must go," she said, "and I've nowhere to go to."

Now as soon as the Princess had been turned out of the palace, the Queen said, "You'd much better have beheaded her for treason." And the King said, "I'll tell the archers to pick her off as she leaves the grounds."

So when she stood up, out there among the oleanders, some one on the terrace cried, "There she is!" and instantly a flight of winged arrows crossed the garden. At the cry Erinaceus flung himself in front of her, clasping her in his arms and turning his back to the arrows. The Royal Archers were a thousand strong and all excellent shots. Erinaceus felt a thousand arrows sticking into his back.

"And now my last friend is dead," cried the Princess. But being a very strong princess, she dragged him into the shrubbery out of sight of the palace, and then dragged him into the wood and called aloud on Benevola, Queen of the Fairies, and Benevola came.

"They've killed my only friend," said the Princess, "at least.... Shall I pull out the arrows?"

"If you do," said the Fairy, "he'll certainly bleed to death."

"And he'll die if they stay in," said the Princess.

"Not necessarily," said the Fairy; "let me cut them a little shorter."

She did, with her fairy pocket-knife. "Now," she said, "I'll do what I can, but I'm afraid it'll be a disappointment to you both. Erinaceus," she went on, addressing the unconscious baker's boy with the stumps of the arrows still sticking in him, "I command you, as soon as I have vanished, to assume the form of a hedge-pig. The hedge-pig," she exclaimed to the Princess, "is the only nice person who can live comfortably with a thousand spikes sticking out of him. Yes, I know there are porcupines, but porcupines are vicious and ill-mannered. Good-bye!"

And with that she vanished. So did Erinaceus, and the Princess found herself alone among the oleanders; and on the green turf was a small and very prickly brown hedge-pig.

"Oh, dear!" she said, "now I'm all alone again, and the baker's boy has given his life for mine, and mine isn't worth having."

"It's worth more than all the world," said a sharp little voice at her feet.

"Oh, can you talk?" she said, quite cheered.

"Why not?" said the hedge-pig sturdily; "it's only the *form* of the hedge-pig I've assumed. I'm Erinaceus inside, all right enough. Pick me up in a corner of your mantle so as not to prick your darling hands."

"You mustn't call names, you know," said the Princess; "even your hedge-pigginess can't excuse such liberties."

"I'm sorry, Princess," said the hedge-pig, "but I can't help it. Only human beings speak lies; all other creatures tell the truth. Now I've got a hedge-pig's tongue it won't speak anything but the truth. And the truth is that I love you more than all the world."

"Well," said the Princess thoughtfully, "since you're a hedge-pig I suppose you may love me, and I may love you. Like pet dogs or gold-fish. Dear little hedge-pig, then!"

"Don't!" said the hedge-pig, "remember I'm the baker's boy in my mind and soul. My hedge-pigginess is only skin-deep. Pick me up, dearest of Princesses, and let us go to seek our fortunes."

"I think it's my parents I ought to seek," said the Princess. "However..."

She picked up the hedge-pig in the corner of her mantle and they went away through the wood.

They slept that night at a wood-cutter's cottage. The wood-cutter was very kind, and made a nice little box of beech-wood for the hedge-pig to be carried in, and he told the Princess that most of her father's subjects were still loyal, but that no one could fight for him because they would be fighting for the Princess too, and however much they might wish to do this, Malevola's curse assured them that it was impossible.

So the Princess put her hedge-pig in its little box and went on, looking everywhere for her father and mother, and, after more adventures than I have time to tell you, she found them at last, living in quite a poor way in a semi-detached villa at Tooting. They were very glad to see her, but when they heard that she meant to try to get back the kingdom, the King said:

"I shouldn't bother, my child, I really shouldn't. We are quite happy here. I have the pension always given to Deposed Monarchs, and your mother is becoming a really economical manager."

The Queen blushed with pleasure, and said, "Thank you, dear. But if you should succeed in turning that wicked usurper out, Ozyliza, I hope I shall be a better queen than I used to be. I am learning housekeeping at an evening class at the Crown-maker's Institute."

The Princess kissed her parents and went out into the garden to think it over. But the garden was small and quite full of wet washing hung on lines. So she went into the road, but that was full of dust and perambulators. Even the wet washing was better than that, so she went back and sat down on the grass in a white alley of tablecloths and sheets, all marked with a crown in indelible ink. And she took the hedge-pig out of the box. It was rolled up in a ball, but she stroked the little bit of soft forehead that you can always find if you look carefully at a rolled-up hedge-pig, and the hedge-pig uncurled and said:

"I am afraid I was asleep, Princess dear. Did you want me?"

"You're the only person who knows all about everything," said she. "I haven't told father and mother about the arrows. Now what do you advise?"

Erinaceus was flattered at having his advice asked, but unfortunately he hadn't any to give.

"It's your work, Princess," he said. "I can only promise to do anything a hedge-pig *can* do. It's not much. Of course I could die for you, but that's so useless."

"Quite," said she.

"I wish I were invisible," he said dreamily.

"Oh, where are you?" cried Ozyliza, for the hedge-pig had vanished.

"Here," said a sharp little voice. "You can't see me, but I can see everything I want to see. And I can see what to do. I'll crawl into my box, and you must disguise yourself as an old French governess with the best references and answer the advertisement that the wicked king put yesterday in the *Usurpers Journal*."

The Queen helped the Princess to disguise herself, which, of course, the Queen would never have done if she had known about the arrows; and the King gave her some of his pension to buy a ticket with, so she went back quite quickly, by train, to her own kingdom.

The usurping King at once engaged the French governess to teach his cook to read French cookery books, because the best recipes are in French. Of course he had no idea that there was a princess, *the* Princess, beneath the governessial disguise. The French lessons were from 6 to 8 in the morning and from 2 to 4 in the afternoon, and all the rest of the time the governess could spend as she liked. She spent it walking about the palace gardens and talking to her invisible hedge-pig. They talked about everything under the sun, and the hedge-pig was the best of company.

"How did you become invisible?" she asked one day, and it said, "I suppose it was Benevola's doing. Only I think every one gets *one* wish granted if they only wish hard enough."

On the fifty-fifth day the hedge-pig said, "Now, Princess dear, I'm going to begin to get you back your kingdom."

And next morning the King came down to breakfast in a dreadful rage with his face covered up in bandages.

"This palace is haunted," he said. "In the middle of the night a dreadful spiked ball was thrown in my face. I lighted a match. There was nothing."

The Queen said, "Nonsense! You must have been dreaming."

But next morning it was her turn to come down with a bandaged face. And the night after, the King had the spiky ball thrown at him again. And then the Queen had it. And then they both had it, so that they couldn't sleep at all, and had to lie awake with nothing to think of but their wickedness. And every five minutes a very little voice whispered:

"Who stole the kingdom? Who killed the Princess?" till the King and Queen could have screamed with misery.

And at last the Queen said, "We needn't have killed the Princess."

And the King said, "I've been thinking that, too."

And next day the King said, "I don't know that we ought to have taken this kingdom. We had a really high-class kingdom of our own."

"I've been thinking that too," said the Queen.

By this time their hands and arms and necks and faces and ears were very sore indeed, and they were sick with want of sleep.

"Look here," said the King, "let's chuck it. Let's write to Ozymandias and tell him he can take over his kingdom again. I've had jolly well enough of this."

"Let's," said the Queen, "but we can't bring the Princess to life again. I do wish we could," and she cried a little through her bandages into her egg, for it was breakfast time.

"Do you mean that," said a little sharp voice, though there was no one to be seen in the room. The King and Queen clung to each other in terror, upsetting the urn over the toast-rack.

"Do you mean it?" said the voice again; "answer, yes or no."

"Yes," said the Queen, "I don't know who you are, but, yes, yes, yes. I can't *think* how we could have been so wicked."

"Nor I," said the King.

"Then send for the French governess," said the voice.

"Ring the bell, dear," said the Queen. "I'm sure what it says is right. It is the voice of conscience. I've often heard *of* it, but I never heard it before."

The King pulled the richly-jewelled bell-rope and ten magnificent green and gold footmen appeared.

"Please ask Mademoiselle to step this way," said the Queen.

The ten magnificent green and gold footmen found the governess beside the marble basin feeding the gold-fish, and, bowing their ten green backs, they gave the Queen's message. The governess who, every one agreed, was always most obliging, went at once to the pink satin breakfast-room where the King and Queen were sitting, almost unrecognisable in their bandages.

"Yes, Your Majesties?" said she curtseying.

"The voice of conscience," said the Queen, "told us to send for you. Is there any recipe in the French books for bringing shot princesses to life? If so, will you kindly translate it for us?"

"There is *one*," said the Princess thoughtfully, "and it is quite simple. Take a king and a queen and the voice of conscience. Place them in a clean pink breakfast-room with eggs, coffee, and toast. Add a full-sized French governess. The king and queen must be thoroughly pricked and bandaged, and the voice of conscience must be very distinct."

"Is that all?" asked the Queen.

"That's all," said the governess, "except that the king and queen must have two more bandages over their eyes, and keep them on till the voice of conscience has counted fifty-five very slowly."

"If you would be so kind," said the Queen, "as to bandage us with our table napkins? Only be careful how you fold them, because our faces are very sore, and the royal monogram is very stiff and hard owing to its being embroidered in seed pearls by special command."

"I will be very careful," said the governess kindly.

The moment the King and Queen were blindfolded, the "voice of conscience" began, "one, two, three," and Ozyliza tore off her disguise, and under the fussy black-and-violet-spotted alpaca of the French governess was the simple slim cloth-of-silver dress of the Princess. She stuffed the alpaca up the chimney and the grey wig into the tea-cosy, and had disposed of the mittens in the coffee-pot and the elastic-side boots in the coal-scuttle, just as the voice of conscience said—

"Fifty-three, fifty-four, fifty-five!" and stopped.

The King and Queen pulled off the bandages, and there, alive and well, with bright clear eyes and pinky cheeks and a mouth that smiled, was the Princess whom they supposed to have been killed by the thousand arrows of their thousand archers.

Before they had time to say a word the Princess said:

"Good morning, Your Majesties. I am afraid you have had bad dreams. So have I. Let us all try to forget them. I hope you will stay a little longer in my palace. You are very welcome. I am so sorry you have been hurt."

"We deserved it," said the Queen, "and we want to say we have heard the voice of conscience, and do please forgive us."

"Not another word," said the Princess, "*do* let me have some fresh tea made. And some more eggs. These are quite cold. And the urn's been upset. We'll have a new breakfast. And I *am* so sorry your faces are so sore."

"If you kissed them," said the voice which the King and Queen called the voice of conscience, "their faces would not be sore any more."

"May I?" said Ozyliza, and kissed the King's ear and the Queen's nose, all she could get at through the bandages.

And instantly they were quite well.

They had a delightful breakfast. Then the King caused the royal household to assemble in the throne-room, and there announced that, as the Princess had come to claim the kingdom, they were returning to their own kingdom by the three-seventeen train on Thursday.

Every one cheered like mad, and the whole town was decorated and illuminated that evening. Flags flew from every house, and the bells all rang, just as the Princess had expected them to do that day when she came home with the fifty-five camels. All the treasure these had carried was given back to the Princess, and the camels themselves were restored to her, hardly at all the worse for wear.

The usurping King and Queen were seen off at the station by the Princess, and parted from her with real affection. You see they weren't completely wicked in their hearts, but they had never had time to think before. And being kept awake at night forced them to think. And the "voice of conscience" gave them something to think about.

They gave the Princess the receipted bills, with which most of the palace was papered, in return for board and lodging.

When they were gone a telegram was sent off.

> Ozymandias Rex, Esq.,
> Chatsworth,
> Delamere Road,
> Tooting,
> England.
> Please come home at once. Palace vacant. Tenants have left.—Ozyliza P.

And they came immediately.

When they arrived the Princess told them the whole story, and they kissed and praised her, and called her their deliverer and the savior of her country.

"*I* haven't done anything," she said. "It was Erinaceus who did everything, and..."

"But the fairies said," interrupted the King, who was never clever at the best of times, "that you couldn't get the kingdom back till you had a thousand spears devoted to you, to you alone."

"There are a thousand spears in my back," said a little sharp voice, "and they are all devoted to the Princess and to her alone."

"Don't!" said the King irritably. "That voice coming out of nothing makes me jump."

"I can't get used to it either," said the Queen. "We must have a gold cage built for the little animal. But I must say I wish it was visible."

"So do I," said the Princess earnestly. And instantly it was. I suppose the Princess wished it very hard, for there was the hedge-pig with its long spiky body and its little pointed face, its bright eyes, its small round ears, and its sharp, turned-up nose.

It looked at the Princess but it did not speak.

"Say something *now*," said Queen Eliza. "I should like to *see* a hedge-pig speak."

"The truth is, if speak I must, I must speak the truth," said Erinaceus. "The Princess has thrown away her life-wish to make me visible. I wish she had wished instead for something nice for herself."

"Oh, was that my life-wish?" cried the Princess. "I didn't know, dear Hedge-pig, I didn't know. If I'd only known, I would have wished you back into your proper shape."

"If you had," said the hedge-pig, "it would have been the shape of a dead man. Remember that I have a thousand spears in my back, and no man can carry those and live."

The Princess burst into tears.

"Oh, you can't go on being a hedge-pig for ever," she said, "it's not fair. I can't bear it. Oh Mamma! Oh Papa! Oh Benevola!"

And there stood Benevola before them, a little dazzling figure with blue butterfly's wings and a wreath of moonshine.

"Well?" she said, "well?"

"Oh, you know," said the Princess, still crying. "I've thrown away my life-wish, and he's still a hedge-pig. Can't you do *anything*!"

"*I* can't," said the Fairy, "but you can. Your kisses are magic kisses. Don't you remember how you cured the King and Queen of all the wounds the hedge-pig made by rolling itself on to their faces in the night?"

"But she can't go kissing hedge-pigs," said the Queen, "it would be most unsuitable. Besides it would hurt her."

But the hedge-pig raised its little pointed face, and the Princess took it up in her hands. She had long since learned how to do this without hurting either herself or it. She looked in its little bright eyes.

"I would kiss you on every one of your thousand spears," she said, "to give you what you wish."

"Kiss me once," it said, "where my fur is soft. That is all I wish, and enough to live and die for."

She stooped her head and kissed it on its forehead where the fur is soft, just where the prickles begin.

And instantly she was standing with her hands on a young man's shoulders and her lips on a young man's face just where the hair begins and the forehead leaves off. And all round his feet lay a pile of fallen arrows.

She drew back and looked at him.

"Erinaceus," she said, "you're different—from the baker's boy I mean."

"When I was an invisible hedge-pig," he said, "I knew everything. Now I have forgotten all that wisdom save only two things. One is that I am a king's son. I was stolen away in infancy by an unprincipled baker, and I am really the son of that usurping King whose face I rolled on in the night. It is a painful thing to roll on your father's face when you are all spiky, but I did it, Princess, for your sake, and for my father's too. And now I will go to him and tell him all, and ask his forgiveness."

"You won't go away?" said the Princess. "Ah! don't go away. What shall I do without my hedge-pig?"

Erinaceus stood still, looking very handsome and like a prince.

"What is the other thing that you remember of your hedge-pig wisdom?" asked the Queen curiously. And Erinaceus answered, not to her but to the Princess:

"The other thing, Princess, is that I love you."

"Isn't there a third thing, Erinaceus?" said the Princess, looking down.

"There is, but you must speak that, not I."

"Oh," said the Princess, a little disappointed, "then you knew that I loved you?"

"Hedge-pigs are very wise little beasts," said Erinaceus, "but I only knew that when you told it me."

"I—told you?"

"When you kissed my little pointed face, Princess," said Erinaceus, "I knew then."

"My goodness gracious me," said the King.

"Quite so," said Benevola, "and I wouldn't ask *any one* to the wedding."

"Except you, dear," said the Queen.

"Well, as I happened to be passing…there's no time like the present," said Benevola briskly. "Suppose you give orders for the wedding bells to be rung now, at once!"

Two poems by
May Kendall

A Castle in the Air

The mansions *they* erected,
    Erected were of brick,
And were by tiles protected:
    The air with dust was thick,
As 'twould the builders smother—
    They built on unaware.
I dreamed of something other,
    A castle in the air!

I said: "Your bricks and mortar
    Are hideous to view;
I'll seek another quarter,
    That shall be free from *you*:
A more imposing dwelling
    You shall see, if you care,
A palace far excelling—
    A castle in the air."

They guarded from disaster
    Their roofs with wooden beams;
They fixed their walls with plaster—
    I fixed *my* walls with dreams.
A dome of high expansion,
    Alight with jewels rare—

That was a *real* mansion
　　My castle in the air.

They never were contented,
　　They fought with spades and tools;
They said I was demented,
　　I said that they were fools.
I built on in my manner,
　　They hardly turned to stare;
I crowned with many a banner
　　My castle in the air.

When ended were their labours
　　They entered in to feast,
They called their friends and neighbours:
　　The wind blew from the east.
To them it did not matter,
　　The gale their walls would spare;
It only chose to shatter
　　My castle in the air.

And now the shadows darken,
　　The wind blows through the rain,
Whereto the builders hearken,
　　Who safe at home remain,
In piles of brick undoubted;
　　Yet mine was far more fair,
My palace that they scouted,
　　My castle in the air!

THE MERMAID'S CHAPEL

Deep in the bay the old church lies,
    Beyond the storm wind's power,
The waves that whelmed it ever play
    In ripples round the tower.
And if you look down through the tide—
    Many and many a time
You may catch the glimmer of its stones,
    Or hear the sweet bells chime.

For they that dwell deep in the sea,
    Below the wind and rain,
The mermen and the mermaidens,
    Have built it up again.
They have made fast the ruined walls
    With their immortal hands,
And strewn its aisles with red sea flowers,
    And with the wet sea-sands.

And when a drifting boat comes back,
    Rock-shattered, to the shore,
With never captain at the helm
    Nor sailor at the oar,
Then down below the stormy foam
    The sweet old bells ring free.
They call upon the mariners
    Who come no more from sea.

Dollie Radford

A Ballad of Victory

With quiet step and gentle face,
With tattered cloak, and empty hands,
She came into the market place,
A traveller from many lands.

And by the costly merchandise,
Where people thronged in eager quest,
She paused awhile, with patient eyes,
And asked a little space for rest.

And where the fairest blossoms lay,
And where the rarest fruits were sent
From earth's abundant store, that day,
She turned and smiled in her content.

And where the meagre stall was bare,
Where no exultant voice was heard,
Beside the barren basket, there,
She stayed to say her quiet word.

When for her tender healing ways,
The women begged her help again,
She answered, "In these bounteous days
I may not let my love remain."

And when the children touched her hair,
And put their hands about her face,
She sighed, "There is so much to share,
I well might bide a little space."

But ere the shadows longer grew,
Or up the sky the evening stole,
She took the lonely way she knew,
And journeyed onward to her goal.

She turned away with steadfast air,
From all their choice of fair and sweet.
And as she turned they saw how bare
And bruisèd were her pilgrim feet.

Through many a rent and tattered fold,
As she went forward on her quest,
They saw the wounds so deep and old,
The cruel scars upon her breast.

They called to her to wait, to learn
How they would ease her pain, to dwell
With them awhile; she did but turn
And wave her smiling last farewell.

And in their midst a woman rose,
And said, "I do not know her name,
Nor whose the land to which she goes,
But well the roads by which she came.

"Among the lonely hills they lie,
Beyond the town's protecting wall,
Where travellers may faint and die,
And no one hearken when they call.

"Far up the barren heights they go,
Worn ever deeper night and day,
By toiling feet, and tears that flow
For some sweet flower to mark the way.

"And down the stony slopes they lead,
Through many a deep and dark ravine
Where long ago it was decreed
Nor sun nor moonlight should be seen.

"Across the waste where no help is,
And through the winds and blinding showers,
Among the mist-bound silences
And through the cold despairing hours.

"Among the lonely, lonely hills,
Ah me, I do not know her name,
Nor whose the bidding she fulfils,
But well the roads by which she came."

Then spoke a youth, who, long apart,
Had watched the people come and go,
With clearer eyes and wiser heart,
And cried, "Her face and name I know.

"And well the passage of her flight,
The starless plains she must ascend,
And well the darkness of the night,
In which her pilgrimage shall end.

"But stronger than the years that roll,
Than travail past, or yet to be,
She presses to her hidden goal,
A crownless, unknown Victory."

WHEN I WAS A WITCH

Charlotte Perkins Gilman

If I had understood the terms of that one-sided contract with
Satan, the Time of Witching would have lasted longer—you
may be sure of that. But how was I to tell? It just happened, and
has never happened again, though I've tried the same prelimi-
naries as far as I could control them.

The thing began all of a sudden, one October midnight—
the 30th, to be exact. It had been hot, really hot, all day, and
was sultry and thunderous in the evening; no air stirring, and
the whole house stewing with that ill-advised activity which
always seems to move the steam radiator when it isn't wanted.

I was in a state of simmering rage—hot enough, even without the weather and the furnace—and I went up on the roof
to cool off. A top-floor apartment has that advantage, among
others—you can take a walk without the mediation of an ele-
vator boy!

There are things enough in New York to lose one's temper over at the best of times, and on this particular day they seemed to all happen at once, and some fresh ones. The night before, cats and dogs had broken my rest, of course. My morning paper was more than usually mendacious; and my neighbor's morning paper—more visible than my own as I went down town—was more than usually salacious. My cream wasn't cream—my egg was a relic of the past. My "new" napkins were giving out.

Being a woman, I'm supposed not to swear; but when the motorman disregarded my plain signal, and grinned as he rushed by; when the subway guard waited till I was just about to step on board and then slammed the door in my face—standing behind it calmly for some minutes before the bell rang to warrant his closing—I desired to swear like a mule-driver.

At night it was worse. The way people paw one's back in the crowd! The cow-puncher who packs the people in or jerks them out—the men who smoke and spit, law or no law—the women whose saw-edged cart-wheel hats, swashing feathers and deadly pins, add so to one's comfort inside.

Well, as I said, I was in a particularly bad temper, and went up on the roof to cool off. Heavy black clouds hung low overhead, and lightning flickered threateningly here and there.

A starved, black cat stole from behind a chimney and mewed dolefully. Poor thing! She had been scalded.

The street was quiet for New York. I leaned over a little and looked up and down the long parallels of twinkling lights. A belated cab drew near, the horse so tired he could hardly hold his head up.

Then the driver, with a skill born of plenteous practice, flung out his long-lashed whip and curled it under the poor beast's belly with a stinging cut that made me shudder. The horse shuddered too, poor wretch, and jingled his harness with an effort at a trot.

I leaned over the parapet and watched that man with a spirit of unmitigated ill-will.

"I wish," said I, slowly—and I did wish it with all my heart—"that every person who strikes or otherwise hurts a horse unnecessarily, shall feel the pain intended—and the horse not feel it!"

It did me good to say it, anyhow, but I never expected any result. I saw the man swing his great whip again, and lay on heartily. I saw him throw up his hands—heard him scream— but I never thought what the matter was, even then.

The lean, black cat, timid but trustful, rubbed against my skirt and mewed.

"Poor Kitty!" I said; "poor Kitty! It is a shame!" And I thought tenderly of all the thousands of hungry, hunted cats who slink and suffer in a great city.

Later, when I tried to sleep, and up across the stillness rose the raucous shrieks of some of these same sufferers, my pity turned cold.

"Any fool that will try to keep a cat in a city!" I muttered, angrily.

Another yell—a pause—an ear-torturing, continuous cry. "I wish," I burst forth, "that every cat in the city was comfortably dead!"

A sudden silence fell, and in course of time I got to sleep.

Things went fairly well next morning, till I tried another egg. They were expensive eggs, too.

"I can't help it!" said my sister, who keeps house.

"I know you can't," I admitted. "But somebody could help it. I wish the people who are responsible had to eat their old eggs, and never get a good one till they sold good ones!"

"They'd stop eating eggs, that's all," said my sister, "and eat meat."

"Let 'em eat meat!" I said, recklessly. "The meat is as bad as the eggs! It's so long since we've had a clean, fresh chicken that I've forgotten how they taste!"

"It's cold storage," said my sister. She is a peaceable sort; I'm not.

"Yes, cold storage!" I snapped. "It ought to be a blessing— to tide over shortages, equalize supplies, and lower prices. What does it do? Corner the market, raise prices the year round, and make all the food bad!"

My anger rose. "If there was any way of getting at them!" I cried. "The law don't touch 'em. They need to be cursed some- how! I'd like to do it! I wish the whole crowd that profit by this vicious business might taste their bad meat, their old fish, their stale milk—whatever they ate. Yes, and feel the prices as we do!"

"They couldn't you know; they're rich," said my sister.

"I know that," I admitted, sulkily. "There's no way of get- ting at 'em. But I wish they could. And I wish they knew how people hated 'em, and felt that, too—till they mended their ways!"

When I left for my office I saw a funny thing. A man who drove a garbage cart took his horse by the bits and jerked and wrenched brutally. I was amazed to see him clap his hands to his own jaws with a moan, while the horse philosophically licked his chops and looked at him.

The man seemed to resent his expression, and struck him on the head, only to rub his own poll and swear amazedly, looking around to see who had hit him. The horse advanced a step, stretching a hungry nose toward a garbage pail crowned with cabbage leaves, and the man, recovering his sense of proprietorship, swore at him and kicked him in the ribs. That time he had to sit down, turning pale and weak. I watched with growing wonder and delight.

A market wagon came clattering down the street; the hard-faced young ruffian fresh for his morning task. He gathered the ends of the reins and brought them down on the horse's back with a resounding thwack. The horse did not notice this at all, but the boy did. He yelled!

I came to a place where many teamsters were at work hauling dirt and crushed stone. A strange silence and peace hung over the scene where usually the sound of the lash and sight of brutal blows made me hurry by. The men were talking together a little, and seemed to be exchanging notes. It was too good to be true. I gazed and marvelled, waiting for my car.

It came, merrily running along. It was not full. There was one not far ahead, which I had missed in watching the horses; there was no other near it in the rear.

Yet the coarse-faced person in authority who ran it, went gaily by without stopping, though I stood on the track almost, and waved my umbrella.

A hot flush of rage surged to my face. "I wish you felt the blow you deserve," said I, viciously, looking after the car. "I wish you'd have to stop, and back to here, and open the door and apologize. I wish that would happen to all of you, every time you play that trick."

To my infinite amazement, that car stopped and backed till the front door was before me. The motorman opened it, holding his hand to his cheek. "Beg your pardon, madam!" he said.

I passed in, dazed, overwhelmed. Could it be? Could it possibly be that—that what I wished came true. The idea sobered me, but I dismissed it with a scornful smile. "No such luck!" said I.

Opposite me sat a person in petticoats. She was of a sort I particularly detest. No real body of bones and muscles, but the contours of grouped sausages. Complacent, gaudily dressed, heavily wigged and ratted, with powder and perfume and flowers and jewels—and a dog.

A poor, wretched, little, artificial dog—alive, but only so by virtue of man's insolence; not a real creature that God made. And the dog had clothes on—and a bracelet! His fitted jacket had a pocket—and a pocket-handkerchief! He looked sick and unhappy.

I meditated on his pitiful position, and that of all the other poor chained prisoners, leading unnatural lives of enforced celibacy, cut off from sunlight, fresh air, the use of their limbs; led forth at stated intervals by unwilling servants, to defile our streets; over-fed, under-exercised, nervous and unhealthy.

"And we say we love them!" said I, bitterly to myself. "No wonder they bark and howl and go mad. No wonder they have almost as many diseases as we do! I wish—" Here the thought I had dismissed struck me again. "I wish that all the unhappy dogs in cities would die at once!"

I watched the sad-eyed little invalid across the car. He

dropped his head and died. She never noticed it till she got off; then she made fuss enough.

The evening papers were full of it. Some sudden pestilence had struck both dogs and cats, it would appear. Red headlines struck the eye, big letters, and columns were filled out of the complaints of those who had lost their "pets," of the sudden labors of the board of health, and interviews with doctors.

All day, as I went through the office routine, the strange sense of this new power struggled with reason and common knowledge. I even tried a few furtive test "wishes" —wished that the waste basket would fall over, that the inkstand would fill itself; but they didn't.

I dismissed the idea as pure foolishness, till I saw those newspapers, and heard people telling worse stories.

One thing I decided at once—not to tell a soul. "Nobody'd believe me if I did," said I to myself. "And I won't give 'em the chance. I've scored on cats and dogs, anyhow—and horses."

As I watched the horses at work that afternoon, and thought of all their unknown sufferings from crowded city sta-bles, bad air and insufficient food, and from the wearing strain of asphalt pavements in wet and icy weather, I decided to have another try on horses.

"I wish," said I, slowly and carefully, but with a fixed inten-sity of purposes, "that every horse owner, keeper, hirer and driver or rider, might feel what the horse feels, when he suf-fers at our hands. Feel it keenly and constantly till the case is mended."

I wasn't able to verify this attempt for some time; but the effect was so general that it got widely talked about soon; and this "new wave of humane feeling" soon raised the status of horses in our city. Also it diminished their numbers. People began to prefer motor drays—which was a mighty good thing.

Now I felt pretty well assured in my own mind, and kept my assurance to myself. Also I began to make a list of my cherished grudges, with a fine sense of power and pleasure.

"I must be careful," I said to myself; "very careful; and, above all things, make the punishment fit the crime."

The subway crowding came to my mind next; both the people who crowd because they have to, and the people who make them. "I mustn't punish anybody, for what they can't help," I mused. "But when it's pure meanness!" Then I bethought me of the remote stockholders, of the more immediate directors, of the painfully prominent officials and insolent employees—and got to work.

"I might as well make a good job of it while this lasts," said I to myself. "It's quite a responsibility, but lots of fun." And I wished that every person responsible for the condition of our subways might be mysteriously compelled to ride up and down in them continuously during rush hours.

This experiment I watched with keen interest, but for the life of me I could see little difference. There were a few more well-dressed persons in the crowds, that was all. So I came to the conclusion that the general public was mostly to blame, and carried their daily punishment without knowing it.

For the insolent guards and cheating ticket-sellers who give you short change, very slowly, when you are dancing on one foot and your train is there, I merely wished that they might feel the pain their victims would like to give them, short of real injury. They did, I guess.

Then I wished similar things for all manner of corporations and officials. It worked. It worked amazingly. There was a sudden conscientious revival all over the country. The dry bones rattled and sat up. Boards of directors, having troubles enough of their own, were aggravated by innumerable communications from suddenly sensitive stockholders.

In mills and mints and railroads, things began to mend. The country buzzed. The papers fattened. The churches sat up and took credit to themselves. I was incensed at this; and, after brief consideration, wished that every minister would preach to his congregation exactly what he believed and what he thought of them.

I went to six services the next Sunday—about ten minutes each, for two sessions. It was most amusing. A thousand pulpits were emptied forthwith, refilled, re-emptied, and so on, from week to week. People began to go to church; men largely—women didn't like it as well. They had always supposed the ministers thought more highly of them than now appeared to be the case.

One of my oldest grudges was against the sleeping-car people; and now I began to consider them. How often I had grinned and borne it—with other thousands—submitting helplessly.

Here is a railroad—a common carrier—and you have to use it. You pay for your transportation, a good round sum.

Then if you wish to stay in the sleeping car during the day, they charge you another two dollars and a half for the privilege of sitting there, whereas you have paid for a seat when you bought your ticket. That seat is now sold to another person—twice sold! Five dollars for twenty-four hours in a space six feet by three by three at night, and one seat by day; twenty-four of these privileges to a car—$120 a day for the rent of the car—and the passengers to pay the porter besides. That makes $44,800 a year.

Sleeping cars are expensive to build, they say. So are hotels; but they do not charge at such a rate. Now, what could I do to get even? Nothing could ever put back the dollars into the millions of pockets; but it might be stopped now, this beautiful process.

So I wished that all persons who profited by this performance might feel a shame so keen that they would make public avowal and apology, and, as partial restitution, offer their wealth to promote the cause of free railroads!

Then I remembered parrots. This was lucky, for my wrath flamed again. It was really cooling, as I tried to work out responsibility and adjust penalties. But parrots! Any person who wants to keep a parrot should go and live on an island alone with their preferred conversationalist!

There was a huge, squawky parrot right across the street from me, adding its senseless, rasping cries to the more necessary evils of other noises.

I had also an aunt with a parrot. She was a wealthy, ostentatious person, who had been an only child and inherited her money.

Uncle Joseph hated the yelling bird, but that didn't make any difference to Aunt Mathilda.

I didn't like this aunt, and wouldn't visit her, lest she think I was truckling for the sake of her money; but after I had wished this time, I called at the time set for my curse to work; and it did work with a vengeance. There sat poor Uncle Joe, looking thinner and meeker than ever; and my aunt, like an overripe plum, complacent enough.

"Let me out!" said Polly, suddenly. "Let me out to take a walk!"

"The clever thing!" said Aunt Mathilda. "He never said that before."

She let him out. Then he flapped up on the chandelier and sat among the prisms, quite safe.

"What an old pig you are, Mathilda!" said the parrot.

She started to her feet—naturally.

"Born a Pig—trained a Pig—a Pig by nature and education!" said the parrot. "Nobody'd put up with you, except for your money; unless it's this long-suffering husband of yours. He wouldn't, if he hadn't the patience of Job!"

"Hold your tongue!" screamed Aunt Mathilda. "Come down from there! Come here!"

Polly cocked his head and jingled the prisms. "Sit down, Mathilda!" he said, cheerfully. "You've got to listen. You are fat and homely and selfish. You are a nuisance to everybody about you. You have got to feed me and take care of me better than ever—and you've got to listen to me when I talk. Pig!"

I visited another person with a parrot the next day. She put a cloth over his cage when I came in.

"Take it off!" said Polly. She took it off.

"Won't you come into the other room?" she asked me, nervously.

"Better stay here!" said her pet. "Sit still—sit still!"

She sat still.

"Your hair is mostly false," said pretty Poll. "And your teeth—and your outlines. You eat too much. You are lazy. You ought to exercise, and don't know enough. Better apologize to this lady for backbiting! You've got to listen."

The trade in parrots fell off from that day; they say there is no call for them. But the people who kept parrots, keep them yet—parrots live a long time.

Bores were a class of offenders against whom I had long borne undying enmity. Now I rubbed my hands and began on them, with this simple wish: That every person whom they bored should tell them the plain truth.

There is one man whom I have specially in mind. He was blackballed at a pleasant club, but continues to go there. He isn't a member—he just goes; and no one does anything to him.

It was very funny after this. He appeared that very night at a meeting, and almost every person present asked him how he came there. "You're not a member, you know," they said. "Why do you butt in? Nobody likes you."

Some were more lenient with him. "Why don't you learn to be more considerate of others, and make some real friends?" they said. "To have a few friends who do enjoy your visits ought to be pleasanter than being a public nuisance."

He disappeared from that club, anyway.

I began to feel very cocky indeed.

In the food business there was already a marked improvement; and in transportation. The hubbub of reformation waxed louder daily, urged on by the unknown sufferings of all the profiters by iniquity.

The papers thrived on all this; and as I watched the loud-voiced protestations of my pet abomination in journalism, I had a brilliant idea, literally.

Next morning I was down town early, watching the men open their papers. My abomination was shamefully popular, and never more so than this morning. Across the top was printing in gold letters:

All intentional lies, in adv., editorial, news, or any other column......Scarlet

All malicious matter......Crimson

All careless or ignorant mistakes......Pink

All for direct self-interest of owner......Dark green

All mere bait—to sell the paper......Bright green

All advertising, primary or secondary......Brown

All sensational and salacious matter......Yellow

All hired hypocrisy......Purple

Good fun, instruction and entertainment......Blue

True and necessary news and honest editorials......Ordinary print

You never saw such a crazy quilt of a paper. They were bought like hot cakes for some days; but the real business fell off very soon. They'd have stopped it all if they could; but the papers looked all right when they came off the press. The color scheme flamed out only to the bona-fide reader.

I let this work for about a week, to the immense joy of all the other papers; and then turned it on to them, all at once. Newspaper reading became very exciting for a little, but the trade fell off. Even newspaper editors could not keep on feeding a market like that. The blue printed and ordinary printed matter grew from column to column and page to page. Some papers—small, to be sure, but refreshing—began to appear in blue and black alone.

This kept me interested and happy for quite a while; so much so that I quite forgot to be angry at other things. There was *such* a change in all kinds of business, following the mere printing of truth in the newspapers. It began to appear as if we had lived in a sort of delirium—not really knowing the facts about anything. As soon as we really knew the facts, we began to behave very differently, of course.

What really brought all my enjoyment to an end was women. Being a woman, I was naturally interested in them, and could see some things more clearly than men could. I saw their real power, their real dignity, their real responsibility in the world; and then the way they dress and behave used to make me fairly frantic. 'Twas like seeing archangels playing jackstraws—or real horses only used as rocking-horses. So I determined to get after them.

How to manage it! What to hit first! Their hats, their ugly, inane, outrageous hats—that is what one thinks of first. Their silly, expensive clothes—their diddling beads and jewelry— their greedy childishness—mostly of the women provided for by rich men.

Then I thought of all the other women, the real ones, the vast majority, patiently doing the work of servants without even a servant's pay—and neglecting the noblest duties of mother-hood in favor of house-service; the greatest power on earth, blind, chained, untaught, in a treadmill. I thought of what they might do, compared to what they did do, and my heart swelled with something that was far from anger.

Then I wished—with all my strength—that women, all women, might realize Womanhood at last; its power and pride and place in life; that they might see their duty as mothers of the world—to love and care for everyone alive; that they might see their duty to men—to choose only the best, and then to bear and rear better ones; that they might see their duty as human beings, and come right out into full life and work and happiness!

I stopped, breathless, with shining eyes. I waited, trembling, for things to happen.

Nothing happened.

You see, this magic which had fallen on me was black magic—and I had wished white.

It didn't work at all, and, what was worse, it stopped all the other things that were working so nicely.

Oh, if I had only thought to wish permanence for those lovely punishments! If only I had done more while I could do it, had half appreciated my privileges when I was a Witch!

Three poems by Elinor Wylie

ATAVISM[1]

I always was afraid of Somes's Pond:
Not the little pond, by which the willow stands,
Where laughing boys catch alewives in their hands
In brown, bright shallows; but the one beyond.
There, when the frost makes all the birches burn
Yellow as cow-lilies, and the pale sky shines
Like a polished shell between black spruce and pines,
Some strange thing tracks us, turning where we turn.

You'll say I dream it, being the true daughter
Of those who in old times endured this dread.
Look! Where the lily-stems are showing red
A silent paddle moves below the water,
A sliding shape has stirred them like a breath;
Tall plumes surmount a painted mask of death.

---

1 Atavism is the tendency to revert to or reproduce an ancestral type. In the context of late nineteenth- and early twentieth-century thought, it was linked to Darwinian evolutionary theory and the notion that human beings still contained primitive or even primate features. Here the atavism could be the narrator's surviving belief that something lurks in the water of Somes's pond—or the creature who lurks, a possible survival from another age.

THE FAIRY GOLDSMITH

Here's a wonderful thing,
A humming-bird's wing
    In hammered gold,
And store well chosen
Of snowflakes frozen
    In crystal cold.

Black onyx cherries
And mistletoe berries
    Of chrysoprase,
Jade buds, tight shut,
All carven and cut
    In intricate ways.

Here, if you please
Are little gilt bees
    In amber drops
Which look like honey,
Translucent and sunny,
    From clover-tops.

Here's an elfin girl
Of mother-of-pearl
    And moonshine made,
With tortoise-shell hair
Both dusky and fair
    In its light and shade.

Here's lacquer laid thin,
Like a scarlet skin
    On an ivory fruit;
And a filigree frost
Of frail notes lost
    From a fairy lute.

Here's a turquoise chain
Of sun-shower rain
    To wear if you wish;
And glittering green
With aquamarine,
    A silvery fish.

Here are pearls all strung
On a thread among
    Pretty pink shells;
And bubbles blown
From the opal stone
    Which ring like bells.

Touch them and take them,
But do not break them!
    Beneath your hand
They will wither like foam
If you carry them home
    Out of fairy-land.

O, they never can last
Though you hide them fast

From moth and from rust;
In your monstrous day
They will crumble away
    Into quicksilver dust.

MADMAN'S SONG

Better to see your cheek grown hollow,
Better to see your temple worn,
Than to forget to follow, follow,
After the sound of a silver horn.

Better to bind your brow with willow
And follow, follow until you die,
Than to sleep with your head on a golden pillow,
Nor lift it up when the hunt goes by.[1]

Better to see your cheek grown sallow
And your hair grown gray, so soon, so soon,
Than to forget to hallo, hallo,
After the milk-white hounds of the moon.

---

1 Not an ordinary hunt, but the Wild Hunt. In European folklore, the huntsmen of the Wild Hunt were variously fairies, demons, or the souls of the dead, riding horses and accompanied by baying hounds. Wylie's is clearly a magical hunt from fairyland.

A HAUNTED HOUSE

Virginia Woolf

Whatever hour you woke there was a door shutting. From room to room they went, hand in hand, lifting here, opening there, making sure—a ghostly couple.

"Here we left it," she said. And he added, "Oh, but here too!" "It's upstairs," she murmured. "And in the garden," he whispered. "Quietly," they said, "or we shall wake them."

But it wasn't that you woke us. Oh, no. "They're looking for it; they're drawing the curtain," one might say, and so read on a page or two. "Now they've found it," one would be certain, stopping the pencil on the margin. And then, tired of reading, one might rise and see for oneself, the house all empty, the doors standing open, only the wood pigeons bubbling with content and the hum of the threshing machine sounding from the farm. "What did I come in here for? What did I want to find?" My hands were empty. "Perhaps it's upstairs then?" The apples were in the loft. And so down again, the garden still as ever, only the book had slipped into the grass.

But they had found it in the drawing room. Not that one could ever see them. The window panes reflected apples, reflected roses; all the leaves were green in the glass. If they moved in the drawing room, the apple only turned its yellow side. Yet, the moment after, if the door was opened, spread about the floor, hung upon the walls, pendant from the ceiling—what? My hands were empty. The shadow of a thrush crossed the carpet; from the deepest wells of silence the wood pigeon drew its bubble of sound. "Safe, safe, safe," the pulse of the house beat softly. "The treasure buried; the room..." the pulse stopped short. Oh, was that the buried treasure?

A moment later the light had faded. Out in the garden then? But the trees spun darkness for a wandering beam of sun. So fine, so rare, coolly sunk beneath the surface the beam I sought always burnt behind the glass. Death was the glass; death was between us; coming to the woman first, hundreds of years ago, leaving the house, sealing all the windows; the rooms were darkened. He left it, left her, went North, went East, saw the stars turned in the Southern sky; sought the house, found it dropped beneath the Downs. "Safe, safe, safe," the pulse of the house beat gladly. "The Treasure yours."

The wind roars up the avenue. Trees stoop and bend this way and that. Moonbeams splash and spill wildly in the rain. But the beam of the lamp falls straight from the window. The candle burns stiff and still. Wandering through the house, opening the windows, whispering not to wake us, the ghostly couple seek their joy.

"Here we slept," she says. And he adds, "Kisses without

number." "Waking in the morning—" "Silver between the trees—" "Upstairs—" "In the garden—" "When summer came—" "In winter snowtime—" The doors go shutting far in the distance, gently knocking like the pulse of a heart.

Nearer they come; cease at the doorway. The wind falls, the rain slides silver down the glass. Our eyes darken; we hear no steps beside us; we see no lady spread her ghostly cloak. His hands shield the lantern. "Look," he breathes. "Sound asleep. Love upon their lips."

Stooping, holding their silver lamp above us, long they look and deeply. Long they pause. The wind drives straightly; the flame stoops slightly. Wild beams of moonlight cross both floor and wall, and, meeting, stain the faces bent; the faces pondering; the faces that search the sleepers and seek their hidden joy.

"Safe, safe, safe," the heart of the house beats proudly. "Long years—" he sighs. "Again you found me." "Here," she murmurs, "sleeping; in the garden reading; laughing, rolling apples in the loft. Here we left our treasure—" Stooping, their light lifts the lids upon my eyes. "Safe! safe! safe!" the pulse of the house beats wildly. Waking, I cry "Oh, is this *your* buried treasure? The light in the heart."

ACKNOWLEDGMENTS

This book would not exist if Christine Neulieb had not asked me, at the International Conference on the Fantastic in the Arts, if I was interested in editing a book for Lanternfish Press. I am grateful to her for allowing me to collect such a strange assortment of stories and poems—which represent, I think, some of the most interesting writing by women at the fin-de-siècle. I could not have done it without her careful editing and guidance. I am also grateful to the staff at Lanternfish Press, including Feliza Casano and Amanda Thomas, for all the work they put into creating and publicizing the final product. I would particularly like to thank Kimberly Glyder for the cover design and Robert Kraiza for the interior illustrations, which capture the spirit of the stories so well. In all these stories and poems, I have tried to accurately reflect the choices of the original authors in their final edited versions, while making a few minor changes to punctuation for easier reading by a contemporary audience. In doing so, I was inspired by the careful editorial practices of my teachers, particularly John Paul Riquelme and Julia Brown, as well as by the students in my course on the literature and culture of the fin-de-siècle, who have such a love for the gruesome, monstrous, and fantastic in literature. Most of all, I was inspired by my daughter Ophelia. I hope that she, and other young women living at the beginning of this exciting new century, will be as fascinated by the work of these women writers as I am.

ABOUT THE EDITOR

Theodora Goss is the World Fantasy and Locus Award-winning author of the short story and poetry collections *In the Forest of Forgetting* (2006), *Songs for Ophelia* (2014), and *Snow White Learns Witchcraft* (2019), as well as novella *The Thorn and the Blossom* (2012), debut novel *The Strange Case of the Alchemist's Daughter* (2017), and sequels *European Travel for the Monstrous Gentlewoman* (2018) and *The Sinister Mystery of the Mesmerizing Girl* (2019). She has been a finalist for the Nebula, Crawford, Seiun, and Mythopoeic Awards, as well as on the Tiptree Award Honor List. Her work has been translated into thirteen languages. She teaches literature and writing at Boston University and in the Stonecoast MFA Program. Visit her at theodoragoss.com.